D1552502

A BLESSED
SNARL

A BLESSE

D SNARL

SAMUEL THOMAS MARTIN

FOR

Samantha, Aunt Jo, Annie Ling, and Annamarie
who have been through fire

In Newfoundland nature is a blessed snarl, humans an imposition.
You have to want to come here; you have to want to fight to stay.
You are not seed on fertile ground. You are a fish washed up on a rock.

— KEVIN MAJOR. *NEW UNDER THE SUN*

I

I t's better to be cheated on than to be ignored. Anne thinks this as she fingers the small bluish bruise on her upper thigh. Patrick is snoring next to her, his wrists crossed above his head. This is how he always sleeps. Like a man in chains. Anne remembers the early days of their marriage, when she would snuggle in to Patrick's sleeping body, her ear on his right arm, bare leg draped over his, hand on his chest, feeling it rise and fall rhythmically. It's been months since they cuddled like that, maybe a year.

Maybe since Patrick brought up the idea of the move.

Pushing her thumb against the bruise on her thigh distracts her from her loneliness. She is thinking that if she had caught Patrick at the computer masturbating to Internet porn, or found he was seeing somebody else, she would at least have a reason to feel the way she does. Resentful. Angry. But he is as faithful as they come. He has never done anything to hurt her. Except forcing her to leave Ontario.

They'd packed up only a few weeks after Anne's uncle Ken passed away and her cousin Debby's boy Kyle shot himself in a shed. Too soon: none of them had any time to grieve. Anne blames herself as much as Patrick for leaving, though. After all, she packed the car. She was the one, in the end, who didn't say anything. Just kept trying to convince herself that the move was a good thing. Breathing on the glass of the passenger-side window on their way through Quebec, watching her fingerprints reappear and fade.

She remembers the ferry and feeling nauseous despite the Gravol she'd taken in North Sydney. Nervous seasickness and it was sleeting outside so she couldn't heave over the rail, not without feeling like she was going to fall overboard into that rolling grey mess. It wasn't the calm sparkling sea she had pictured when Patrick told her they were moving to Newfoundland.

Yes, *told* me, she remembers whispering on the boat.

A decision for the *man* of the house.

He could've asked what I thought.

She recalls the young mother in the stretched white V-neck, holding her crying baby against her big belly, staring at Anne quizzically. That's when Anne realized she had just puppeteered that whole conversation with her hands.

Her right hand is the ornery one, and Lefty always tries to reason with Righty. She's done it since she was a kid, but somewhere in high school she learned to pocket those conversations so that Dave Collins, the only boy she'd ever had a serious crush on, would stop tossing condoms at her and saying there were better things to do with her hands.

At the time she'd thought it was probably the Gravol making her dopey. For once she didn't care that her hands were chatty. At least it kept her mind off her sloshing stomach.

Lefty: You hear that?

Gurgle.

Uh-oh.

Crap.

Exactly.

The big woman across from Anne had snorted and smiled. Missus, she'd said, pulling a strand of hair out of her mouth and hefting the screaming kid, Don't know if you're kiddin or crazy but if you needs the washroom it's just that way.

Anne had smiled, and Righty said Thanks.

No worries, my love. Mind if I feed him?

Lefty: Knock yourself out.

But instead of pulling out a bottle she'd heaved her V-neck down, tugged out a big veiny boob and stuck it in the baby's mouth. Then it was like Anne wasn't there: Bertha just humming and staring out the window.

Righty: How do you know her name's Bertha?

What was that? The woman had asked, glancing back.

Anne remembers sitting on her right hand to shut it up. She'd gone red and smiled weakly, her face suddenly hot as the whole cabin heaved. She'd seen Patrick coming toward her, strolling back from the canteen with coffees. He'd been strangely sure-footed in his Sunday shoes.

Anne had jolted past him on her way to the washroom, clenching her teeth to keep the Tim Hortons chili down as she ran. She'd made it before puking, and flushed the first Gravol before taking three more. She'd washed her mouth and the side of her face, the smell of pink soap doing nothing to settle her stomach. She remembers swaying as she'd walked back past the gift shop and the TV lounge to where Patrick and the lady were chatting. The young mother had re-tucked her boob, and the baby was drooling down her arm as she sipped the coffee Patrick had purchased for Anne.

Anne rolls over in bed, picturing Patrick's smile that day, hearing him say: Didn't think you'd want it after the big heave.

That's fine, she'd said. I'm going to find an empty chair. See if I can sleep.

You seen Hab?

No. You?

And then she doesn't remember much until Patrick had shaken her awake and she'd surfaced out of a thick fog only to get in the car and drive off the ferry into a thicker fog. She couldn't tell at the time if it was the pills or being over-tired or if it was the sudden gut-punching memory of Debby's son's suicide that had started her crying.

Kyle. The kid she used to babysit when she was pregnant with Hab and spending time with her mom up on the lake. The boy she taught to catch muskie under the St. Olga Bridge by hooking a field mouse in the skin above its tail and letting it swim out into the river, like her dad had taught her. She'd once

handed Kyle her slack line when they were out in her father's bass boat and he'd wound up wrestling in a three-pound burbot ling, its mottled flanks dark olive and its belly black against Kyle's little white hands. Kyle had looped a cord through its gills and tied the other end to his wrist; then he had let the strange fish down into the water alongside the boat, watching its cream-coloured fins wimple and its single-chin barbell twitch. Anne hadn't seen a ling before, or since. Her father told her they were a dirty fish and not much sought after by *real* fishermen. She only knew that its white meat, grilled with ground peppercorns, flaked beneath her fork and that she and Kyle had licked the bones clean.

When she thinks of Kyle she thinks of this strange north-water cod in its deep lakes and cold rivers, making its home in rock-pile crevices and submerged logs. A mystery fish known by many names yet seldom caught; she has learned its names, like a shaman chant—Cusk, Dogfish, Eelpout, Gudgeon, Lawyer, Ling, Loche, Lush, Maria, Methy, Mother Eel, Mud Blower, Spineless Catfish, Swe—but she has never hooked one herself, never felt its eely fight, only seen the rod tremble and bend in Kyle's white-knuckled fists. She called him her *ling-catcher* until he told her it was embarrassing and that the ling was not a real fish like bass, trout, or salmon. But she never forgot the look on his face when he pulled it in, not knowing what he'd caught, only that he had to hold it tight so it wouldn't fight free of his slick grip.

Anne does not have such memories of her own son, though she has always meant to teach Hab outdoorsy things—take him camping on the island at the butt end of Little Salmon Lake. But once Hab was old enough to swing a bat Patrick had him in Little League, which kept them in Peterborough most weekends of the summer. That, and Hab was prone to carsickness, so driving *anywhere* was a pain, let alone making the two-and-a-half-hour trek to Lemming's Lake.

Hab, now eighteen, had fed himself Gravol every few hours during their long, wet, and winding drive out East.

Anne remembers her son snoring in the back seat as Patrick drove out of Port aux Basques. She could hear him breathing heavily and could not stop thinking of her cousin Debby—her close friend since childhood—at Kyle's closed-casket wake, of how she had given Debby her seven-eyelet flex rod with the closed-face Zepco reel, the one Kyle had once jokingly asked her to leave him in her will. The memory of Debby's tears, and her own that day, made Anne cry harder in the car, and she couldn't stop until Patrick pulled off onto a side road that wound out to a cape where the houses looked like they were huddled together.

Hab had shifted in his seatbelt but didn't wake when Patrick stopped the car.

Anne looks at her bedside clock blinking 3:13 a.m. and thinks of Patrick leading her by the hand down along the craggy beach, unlike any beach she ever knew in Ontario, their feet sliding on smooth stones and gravel. Patrick took her down and down again until she said something about the surging sea and he laughed, bent over, picked up a perfectly smooth stone.

Copper-veined and purple.

A worry stone, he had said, to rub when you're upset.

The salt wind stung her lips and she didn't say anything on the long, winding drive back to the highway, hills slooping up and disappearing in cloud. Everything mizzly and grey. Water beading on her window and Hab groggy in the backseat. She doesn't remember falling asleep. Doesn't remember any part of that leg of the journey.

Until Deer Lake and the roadside hotel.

She knows now that what she was feeling that day was lone-liness, but under the cracked yellow Super 8 sign she couldn't tell if it was a Gravol hangover or carsickness or what. But Kyle's face wouldn't leave her all that long night as she lay in a strange bed, wide awake because she had slept through most of the day. Patrick had snored, his wrists crossed above his head—just like they are now. And the sheets had smelled like medicine and bleach.

That was Anne's first day in Newfoundland.

She remembers it still, even after settling into their new home and unpacking. She played an inaugural game of *Taboo* with Hab while Patrick was away at the new church office. She remembers Hab being quiet, and she wondered if he was thinking of Uncle Ken or Kyle as well. They hadn't really been close, Kyle and Hab. Hab was always the city boy, the preacher's kid—*PK*, Kyle had called him back when he hung around Anne's father's dock in the summer. Back when he would teach Hab how to catch crayfish and Anne would take the boys out in her dad's bass boat to go fishing. Kyle always caught something. Hab couldn't be bothered to watch his bobber: too busy zipping his hand through the water and making motorboat noises. Kyle was as strange as a mudcat, always telling Hab to *shush*. That was when they were boys. Eventually he stopped coming around, and Debby would tell Anne over morning coffees in August that she thought Kyle was into drugs. That she'd caught him snorting a line and he'd laughed at her and giggled as she smashed the powdered shaving mirror and cut her hand on the loose razor blade.

I shouldn't have done that, Debby had said to Anne afterward. I shouldn't have done it, but I was so furious.

Anne thinks of Debby's palm as it must have looked when Kyle laughed at her. Before she and her husband, Nick, kicked him out of the house. Chalky white and blood rivering her palm; the fingers of her other hand clenched around her wrist. Like Christ, she had thought. But what did that make Kyle?

Judas?

No, Anne thinks, *no*. But she does remember feeling betrayed by the boy she had loved—the sun rising over the hills behind them on that long-ago summer morning, splashing the lake's liquiglass surface.

Anne knows that they had left too soon after the funerals. She knows this now, but she couldn't say it to Patrick then because the ferry had been booked and the travel plans made. She wasn't over her shock before she was packed up and moved

A BLESSED
SNARL

to a strange island in the North Atlantic.

And forgotten.

The move to Paradise, a suburb outside St. John's, was Patrick's idea, his dream to move back *home* and start a Pentecostal church plant. And what was Anne to say when he called it his dream? The language of dreams between them was tied to faith and was beyond questioning. Anne had been raised by a Pentecostal evangelist, a travelling minister, and she didn't question dreams, at least not when they came from a man of God. And Patrick was a minister, ordained by her own dad. After the formal service her father had taken Patrick down to the beach at Lemming's Lake, her childhood home, and they had waded out into the lake in their good suits until the water was up to their chests. Then her father uncorked the bottle of olive oil he had with him and poured the whole thing over Patrick's head, Patrick weeping and allowing her father to place both hands on his head and submerge him—rings of oil rainbowing as he uttered a blessing. But from where she stood on the shore, Anne couldn't make out what they were saying.

Life with Patrick always involved waiting: waiting for him to finish Bible College before they could be married; waiting to kiss him until their wedding day; waiting five years before trying to have children, and another two before Anne finally conceived; waiting three months after the baby was born for their son's name to be revealed to Patrick in his morning prayer time; waiting on God's direction for *their* ministry. All while Hab was growing up and Patrick was serving as Associate Pastor in a string of churches in and around Peterborough.

But Anne did not always feel ignored by Patrick. There were times when he was as free and flowing as the oil he poured over their naked bodies on a blue tarp he had spread over their bed on that long-ago summer afternoon when Hab was conceived. Words like *blessed* and *holy* came jumbled from his wet lips with things Anne has never been able to repeat. And it wasn't just fun sex—*carnal anointings*, Patrick had joked as he reached out for her, grinning like a puppy—it was all of him Anne loved.

And he loved all of her right back: even her stupid talking hands.

Anne had always enjoyed being with Patrick. Saturday morning coffee at their kitchen table, sometimes with his scrambled eggs and toast, other times with her homemade pancakes drenched with real maple syrup. But now there is no real maple syrup, not here in Newfoundland. There are no real trees——no maples or beech trees, except in the wealthy downtown areas of St. John's. There are birches here and there, like golden fall flowers in a weed bed of pine and balsam. Anne has been told bakeapple jam is the next best thing to syrup, but she doesn't like its grainy, tomato-seed texture on her pancakes. She misses boiling the syrup down into maple sugar.

Patrick used to dip his finger in his coffee and then in the bowl of maple sugar and offer her a taste. She misses their midmorning flirtations, how at-home they made her feel in her own skin. Anne feels out of place here, out of *her* place, like a tamarack tree in November, choked in a thicket of pines. The persistent green here, the frustrating island stubbornness, the weird resilience to all types of weather—all this makes her fear and loneliness more yellow, more apparent.

Rolling onto her back in bed, she thinks of her big scrawl looping next to Patrick's neat signature in the church guest book.

The new pastor's wife is from away.

She can't hear the church ladies' whispers but she sees them leaning into each other, and she knows they see her wrinkled nose when they put salt beef on her plate at church potlucks— the red boiled meat stringy, salty, and ringed in fat. Anne can only imagine what they would think of her if she stopped sitting on Righty and let her hand say what it wants to say about jigg's dinner.

But she keeps her hands quiet because people watch her closely here, sitting as she does in the front pew on the left side of the aisle. She thinks often of St. Paul's letters to the Corinthians and how her life is a paraphrase: The pastor's wife should be seen and not heard.

She has spent her life sitting in the front pew while her father preached, serving dinner in her parents' home to guests and relatives, has long gone unnoticed as Pastor Wiseman's wife. Suddenly she is as visible as a broken bone punched through torn skin, and being classed a Come From Away every time she says anything makes her blister inside. She tries not to speak at all, but that makes her stuck-up, snooty: too good for her own good.

She hates that she can never tell anyone that she is still not over her Uncle Ken's death, even though he had Alzheimer's and had no idea who Anne was in the months before he passed. She hates even more that she has trouble sleeping because Kyle comes to her in her dreams and asks why she has gone away. She's dreamt him under the St. Olga Bridge, hooking a tomcat through the neck while it clawed the dead skin off his cadaverous arm. Pastor's wives don't talk about such things: watching a ghost boy turn and seeing the back of his head blown off. Anne has wondered if it is demon possession. Or oppression. She's never been able to keep those two as theologically separate as her father has. She wonders if the nightmares have anything to do with her Facebook messages to Dave, if they are a punishment from God, a way of keeping her up at night so that she is forced to see the sleeping face of her husband, who she is sure she's cheating on with this Internet connection. But she feels nothing when she looks at Patrick's face in the red glow of the alarm clock. She feels hollow.

And alone.

She smiles at church so she doesn't stand out as the lonely, glum pastor's wife from away. But she feels conspicuous and fake.

Not like Patrick.

Patrick blends in so smoothly here that if Anne closes her eyes at a church social she can't tell his voice from those around her. His accent, something she had never known he had, suddenly taking his words and setting them to music she doesn't know and can't keep time with. His voice, once so distinctive to her, fades out in

a group, just as he has faded out of her life, out of their house—always away at the church office answering phone calls, meeting with people and other pastors in St. John's, pestering the Pentecostal Assemblies of Newfoundland for more money.

She remembers once hanging on to Patrick's every word while he preached. He had such a way of opening up the Word—not just peeling away layers of obscurity like you'd peel an orange, but explaining the layers, scraping the vitamin-rich pulp off the inside of the peel and feeding Anne even the bitter parts of scripture with a tenderness she adored.

Anne can't recall the last time she actually heard one of his sermons, even though she sits in the front row—feeling everyone's eyes on the back of her head.

She doesn't remember the last time Patrick actually looked at her since they'd moved here. She doesn't even think he looked at her, really looked at her, when he said they were moving *home* to Newfoundland. For months now Anne has been angry at herself for feeling as if she needs him to look at her. She has told herself repeatedly that he does still see her: that he still wants her.

But she has dumped more cups of cold coffee down the sink in their house in Paradise on Saturday morning after Saturday morning than she cares to count. But she has. *Twenty-eight*. Twenty-eight times she has watched Patrick's cup steam and then grow cold sitting on its coaster across the table from her. She'd bought the coasters downtown at one of the tourist shops. They're red clay with a Celtic swirl. Anne is sure it has another name, some story she hasn't been told, some significance she won't get because she's from away. Or maybe it's because she's bitter. She can't bring herself to say *rotted*, like they do here, even though that is exactly how she feels when she pours yet another cup down the sink.

Hab has started his first year of university. He hasn't declared a major yet but says he likes the local art. Anne tries to pay more attention when he shows her images online, but when she sits in front of the computer on her own, trying to remember the artists he has mentioned so that she can Google them and take more of an interest in her son's life, she can't recall a single name. She was doing that earlier today: sitting in front of a blank screen for an hour before opening up Facebook again. The only thing that registered in that hour was the date in the bottom right-hand corner of the screen. November 5—another empty day. And her mind on fire thinking about Dave.

The other day, Hab put the *Taboo* board game on the top shelf of the closet in the basement computer room. *Did he do it so I would see?* They used to play it a lot when Hab got home from school, ever since the move. Before they would begin making supper together, or Hab would start scribbling away at his homework on the couch in the living room while Anne peeled potatoes.

Anne thinks about preparing those dinners: boiled potatoes and pork chops baked in mushroom soup. Then she thinks about the laundry she has to do tomorrow.

The room is flashing red and the man beside her in bed is snoring. Everything is muted and dim, unreal, until Patrick shifts in his sleep and gulps. She has taken to sleeping on the couch some nights, to see if Patrick wakes and comes to find her. Sometimes just to be alone so her crying doesn't disturb him. She wants him to hear her and she doesn't. She doesn't know what she wants.

Anne listens to his breathing even out again. And she thinks of when she signed up for Facebook over a month ago. It was after Hab had caught her staring at a blank Google page—after she'd spent an hour looking up used Zepco reels on Kijiji—and she couldn't admit she was trying to remember the artists' names he'd been telling her about. He asked if she wanted to set up an account and then he showed her how. He said that this way she could keep in touch with people from back home. He didn't say, This way you won't be so lonely, but Anne felt the pity in the way he gently rubbed her back before heading up the stairs and out the door on his way to catch the bus into St. John's.

She began searching for people to invite to be her friends,

feeling foolish and awkward like she was in grade school again and *she* was the PK. Little Miss Goody-Good. Crazy over there with the talking hands. Alone. Sitting in her dark basement, in the blue light of the computer screen—flickering window elsewhere—scanning profiles of people she knew or had known. Peggy Townsend from St. Lola. Her cousin Reece. Kim Delehunt from Peterborough.

Dave Collins.

She sent out her invitations and sat back. Dave answered back almost immediately, and Anne was shocked by the sudden response. Like knuckles rapping a window she was leaning her forehead on. *Hi there, Anne. Haven't seen u in ages. How r things with u?* She answered the message, unsure of whether to write you or u. And then she spent an hour chatting with Dave.

It seemed like five minutes.

Anne didn't mention the condoms he'd thrown at her in high school, before she really knew what they were. She didn't say how she'd hated him but could never stop thinking about him. How she'd watched him play rugby from underneath the bleachers. He was the reason she had tried to join the girls' team—maybe he would watch her play, though he never did. All these memories of him were like the bruises she had discovered on her body when taking a bath the night after her first practice in grade ten. Finger scrapes on her ribs from a rough tackle. Cleat marks raked across her legs. A gouge from a fieldstone dug into her knee.

Remembering Dave as she sent messages to him on the computer was as painful and intriguing as exploring her body that night in the tub, the first time she had ever locked the bathroom door. She still remembers her father rattling the knob and saying he needed to use the toilet.

Why is this door locked? We don't lock doors in this house. Anne? What are you doing in there? You'll become a prune. Anne!

After that initial online chat with Dave, Anne had gone upstairs with a basket of laundry. She'd folded socks and rolled

underwear, her fingers numb and her mind shivering from one memory of Dave to the next. She hadn't realized the air cooling around her like bathwater left too long. That is, until Hab returned and asked why the thermostat was turned so low. It was evening and the temperature outside had dropped below zero.

Mom, it's frigid in here. Your lips are blue and you're shaking.

She had not started supper. And the laundry—except for the mismatched socks and tightly rolled underwear—was still unfolded in the basket beside her.

Meet any old friends on Facebook, Mom?

Yeah, she'd said. But she hadn't told Hab any more than that. She did not say that she'd laughed at something Dave had written to her in their online chat—the first time she had laughed since before the funerals and the move. And she did not say Dave's name along with Peggy's, Reece's, or Kim's. Since that day, Anne has kept Dave's name to herself, like the purple worry stone she's kept hidden in her pocket, though it digs into her leg sometimes and leaves a thumb-sized bruise on her thigh.

Now, lying in bed, listening to her husband's breathing, she fingers the bruise and presses it hard with her thumb so that it doesn't fade.

Natalie remembers thinking Biz was a rapist on top of her that night. Biz's hands all over her. But it was Biz's shaking that jolted her from a nightmare to the reality of choking smoke and Biz's hoarse screaming that the building was on fire.

Come on, Natalie! We gotta get out!

Wha—?

Fire! The building's on fire!

Natalie could smell the smoke then, acrid and thick, like vomit on a hot sidewalk—making the dark room darker.

Quidi Vidi's heavy fog makes Natalie recall that night when her Toronto tenement building burned. The pea soup is so thick she can't see out the Gut to the sea. She wouldn't even know it was the sea in front of her if she opened her eyes and this was her dream and Toronto her reality, because she hasn't been able to smell a thing since that night, nor taste anything.

She stands alone in the wet grey, sometimes hearing the waves and the suck and scroll of stones on stones, sometimes hearing nothing at all. Sometimes hearing Biz's voice and feeling the fire hot on her belly. Heat through the floor. Ants crisping on campfire rocks. Crawling toward the door to the hall.

Her hand gripping Biz's ankle.

Anyone watching Biz lift her pant leg in the airport might have thought she was showing off a new pair of shoes, orange Crocs bought to replace the ones that nearly melted to her feet as she and Natalie ran across the roof of the building. But she was showing Natalie the claw marks she'd left, Biz's gashed ankle red and shiny with ointment. That was their goodbye hug. Natalie's saviour showing her wounds and Nat turning her back on Toronto and their life together as friends—flying as far east as health insurance would allow.

It has been a beautiful St. John's summer. But now it is a Newfoundland November. Rain or fog every day, so that often Natalie doesn't even feel like leaving the apartment on Merrymeeting that she shares with Gerry, an English Lit student from the university, and Lisette, a nineteen-year-old girl from Bonavista who wants to make a career out of waitressing.

In warmer weather the three of them sit out on the sidewalk in front of their place and talk—Lisette chain-smoking, and Gerry and Natalie drinking most of the wine. Gerry's a writer, he tells them, but he can't get a damn thing published.

You have to write about outports, the Beothuk, Joey fuckin Smallwood, or being stoned out of your tree if you want a story published here, he said once, his thin lips purple, a glass of wine balancing on his bony knee. Lisette calls this his pontificating posture.

Gerry: Local readers want their heroes high and their priests dirty. I got stories about cocksucking priests and people fucking in George Street alleys. I got 'em jumpin off the TD building and splattering all over tourists on Water Street. That's funny shit. But can I get anything in print?

Lisette: No. But you also don't send your stuff anywhere but here.

That's 'cause I know what the outcome will be. My point is that I'm not the only one with this problem.

Oh?

All the greats suffer. You know who else couldn't get anything in print because he was too brilliant for his own time?

James fuckin Joyce.

Yes.

Maybe you need more sex, Natalie had piped in.

In the stories?

No, Lisette had said, blowing smoke out her nose. In real fuckin life, Gerry. Try getting laid. Blow off some of that artistic steam.

Maori artists never have sex when they're workin their craft.

And a Maori is?

A New Zealand native.

Oh, that's you to a T.

Shut up, Lisette.

Blow me.

Gerry never gets the last word with Lisette. To hear them go at it you'd think they hate each other. But Natalie knows Gerry has waited up till five in the morning to make sure Lisette gets home safe from downtown. And Natalie saw Lisette hand-scrub a shirt that Gerry puked all over the night the three of them went dancing. Gerry's even let Natalie read one of his stories, but when she asked him if the bit about the dog and the cinder block was true he snorted, took the story back, and hasn't let her see one since.

When the weather turned, Natalie started walking to the university with Gerry and spending most of her days surfing the web on the library's wireless, using Lisette's laptop when she was at work or at home sleeping. Natalie often Googled the photography school in Toronto that she'd dropped out of after the fire. She'd photographed fire obsessively when she was there. Setting her camera on a tripod in front of a trashcan blaze she'd built up in an alleyway, setting the shutter for exposures of one, five, and fifteen minutes. Occasionally she would walk between the open lens on the tripod and the burning trash and smashed skids sparking-up six feet behind her—her presence a shadow smear. She would wait for the click and then reset the camera to capture the red-lit infernal alley, her long shadow ghosting all the way to the darkened street. The lamppost light: a lone phosphorescent moon.

Natalie remembers all the photos she took during her time in Toronto with Biz. All her friends at the school were into portraits or washed-out cityscapes. There was a lot of talk of irony, peeling away façades, deconstructing the flashy visual utopias of downtown advertising. Contrast: Bay Street businessmen walking past homeless teens sleeping on air vents in the sidewalk; Armani and greasy plaid. But Natalie wanted to paint with her camera. She hated focus and adored movement, obscurity, ghosts.

Flames.

The figures in her photos looked like they were on fire. This made her wonder if her Pentecostal upbringing subconsciously sparked her searches for unlikely altars across the city, on side streets and in forgotten spaces where weeds pushed up through cracked asphalt. In the heat of an alley in August she would remember a summer revival meeting on the island at Lemming's Lake. Old Gurney Gunther pacing the platform, lashing the microphone cord in front of him as he marched, as if he were driving demons before him, talking about fighting fire with fire. Holy Spirit fire that purifies against hellfire that destroys. *Which will you choose?*

Natalie would see her shadow in a photo, wreathed in sparks, and she would remember Gurney Gunther's white dress shirt translucent with sweat and clinging to his large belly. His hoarse voice calling out: *Like Wesley I'm a man on fire. You've come to see this body burn away so that the Spirit can fly.* In their stifling Toronto apartment she would remember the heat of the alley and the humidity of the old log tabernacle in June—spit flying from Gurney Gunther's lips. *Jesus shed his blood so that we would not have to face the flames of Hell. His death brings us life, and to tell another person of Christ's sacrifice is to offer their hell-bound soul a cup of cool water. If you could only imagine hell in its fury you would surely tell everyone you know, everyone you love, how they can be saved from it.*

Natalie never told Biz about those meetings: how she would go to the front for every altar call and wait in line to be prayed for. She never told Biz that she did this to get out of her seat and away from her parents who sang beautifully in church but argued bitterly at home: that she prayed until her body shook;

SAMUEL THOMAS MARTIN

27

stamped her feet and cursed the devil; called on the name of Jesus. She never brought any of this up because her parents got divorced shortly after she moved to Toronto. That's when her father went back to long-haul trucking and stopped going to church. Natalie never told Biz that she thought her father might be going to Hell: that she was terrified of that place and its fury and of the God who would send people there. She never mentioned any of this to her friend.

But she did stand in a cold shower once, fully clothed, with Biz, during a summer heat wave. Afterwards they sat out on their fire-escape in the evening, hearing the drips from their sodden clothes ping on the metal ladders beneath them as they laughed and passed a cigarillo between them, drinking Barefoot Merlot from a chipped wineglass.

She remembers breathing easy then.

Knowing, in such moments, what it was like to be at peace and unafraid.

Feeling refreshed, fireproof, loved.

On evenings like that she would show Biz her photos. Arsonist, Biz coyly called her once, leaving a lipstick stain imprinted on the wineglass rim. Just a taste, she'd said, before getting up and going to the fridge for a green-bottled pilsner. You're going to burn down the whole city, block by block, making your art, aren't you Natalie?

In cooler weather they would pull every cushion and pillow they owned onto the floor between their milk-crate coffee table and ratty green couch. A fat, three-wick candle sat on the crates. The candles were always Natalie's idea. The cushions on the floor were Biz's. And they'd talk: long hours into the night, sirens on Spadina nearby, intermittent in the dark like distant cries. They talked sometimes until the skyline out their window began to glow: the sun blood red on the horizon and the wind hot on days calling for thunderstorms.

As much as Natalie loved fire and clear night skies purple with city lights, she hated—hates—rain. Rain's only redeeming feature is thunder and lighting but there is little thunder here on the edge of the North Atlantic, and next to no lightning. It frightens Gerry when it comes: sends him indoors, where he sits on the couch with his rubber boots on. But it makes Natalie remember that day as a girl in that faraway field next to the crabapple tree up from Lemming's Lake when the wind went dirty and bent the old trees' branches in her direction, even as she felt her skin tingle and she reached up to feel her long hair all standing on end—just before lightning struck a hydro pole across the field by West Coon Lake Road. And then the deluge came. Something that hasn't really stopped since September passed in St. John's, some five months after Natalie moved here with little besides her camera and a backpack of clothes bought at Value Village.

People gave so much after the blaze: church groups and charities and old women living in apartments nearby. But nothing they gave Biz or Natalie was what either would ever wear. Old feather boas, neon-green tank tops, a paint-stained hoodie, three pairs of enormous granny panties. It was like the disaster was a good chance to empty closets of all the old junk and give it to someone who had nothing because, well, something is always better than nothing, and beggars can't be choosers.

And, at that point, they were beggars. Everything was gone. Natalie's computer, her cameras, journals and books—even her portable hard drive that she had bought to back up everything on her computer in case her Toshiba laptop was ever stolen. In place of six thousand dollars' worth of computer and camera equipment, Natalie got a hand-knit woollen sweater that smelled of mothballs and old man from an old Hungarian woman who said it kept her husband warm even on his deathbed, so it should keep her warm as well.

Thanks, Natalie said as she balled it up in her arms, knowing by the feel of it that she'd never be able to wear the sweater without breaking out in a rash. She kept it, though. It was in the bottom of her backpack when she landed in St. John's. She'd pinned it to her bedroom wall as soon as she'd found this place to live through Kijiji. A memento. A woollen icon of absence.

Lisette asked if she had bought it in one of the downtown shops as a souvenir. Said Natalie should've asked her first, 'cause she's got a Nan who knits and would give her a sweater for free instead of paying a hundred bucks on Water Street. Then Natalie told her the story and she kept saying *my love, my love* with her hand over her mouth and her eyes watering up. She called herself a *sook* and Natalie *a poor thing* and then she said: So that old lady gave you the sweater her husband died in? Sent his ghost along too to give you back rubs, I'll bet.

Natalie laughed: the sound shocking. Like a crow's sudden caw catching in her throat. And she kept laughing. She laughed a lot with Lisette after that because Lisette would tell her stories of her family up on the Bonavista. Like how her Pop went to cut firewood in the bush one winter's day and ended up chopping off three of his fingers, and how the priest was more concerned with burying the severed fingers in consecrated ground than in getting her Pop to a doctor. And then years later, the wild Pentecostal evangelist from the mainland who prayed for her Pop's gnarled hand and felt two of the three missing fingers grow back—the old man's paw pressed between the preacher's fleshy oil-slick palms.

Two-thirds of a miracle, her Pop would say, laughing and jinking the tiny ice cubes in his empty rum tumbler. Crafty Christ makin sure I shows up on Judgement Day for the roll call to collect my middle finger!

Lisette's favourite stories were from before Resettlement, when light smoked and guttered and electricity hummed only in rumour.

Gerry's family had always been townies, so they'd never experienced Resettlement but through old photographs of full houses being floated around headlands and across the water to newer modernized towns.

And now we sells the pictures to the fuckin tourists who loves our bleedin-heart history, Gerry said one night in his thickest mock accent.

Natalie did not want to tell him that she had bought one of

those pictures her first week here. She was going to hang it on the wall beside her dead man's sweater, but she didn't have a nail so she didn't hang it. By the time she had gotten a nail and hammer, though, she had also heard Gerry's opinions on what should be done to the stupid tourists who think they can buy such a simple picture and carry a nation's grievance in their back pocket. And to him Newfoundland was certainly a nation still.

So Natalie hid the photo she had bought at Piper's, but would pull it out on nights after she had downed a tetra pack of wine by herself and sat out with Lisette on the stoop: Lisette chain-smoking and telling Natalie stories to make her laugh and forget. But each time Natalie pulled out the picture of Mr. Malcolm Roger's house being towed across the water behind a Rodney loaded with the cut poles used to roll the house along the shore—each time she held that image in her hand of three children, a boy flanked on either side by two girls, looking out to the saltbox house sitting square on the water—she thought of pulling her life, the life she had before the fire, behind her to this new place. Mr. Malcolm Roger's move from Silver Fox Island to Dover, Bonavista Bay, became a mirror in which Natalie could look at her move away from Toronto, away from the night she lost her sense of smell and her best friend.

Biz tried to hold Natalie that day after the fire, after they had watched the tenement building burn for seven hours. But Natalie wouldn't let her. Her friend was strange to her. Like those memories of the night before and the two of them reaching down through the bars of the fire escape to grab the little hands of infants and children ferried up to them from frantic parents below whose own bare feet were sizzling on the hot iron—the fire mere feet from them through the broken windows of that floor below. They passed along children like bags of sand until their shoes began to melt and the people below them stopped trying to scramble up the burning fire escape because they couldn't go down for the flames. And those people started jumping ten storeys to save themselves. *Funny*, Natalie thinks, *I remember the sound of cracking shins over the roar of the fire a few feet below.* She remembers running across their rooftop chasing after Biz and almost faltering as Biz jumped the six feet to the next building and she came flailing after. Natalie knows they must have passed through the smoke-filled hall, but she doesn't remember it. She only recalls Biz's ankle and her fingernails digging into Biz's flesh as her friend pulled her along to another apartment where they knocked out a window and crawled out onto the fire escape.

That is all she has. That, and Biz trying to hold her after seven hours of watching the building collapse and hearing reports around them that twenty-three people were unaccounted for. One woman unhinged and screaming in Cantonese, wailing for someone lost in the fire, perhaps: her mother or father or her child gone back into the blaze for a toy. Natalie tries not to speculate. She tries not to fill her memories with stories.

But she cannot help doing so. She remembers three children, a boy flanked on each side by a girl, staring across the street at the inferno: watching for their home to come to them out of the burning deep. Not knowing that only blackened steel beams would remain by 8:00 a.m. when finally the fire was doused.

It seems unreal, the fire, even now, even after replaying it over and over in her head, trying to separate it from her imaginings of Hell and her ten thousand photos, lost, of fire and furious light. But she cannot. She can't even remember if she pulled away from Biz or if Biz pushed her away because she would not let her friend console her. She wandered. Or maybe it is that she is wandering now in her deep subconscious, so like the subway under Spadina where she wandered and wanders still—looking out into grey fog, smoke, speeding grey trains and swirling mist—unsure of where she is save that she's on a concrete platform looking out to sea for Mr. Malcolm Roger's boat to slip into view.

There were people in that fog and they had ash on their foreheads, and that's when Natalie reached her hand to her long hair now cut short and felt the ash and wondered *Why can't I smell it? Were all these people in the fire, or are these their ghosts?*

Then a flicker, a witchlight on the water, the flash of a television screen above the crowd on the subway platform, and images of her apartment building in flames, and she found it strange to see her nightmare played out on TV, to see herself onscreen talking to herself, looking out at herself, a City News microphone resting on her chin as she, clearly stunned, recounted what happened. And all the while people with ash on their heads, smeared across their brows, were streaming past and she lost sight of herself but heard a voice saying an old tenement building near Toronto's Chinatown burned to the ground this morning as thousands walk the streets marked with the sign of the cross on this Ash Wednesday.

Natalie turns and heads back to the apartment, thankful for a place where the language and stories somehow cradle her memories in a way that she would not let Biz cradle her on that Wednesday last winter. She is afraid to speak, as she is fearful to again take up her camera, which she bought with the money that a few people were smart enough to give her instead of their hand-me-down sorrows. For this is not her home, and Gerry inadvertently reminds her of this every time he rants about mainlanders and those who come from away because they want to live in a dream world—shot in sepia tones—of men in sou'westers and rubber boots and women always looking out to sea. He is right; she knows he is right. She is a CFA, a Come From Away, and she does want that world.

Not so that she can hold it in her back pocket in place of the ten dollars she paid for that photograph taken on a beach in Bonavista Bay in the sixties. Not so that she can own the image and claim to know the history. But so that she can sink into the image and let it creep into those empty crevices where there are no memories of what happened nearly a year ago. Let it fill her emptiness, with fog: *that scentless ocean smoke rolling off ships burned and sunk offshore here for hundreds of years.* Gerry wrote that and she told him it was good, but he only laughed and shook his head: said he was going to help Rod, their neighbour, load up his shopping cart of recyclables.

Natalie recalls his words, though. Even as she walks the trail up from Quidi Vidi past Cuckhold's Cove, halfway up Signal Hill and down past the hotel to the road that leads past the big grocery store that Gerry tells her used to be a hockey arena. She takes the trails from there to Bonaventure and then up the hill to Merrymeeting and home. It *is* home. *Now.* Lisette's there and makes Natalie a rum toddy as soon as she walks wet through the door—her clothes pasted to every curve of her body, which she can hardly feel for the cold.

While she warms in her pyjamas and wool socks hand-knit by Lisette's nan—the hot rum cupped in her red hands—she feels her skin tingle.

Out for a walk on this fine day, Lisette says smiling. And Natalie says yes and they drink their hot rums on cushions pulled from the couch. Gerry walks through the room and says they had better put those back when they're done, 'cause he will not live in a pigsty.

Too late, you townie, Lisette calls after him. You live in St. John's, remember, where we still flush our shit into the harbour!

And they laugh, blowing the steam off their mugs.

Later, after Lisette's gone to work downtown and Gerry's curled up on the couch with a new novel, Natalie slips into her room and pulls that photo out from under the bed. She lays it out on her rumpled sheets and takes the lens cap off her camera. Then she zooms in until the camera swallows the picture's frame and all she sees is a boat pulling a house over the water, like in her memories of standing on that shore with the sound of trains gone in the stillness ebbed only by her breath slipping out of her. This is how she remembers it.

Click.

H e is hoping to see her again today, the girl with the pale face and buzz-cut hair, wearing a heavy green army jacket that's three sizes too big for her. The QEII Library is packed this morning, but Hab has slunk his way into his usual spot near the back wall where he can see her if she shows up. He keeps thinking, *Just talk to her*, but what would they talk about? That his dad moved them to this frigging island right after his Great Uncle Ken's funeral and his cousin Kyle's closed-casket wake? Or maybe he could start by saying that his grandfather is famous in some circles as the wild Pentecostal evangelist who raised a girl from the dead.

Hab thinks that would probably be a clear conversational exit sign for her. But sometimes he wonders if she might show some interest and he'd have a chance to tell her that the resurrected girl was his mother, Anne.

His mom being raised from the dead was the myth that filled his head as a little boy, and it was a bragging right that none of his friends possessed. As he grew up, however, he'd tell the story not to impress people but to make them uncomfortable, conscious of their cadaver-cold skin, their palms clammy as fish flanks. Sometimes he would picture himself as an old-time prophet: cooking over a fire of smouldering dung, walking naked into the temple, sleeping for forty days with his face to the wall. He knew all the biblical stories in which it was the outcast who heard the voice of God, and he had thought maybe *he* would hear that voice someday as well. But that thought was blown away by Kyle's suicide, a few short weeks before they moved.

Sometimes Hab feels like his skull has been blasted out. Other times he doesn't feel anything at all, only a spreading numbness in his joints and an ache in his throat like he's parched for water.

Everything's been a blur for him since moving to St. John's. Paradise, actually, which he thinks is a pretty lofty name for a suburb. Hab tries not to think too much about Kyle, and being in school helps. He is not sure what he wants to do yet, degree-wise, but he enjoys his art class and likes surfing for images by local artists, the darker the better. Grey colouring that seems cold to some people smells like wood smoke to him when he looks at these paintings, and feels warm in his own skin. Not like when his sociology professor called his name and half the class smirked.

Habakkuk.

Hab for short.

His dad is a Pentecostal preacher so he gets the biblical naming business, but he is convinced Ezekiel or Zechariah would have been better picks. He was called Have-a-Cock in high school. Which pissed him off until something clicked and he became jaded and sarcastic—*I know I have a cock, dimwit*— and also, because of that, withdrawn.

He likes libraries. Not like his cousin Kyle, who preferred the bush. Hab knows he has a cousin here in Newfoundland who he's never met, his dad's brother's son. Hab doesn't even know his name, only that he's a handful since his parents split. Apparently blew up a shed out back of their house. That's what Patrick told Anne after a call from Hab's grandparents out in Fawkes Cove. They didn't say whether it was an accident. There wasn't a word after, though—typical of Patrick's side of the family. Hab and his parents don't talk about the Wisemans much. Either way, this cousin he doesn't know can't flush Kyle out of his mind. Hab sometimes thinks about hunting when he's in the book stacks because they bring to mind the quiet forests around Lemming's Lake and the backwoods shed where Kyle killed himself. That's why Hab spends more time in the common area at a computer: so he's surrounded by people, though he doesn't talk to anyone. Only looks up art online and watches for that girl with the buzz-cut hair who comes around everyday about this time.

He feels drawn to her but he's not sure if it is attraction so much as gravity. Even though when he first saw her he thought she must be gay or a cancer patient because of her shaved head.

She has become Hab's distraction, his only distraction since his dad moved them here last March so that he could take up a senior pastor's position at a new church down Kenmount Road, between St. John's and Mount Pearl. They meet in a little unfinished strip mall—*New Life*, the sign says. And Hab thinks that is kind of ironic because he wants nothing more than his *old life* in Peterborough back, and for Kyle to still be alive. Sometimes he Googles Kyle's name but nothing comes up. As far as the Internet is concerned, the kid who once made Hab put a whole frog in his mouth never existed.

When he searches his dad's name, the church website appears—a splash of blue behind his dad's picture, which makes Hab think of what his mom said. That marrying a Newfound-lander is like marrying a salmon—eventually they swim home. There was an edge in his mom's voice when she said it, half laughing, like she might cry. Hab tries to think of her words minus her tone but they float away, as if his mom is trying to speak under water.

Sometimes Hab thinks of swimming the sea, diving down, and in his mind he can see things clear as glass beneath the waves. Like an image he saw online of two tiny figures being sucked along in the tow of a great black whale larger than the cathedral-sized iceberg buoyed up and glowing in dark waters.

But the magic glow hisses and goes out like a cigarette dropped in water, and he wakes to the wet drizzly memory of moving here, a memory not of swimming but submersion. Like this image he has of his dad baptizing him and his mom. He

knows that this never happened but he feels like it did: his dad holding them under in the frigid salt water. That's when he thinks of that painting online, of the whale and the iceberg and the two drowning men, and he finds himself gut-hooked and hauled flailing into a strange peace. Same as how thinking of Kyle sometimes makes him feel less lonely.

Hab is Googling more paintings online now, thinking about a possible art minor, when he looks up and sees the girl in the big green jacket. She brings her laptop every day. And she drinks something dark from a Nalgene when she thinks nobody is watching.

She's looking for a spot now. The library's pretty full today, and her usual place, against the wall where the art hangs, is taken. Hab sees her look his way.

There's a horny couple sitting next to him. The girl's been grinding her hips against her boyfriend's pelvis as she sits on his lap, searching sociology topics—apparently oblivious to the fact that this outer-course is visible to the people sitting beside them.

Hab glances up again at the girl in the green jacket, who looks about ready to give up on finding a seat. Without thinking he turns to the copulating couple and says, Have you guys ever considered a threesome?

Why were those two so pissed off? the girl in the green jacket asks as she takes the vacated seat next to Hab.

I propositioned them, Hab says blushing. Apparently they're monogamous.

And you're a bigamist?

If it stops them from having sex on that chair.

This chair? she says.

Don't worry. I stopped them. Before … you know.

Thanks for that.

Hab turns back to his screen and wishes it would just suck him in. He can see her pull out her laptop—an Acer with a Republic of Newfoundland flag stickered to it. He is trying to be okay with the fact that he obviously killed the conversation and blew his only chance at talking to this girl when she turns back to him and says, Hi, I'm Natalie.

Natalie greets him at the door of her apartment on Merry-meeting. She's wrapped in her big green coat, her feet in wool socks pulled up over striped pyjama pants. She cups a wineglass in her hand, its broken stem jutting out between her fingers, making it look like her hand is pierced by the glass. She sees Hab eye it and says, Gerry broke it doing dishes yesterday.

That's a load of crap, Nat! a voice calls out from the living room.

Gerry? Hab asks, grinning.

Yes, Natalie whispers, flourishing the broken glass.

Hab can see that there's only a sip left in it and that Natalie's lips are purple. This is his first time at her apartment, and all he can think about is kissing her.

Thirsty? she asks, offering him the cup.

A little early, isn't it?

She shrugs, sips: You like ninja movies?

Sure.

Come on, we're watching *Drunken Master*—

The Legend of Drunken Master, Gerry calls from around the corner. Hab wonders as he kicks off his shoes who this Gerry guy is and why he's here in Natalie's apartment. He follows Natalie into the living room, where he sees a girl lounging on a green couch, her hair bobbed in a scrunchy, beside a wiry guy in a grey track suit with his bare feet up on the couch, balancing a beer stein on his knee. The room smells like Saturdays: sweat and coffee, with a winey tinge.

Gerry and Lisette, this is Hab. Hab, my roommates.

Hi, Lisette says.

Hab? Like the hockey team?

Like the Old Testament prophet Habakkuk.

Your parents hate you or something?

Lisette: Gerry, stop being a cunt.

You're being the cunt.

Not like your mother, hey.

What do you know about my mother's vagina?

I knows it egg-shaped your head.

Fuck off.

Love to.

Gerry and Lisette do not look at each other once during this exchange. Their eyes are fixed on the wobble and sway of Jackie Chan's inebriated martial arts as Chan's character crawls backward across a bed of coals.

Hab settles into the couch and eyes Gerry—trying not to be jealous of the guy's comfort here with these girls, with Natalie. But Gerry's gaze is fixed on the television screen, even as Natalie sheds her big green coat, spreads it on the floor, and plops down cross-legged in front of Hab.

There is a crash outside. The four of them can now hear men shouting over the television. Lisette pops up on her end of the couch and peers out the window.

It's that fat guy who lives above Rod next door, she says, cupping her hands around her eyes. Holy shit! He just cranked the guy with a metal bar! Nat, get the phone.

What is it? Gerry asks, scrambling for the window. They all pop up and peer outside just in time to see a man jump from a second-storey landing and crash onto the frozen snowbank below. They can hear their angry neighbour yelling *and tell them I fuckin told you so* as the other man runs away, kicking up slush behind him. They watch the big man, shirtless in the winter cold, spit over the rail and then drop something heavy into the snow below before going inside and slamming his door.

Should we still call them? Hab asks, his words fogging the windowpane.

Nobody died, Gerry says.

Natalie: Gerry has rules about calling the cops.

Gerry looks at her: That shit comes back to you. That's all I'm sayin.

See what I mean?

Just as they are about to sit back down, Gerry, Natalie, and Lisette see their other neighbour, the guy who picks up their recyclables, stick his head out of his basement apartment. He looks both ways, then peers up through big pop-bottle glasses at the porch above him before stepping out into the snow and picking up the big metal hook that the shirtless thug dropped.

They watch him carry the thing—a tire iron, maybe—back into his basement apartment and shut his door. Then Lisette drops back into her seat and says to Hab: Welcome to the neighbourhood. We'll understand if you can't stay.

Gerry snorts and Hab says he'll definitely be staying.

Nothing like this happens in Paradise, he says as they all settle back down into their seats and Gerry presses rewind on Chan's antics.

Natalie is sitting between Hab's knees. Her shirt is a swirl of colours, and Hab can see that she isn't wearing a bra. He also notices that this doesn't draw even a passing glance from Gerry, who seems to have no interest in Natalie, or anyone else now that the movie is back on. And that makes Hab more comfortable. So he snuggles in and they watch the film, Hab wondering if maybe they should have called the police about what they just saw. But his attention drifts back to Natalie's shoulders between his knees; they shake when she laughs and he can see the lines of her collar bones through her tie-dyed T-shirt.

Winter comes on, and they fall into each other like kids into new snow. Hab helps Natalie find a job at a group home through Workopolis and she reads aloud to him from a book of poems he came across in the QEII Library, her body tucked in behind his on the couch, his thumbs rubbing the arc of her feet, making her toes squirm inside rough-knit wool socks.

They're from Lisette's nan, she says. Made from boiled wool.

Hab's hangnails snag fabric tendrils. He loves the feel of Natalie's feet in his hands, the arch between ball and heel, her toes.

She makes him almost forget the cold feeling he's had since moving here, and her easy laugh puts Kyle at rest in his mind. He has often tortured himself since the funeral, wishing that he had made more of an effort to hang out with his cousin—fishing and hunting, doing the things Kyle liked to do. But he knows, deep down, that he and Kyle always lived in different worlds—a deep, quick-flowing river always rushing between them—and that it was not for lack of company that Kyle did what he did. Hanging out with Natalie makes Hab more aware of his own world, the one he is in now, which he feels newly born into—everything fresh, shocking and vibrant. The more time they spend together, the better he feels. No longer wishing he'd been more like Kyle, but missing him all the same.

He feels full and happy when he is with Natalie. They often split blood oranges between them, and she always tries to rub her sticky fingers over his face. Sometimes he lets her, after they wrestle themselves off her bed.

Her room is always dark because she keeps a sheet pinned over her window. She has no pictures on the wall, only one under the bed that she doesn't like to talk about. The only decor in her dark little room is a big woollen sweater stretched and pinned to the plaster. Hab doesn't ask about the sweater, and they talk of other things—of Gerry's writing and Lisette's new job at the Shamrock, on Water Street. But Hab wonders about it, the sweater, as he sits on her bed while Natalie is in the kitchen uncorking yet another bottle of wine.

Hab is not used to drinking, and the wine—the first he's ever tasted—is making him lightheaded and wobbly. Natalie finally got him to try it today, and he was surprised at how unlike grape juice it was. He gagged at first, but after a few swallows his cheeks started to burn and he felt blinky and loud. Natalie laughed, her voice rich, full. Hab wants to hear her laugh again, so he gets the idea to unpin the sweater from the wall and put it on and hide behind the door. Then maybe she will explain its significance to him, why she keeps it pinned to her wall.

The old sweater smells funny and he begins to sweat in his

hiding place, eyes darting from the rumpled bed to the pinholes in plaster where the sweater hung moments ago. Natalie is talking to Gerry in the living room down the hall and she laughs at something he says about their scroungy neighbour. Her laugh is full-bellied and rich—it rings like struck crystal. Hab can hear her singing now in the kitchen. He hears the clink of glasses. What he wants to do is startle her, make her jump and laugh, see her smile.

So he holds his breath when he hears her coming down the hall. He crouches behind the door, swallows a cough, and yells *Whaaa!* when she passes by.

She starts and almost spills the wine. Her eyes flash and spark as her face twists.

Get out, she says, inhaling, not looking at Hab but at the sweater he's wearing.

Hab stands there, stunned.

Wha—?

Get out! she says.

Nat?

I said get the *fuck* out!

There's no joking in her voice. Hab's face is burning and he's embarrassed, angry, confused. He peels the stupid sweater off and drops it on the floor, wondering what the hell got into Natalie. She is standing there shaking, a glass of wine trembling in each of her hands. She does not have to say it again because he leaves. He staggers down the hall and kicks his shoes on by the door, not looking at Gerry who's peering over the edge of his book. Then he stumbles and trips out the door.

The wind freezes the tears in his eyes as he tries to stop the pavement from tilting under him.

Days turn into weeks, and Hab cannot bring himself to phone Natalie or visit her apartment. He has no idea why she freaked out on him, why she threw him out. All he knows is that spending so much time in his own house in Paradise is driving

him mad. His mom is acting weird and doesn't really talk to him anymore when he returns from school.

Some mornings he has found her sleeping on the couch and wonders what is going on between her and his dad. He has even, more than once, found the computer on from the night before and a Kijiji page open listing fishing rods for sale. He's wondered at those times if he should get his mom a rod and reel for Christmas, or suggest this to his dad. But he often forgets about this during the day.

There was a time when maybe he would have told his mom about Natalie, but not now. He has put the *Taboo* game away in the closet downstairs because his mom doesn't seem interested in playing, and he's worried that she seems interested in little besides checking her Facebook page and typing away to her friends, or looking up fishing gear online.

He thinks she misses the mainland, Peterborough, her friends and family. He misses his Grandma and Grandpa Gunther and their small house on the hill overlooking Lemming's Lake. One day he finds his Grandpa Wiseman's address on an empty envelope in his dad's desk and looks it up on Google Street View. He scrolls the mouse up the street, waiting for the image to adjust and clear before advancing again, until he sees the house his father was born in, the match to the address on the empty envelope that he had written on the back of his hand. He sees a man in the yard, a thin man in blue work pants and a striped, collared shirt, but his face is blurred out.

Now that Hab thinks of it, he has never seen a picture of his Grandpa Wiseman, and he wants to see him—he wants to meet the man. So he prints off directions, asks if he can borrow the Malibu and he drives out along the Outer Ring to Torbay Road and north to Fawkes Cove, where his grandparents live at the top of Noseworthy Drive. He finds the house, recognizing it from the Internet, and he sits in the car waiting to see them sit down to dinner through their ground-level kitchen window.

When he sees his Grandpa Wiseman come in and sit down he gets out of the car and sneaks across the road, ducking his head beneath the windowsill. He works up enough courage, eventually, to peek over the sill and he sees his grandparents laughing, listening to a story Hab cannot hear. A man near his dad's age sits at the table with them. He wonders if this is his infamous Uncle Dale, who apparently dropped some acid as a teenager and wore out a pair of shoes running all the way from Fawkes Cove to Torbay, thinking he was being chased by accordion-playing pterodactyls.

He leaves before they are finished and drives home, wishing he could either turn around or head straight to Natalie's. He wants a place where he can laugh. He wants to share a meal with people who sit around the table and talk.

He wants a glass of wine, and for God to answer his prayers.

What he desires most is that hair-raising presence like a breath inside his breath that he has not felt since Kyle's death: that surging of the Holy Spirit in him that he could call up so easily as a kid in camp meetings, when he would spin around and dance and shout for rivers to be divided and walls to come crumbling down.

As he merges onto the highway and presses the gas pedal, he feels as if his body is falling away, being pressed back into the car seat. He feels for a brief second—the speedometer ticking past 140, the highway dark around him and headlights switched off—that this is what it will feel like on the last day, when the trumpet sounds and the faithful are enraptured and launched into eternity.

He takes his hands from the wheel, imagining the weight-lessness he will feel if his car flies over the embankment—like blowing out half his air and floating below the surface of Lemming's Lake, down from his Grandpa Gunther's place.

Drifting.

That's when the cop on the Allandale ramp clocks him at 143 and suspends his licence. You're from Ontario? the cop asks, looking at his card. Well this isn't the 401, kid. You hit a moose out here at that speed and its ass will take your head clear off. The officer tells Hab he's lucky the car won't be impounded.

You'll have a hard enough time explaining this to your parents, I imagine.

True enough: but aside from his dad's brief freakout, the repercussions weren't as bad as he anticipated. His parents don't seem to have the energy to pay much attention to him. They just grounded him for a month.

He didn't tell them he had half hoped to hydroplane.

But the months following are like prison, with brief parole stints to the university just to attend classes. Most days, his body feels heavy and numb and he thinks of himself as a fish in the gravel, flopping but going nowhere.

It has been four months now since Hab left the Merrymeeting apartment, staggered to the bus stop and returned home drunk for the first time in his life. Four months, and now he finds himself at the Sobeys on Merrymeeting, thinking that he needs to try and talk to Natalie again. Try and understand what happened that night he was buzzed and she freaked.

He is picking out two fresh blood oranges, trying to recall when it was that the thought to kiss Natalie first came into his head—her purple lips, the smell of the apartment, the broken stem of that chinked wineglass between her second and third fingers. He doesn't remember anything about the months since he last saw her. Except that he lost his licence and forgot to buy his mom a fishing rod for Christmas.

All he really recalls is sitting quietly in the corner one night after school and watching his mom stand catatonically with a sock in her hand over a laundry basket for five minutes while the potatoes boiled over on the stove. He eventually got up, but even his shuffling and clanging in the kitchen didn't move her. She just stood there. Frozen. Until the fire alarm went off.

Standing in line now with his two oranges, he remembers how, when he would come home from school, his mom used to ask him all kinds of questions about his day. They would talk, play *Taboo*, or cook supper together—slicing onions, peeling

A BLESSED
SNARL

potatoes, pouring mushroom soup over the pork chops—waiting for his dad's tired smile to appear in the front-door window. But his mom slipped into silence with the darkening autumn nights and stayed there through the winter. Lately Hab has found her wrapped in a quilt on the couch, shivering.

The magazines on the rack by the cash, which he usually scans for juicy headlines, say nothing to him today. His eyes are restless, looking for something meaningful, and he recalls that day, searching Newfoundland artists on the Internet, when he found an image of a lithograph by Gerry Squires. The bestial burst of white on pitch made him sweat suddenly so that his clothes stuck to the contours of his body, like that day in Natalie's bedroom months ago when he took down that old sweater from the wall.

He hadn't thought that any piece of clothing could mean more to her than her army jacket. But now he knows he was wrong. It has taken him these winter months to bring himself to the point where he feels he should try to talk to her again, even though she may not want to have anything to do with him.

He pays cash for the oranges and as he steps out into the piercing wind, pushing his hands deep into his coat pockets, he thinks of how he rarely saw Natalie without that oversized jacket, even in the warmth of her apartment on Merrymeeting. She said it was the first thing she'd bought when she came to Newfoundland, after she'd told her first taxi driver that she wasn't visiting but had come to live and he'd said, You'd best go straight out and buy a nice thick coat, my love.

Hab remembers her holding that thing tight around her body the first day they flirted in the library. He recalls how it hung open as she stooped to give him his first cup of wine—the shirt underneath the coat bright red and breathtaking. And he can see her even now slipping the coat off her shoulders when she went to the kitchen to open another bottle of wine, saying something about herself and the Holy Spirit in the eyes of a preacher's kid.

The snow is higher than Hab's boots and the wind wet in his face as he walks down Merrymeeting toward her house. He hates that there are no sidewalks in this frigging city in winter, just mammoth snowbanks that force him to walk warily against the traffic. At least he can see down the road a ways if any buses or trucks are coming. His fingers fisted around the two blood oranges are frozen, and he's wondering if she even still lives on this street.

Lisette answers the door. Her look goes from *yes* to *oh* as soon as Hab pulls his scarf from his face.

She's not in now, Lisette says.

Do you know where she's at?

She's workin. Downtown.

Whereabouts?

The Crazy Horse.

The strip club?

Yes.

Lisette looks at him hard, arms crossed, when he asks if he can come in and wait for Natalie to get home. She tells him that Natalie's not actually working at the Crazy Horse and that she just said that to see if he'd get all righteous and bugger off.

She waits, sees that Hab is not going anywhere despite her comment. Then she says: I thought first you might want to stay *'cause* I said she was workin down there. Come to think of it, it's not the most deterring lie, is it?

I did genuinely come to see her, he says.

You lose track of time?

What?

It's been four months.

Hab tells Lisette he wasn't sure if Natalie wanted to see him. He didn't tell her he had been stewing in his own stupidity all winter or that he had been swallowed by the discovery that his mom was having a cyber affair with a guy on Facebook. She'd left her browser open one day, on the computer in the basement, and he'd come home from school early while she was out running his dad to a church meeting because they only have the one car. He read her most recent unsent message to *Dave*. There was nothing graphic in the email but it was full of fondness for this man who was not Hab's father, who apparently *understood* his mom in a way that his dad did not—not since moving to this *stupid godforsaken rock*. She told Dave about the endless grey days and the smothering fog and the poor customer service and how everyone seemed nice when they thought she was a tourist but turned cold and distant when she told them she had come to stay. I wish I wasn't here, she wrote, and I wish for all the world I could just be with you now.

Hab was nearing the end of the email when he heard his mom pull in the drive. He had met her in the driveway after running from the basement and out into the cold. Her cheeks flushed red when she saw him.

You're home?

Yeah. Class was cancelled. I took the bus.

Where are you going?

For a walk.

How long have you been home?

Two minutes, he lied.

He couldn't look her in the eye when they spoke, and they hugged like two marionettes. She never left her browser open again. But the search history on the computer read Facebook from the top of the screen to the bottom.

Five to six times every day.

Who is this guy?

Why him?

Why someone other than Dad?

For fuck's sake!

What the hell is she thinking?

I mean, what in hell is she thinking?

He wished his mother was computer savvy enough to know how to delete her search history. He wished he had not found out, that her affair had remained *her* secret and not *their* secret. He hated being complicit in her indiscretion. Yet he couldn't say anything to his father.

He saw the distance between his mom and dad stretching wider, like the sea between the ferry and North Sydney that day they pulled away from the mainland, almost a year ago now. He saw it happening but wasn't sure if his dad did, because he was so busy with the church and happy enough with silence at home after seeing people and answering phones all day. Pastor Wiseman: none the wiser to his wife's longing for another man from away—*from home*.

Hab is deep inside himself when Natalie walks through the door, shucking off her scarf, mitts and boots before she sees him on the couch, staring back at her dumbly. He stands, still staring at her face. Her hair is growing in now and curling around her ears. Lisette strolls into the room and says: He comes bearing oranges.

Hab weakly holds one up and forces a grin.

Natalie looks at the calendar on the wall by the coats, marked red on dates that Gerry has assignments due, March looking like a scrawling massacre from across the room where Hab stands.

Thought you'd crawled off into a prayer closet somewhere, she says, her sarcasm steaming like the top of her head after she takes her toque off.

He wants to tell her that it was she who did the yelling and he who did the fucking off like he was told. But he bites his tongue, wondering, hyperventilating, fingernails digging into his palms.

And suddenly he doesn't know where he is, only that Natalie moves toward him and he crumples and buries his face in her neck and he's screaming inside—his hands clenched and sticky, the air sharp with the citrus sting of oranges.

When he comes to himself, Lisette is gone—to her room or outside for a smoke, he doesn't know. It's just him and Natalie. And there is no closeness between them. She's on one end of the couch and he's on the other—the space between them filled with

cushions and a dog-eared novel. She takes the crushed oranges from his hands and sets them on the coffee table, dripping. And then she gets up to fetch him a wet cloth to wipe his hands. And he says *sorry* when he receives it.

Mind telling me what's going on, Hab?

He tries to step around it with talk of the two oranges he hand-selected from the grocery store, of that book of poetry they'd read together and his cousin Kyle and the lithograph by Gerry Squires of what looks like a split cod—tortured flesh splayed out and flying. Natalie lets him talk and he drinks the wine she offers until he is drunk and soppy, tripping over his shoes as he tries to put them on, falling against the wall, saying that he has to catch the last *bluss* as he lunges through the door and feels the ground wonk out from under him.

When he wakes up, he's itchy all over from a coarse woollen sweater he's wearing. He is lying on Natalie's ratty green couch, stretched out and shivering. And then he sees Natalie come into the room in her pyjama bottoms, wrapped in her big green jacket—half her face red and wrinkled from her pillow—and she smiles. He knows now that the sweater is her apology. He can smell the citrus remnants still in the air, the surface of the coffee table moist and sticky still.

His head pounds as she sits down, pulls her knees up under her chin at the other end of the couch. She tells him the story of the sweater. A dead man's sweater, given to her by an old woman in Toronto after a fire destroyed everything else she owned. She tells him of wanting to throw the sweater away but being unable to. She didn't know why the sweater was sacred to her, but it was. That's why she yelled at him that day she saw him wearing it. They sit for a bit in the morning chill, shivering. The throbbing in Hab's head lessens and they begin to relax— make small talk.

So, how's the group home? he asks. Fun?

Terrifying. There's this psychotic kid.

SAMUEL THOMAS
MARTIN

51

Hab wonders what she means but she doesn't elaborate. Silence settles in and sweetens. There are half smiles and glances elsewhere. Slowly he becomes comfortable just sitting there. Then she gets up and walks to his end of the couch and tells him to scooch down. She slides herself in behind him like she used to do, and he feels her open the flaps of that big army coat wide, as if they were her wings, and wrap them around his shoulders. His back to her torso and not a word passes between them for a long time.

H*e's a queer old goat*, Gerry thinks of their scroungy neighbour, Rod, who has just come by in his bright-orange coveralls and pop-bottle glasses, pushing a shopping cart, to ask for their recyclables. Gerry is expecting Natalie home from work soon, wondering where she hid the remote this time. *For frig's sake, Nat, how am I supposed to watch the news?* He runs his hands around the couch cushions, finds a loonie and an empty Bic lighter before spying the remote half-hidden under the novel Natalie is reading. He turns and clicks, and hears Rod's voice over the old TV's low hum, calling for his cat outside:

Snuggles!

Gerry loves the juxtaposition of Rod's pockmarked face, scruffy beard, and bleary, magnified eyes with his cat's cuddly name. What a guy, he mutters as he heads back into the kitchen to make himself a cup of coffee.

Waiting for the kettle to boil, he thinks of Rod telling him about some punks who had spray painted the word RAT in big black letters on his door the night before. They think I'm somebody else, Rod kept saying, looking away and patting his pockets for cigarettes that weren't there. So Gerry gave him their pop cans and wine bottles and one of Lisette's cigarettes from her coat hanging by the door.

The kettle whistles and Gerry pours the scalding water over the grounds in the French press, stirs the froth, and caps the contraption.

He can hear the TV popping as it warms to life in the other room, even while his head is stuck in the fridge looking for a can of condensed milk.

After he walks into the living room it still takes three minutes for the screen to brighten. Piece of junk, he mutters. But he can hear the weather report, even though the picture is hazy—snow and blowing snow for the Avalon, Mary's Harbour, Clarenville, Grand Falls–Windsor, Deer Lake, the Wreckhouse and Port aux Basques.

He stirs in three lumps of sugar as a story comes on that sours his mood. But it hooks his attention, so he keeps clicking between CBC and NTV to get all the details: Heathrow; a seized laptop; 783 child porn photos.

For Christ's sake, he thinks. *Again?*

The more he watches, the more he boils inside, swigging his coffee, rocking back and forth, transfixed.

Natalie walks through the door just in time to hear Gerry yell at the TV: I catches one, I'll kick him till he pisses blood!

The thought of Gerry kicking anyone to death makes Natalie snicker. The guy is five foot two, a hundred fifty pounds, and as unthreatening as a llama. *All he can do is spit at you with words*, she thinks.

He is a scathing critic when it came to writers he doesn't like, sure.

But violent?

Not so much.

Gerry is always giving Natalie the gossip on his favourite writers in town, telling her why he thinks poets should be interred before being read, and going on and on about which red wine went with which Stephen King novel—Chianti for *Carrie*, cabernet for *The Shining*, and burgundy for *The Stand*. So the outburst doesn't really shock her. She just says hello and gets no response as she settles into the couch with her book. Nothing new there: Gerry doesn't talk to anyone when he watches the news and drinks his coffee, but the dark mood he is in makes her watch him over the edge of her book.

He flips between two news broadcasts for the next hour—searching for what, Natalie doesn't know—all while swigging strong coffee from a beer stein until his hand begins to shake so badly he has to put the mug down and cross his arms.

When the news ends at seven he shoots upright, puts on his jacket and boots, and steps out into the winter night, slamming the door behind him.

Natalie gets up, goes to ring Lisette at work, or Hab, but puts the receiver back in its cradle. What is there to say? *Gerry's mad.* She can imagine their responses.

Lisette: Well, will the wonders of Jesus never cease?

Hab: So Gerry's being Gerry.

But uneasiness pricks at the back of her neck—a needle stitching with every tick of the clock.

On Elizabeth Avenue, Gerry comes across Rod trying to push his shopping cart loaded like a pack horse with bulging bags of pop cans and glass bottles. He's on his way to the Evergreen Recycling Depot. Rod once told Gerry he could get fifty to seventy bucks on a regular outing: enough for a couple of forties of rum. Gerry asks Rod if he needs any help pushing the cart.

Yes, b'y. That'd be good now.

And they push the cart, the two of them, down Elizabeth from Bonaventure to the depot. Gerry flags traffic to stop so Rod can cross: the old drunk walking gingerly on his left foot because of a bunion.

Gerry watches Rod count his earnings as he empties the cart, sorting tin from glass. And he thinks of helping his father do the same thing when he was a boy. Regatta Day in August was always his dad's big haul. Quidi Vidi Lake would be jammed with vendors selling everything from popsicles to hotdogs to vindaloo. He remembers following his dad around, dragging a clear plastic bag behind him, picking pop cans out of trash bins, off the grass by the bandstand, out from under bushes along the

lakeshore. All day collecting recyclables under the hot August sun, hearing the gun go off occasionally to signal the start of a new race, then the announcers broadcasting the results above the din of the crowd.

Rod's greasy hair spiking out from under his beanie, his wrinkly red neck, reminds Gerry of his dad's unwashed hair matted beneath a mesh-backed Irving hat with a Kiss button through the I. When he sees Rod collecting the money he remembers his dad each year promising him a swim in the lake after the races and a hotdog for helping out. Standing in the recycling depot, rank with the syrupy smells of stale Coke and flat beer, Gerry thinks of that old shepherd dog with the gamey back legs lunging stiffly into the lake after the ducks. He's twelve and chasing after the dog, splashing into the lake, ducks scattering, taking flight; and his father's hand is on his collar pulling him back up the shore and cuffing him for getting his shoes wet. He never did get a hotdog at the Regatta, except the one he picked out of the trash, half the wiener missing and the end of the bun soggy with Sprite.

Gerry sees something in Rod though that makes him think *This man is not like my father*. His dad: charged with assault on nine-year-old Trudy, Gerry's childhood playmate in Buckmaster's Circle. He's not sure if he imagines more than what happened but he has these snapshots in his head. His dad patting Trudy's blonde hair twisted in a rough ponytail. His dad giving Trudy a twenty-dollar bill so she could get him smokes at the store and a chocolate bar for herself. His dad catching Trudy in his arms and hauling her up onto his lap and pinching her armpits.

But after the Troke boys began taunting Gerry, calling his dad a pervert, saying his dad had fingered Trudy under her dress and that it was good the bugger was in prison, he started to wonder if his dad's kindness was a way of buying his love—making his dad appear like a normal father when he really wasn't like that at all.

Gerry hasn't spoken to his dad in years. But when he sees Rod he sees the good that he remembers in his father: the goofy grin, the hoarse voice, the joking manner. He thinks Rod is too gentle to be like his dad—at least, how he imagines him to have been—even though Rod has on occasion ribbed him and asked him if he's getting any.

Any what, Rod?

Pussie, b'y. I knows this whore down the road.

I live in a house with girls.

Oh. This one, she'll do ya in the graveyard.

The what?

Provides her own condoms for a toonie.

Gerry had thrown up a little in his mouth then but he had let Rod write out the woman's number on the back of his hand. He'd even given it a ring at three in the morning and heard a smoker's cough on the other end and a baby crying. After that he went and washed his hands with bleach to get the number off. Still, knowing Rod had done God knows what with that lady, Gerry couldn't compare him with his dad. There was a line there somewhere. And he knew he'd done things he would rather stayed hidden. Like Rod's prostitute: as long as Gerry didn't see her, didn't know who she was, she could remain a crude joke, the subject of a weird conversation with a drunken cripple—a smoky voice on a staticky line. But Trudy had been real. He'd felt her sweaty forehead pressed against his when they sat cross-legged from each other in the crawl space between their houses and she had said, Just let's sit like this till you're ready to kiss me then. Trudy's hands had held his. And his father had held her squirming little body next to his sunburned chest: Tigger tattooed over his left breast, the cartoon tiger wearing a pirate's hat and eye patch; a plastic rosary he wore as a necklace.

She's done, b'y! Rod's voice nets Gerry's attention.

Where to?

The old man looks at him through thick glasses, brown eyes sunken but gleaming soft like Labradorite stone in clear water.

To Sobeys, I guess.

The grocery store is code for liquor, Gerry figures as he walks with Rod in the darkening cold—the clatter of cart wheels on

SAMUEL THOMAS MARTIN   57

pavement driving them inside themselves so that when they reach the liquor store and Gerry asks Rod what he wants, Rod stalls.

I ... I ...

Rum?

Yes.

Rod smiles crooked as a broken finger and Gerry ducks inside to buy a forty of Lamb's, leaving Rod's earnings in the old man's pockets.

The wet cluck of Rod's tongue after a deep slug of the rum makes Gerry a little squeamish about taking the bottle Rod offers on their walk home along Merrymeeting, pushing the cart, dodging traffic and puddles.

He nods as he takes the bottle, telling himself the warm brown liquid running down the side onto his fingers is liquor, not saliva. He swigs deep and hands the bottle back to Rod, who is grinning, gap-toothed.

Rod's apartment is small, a split basement smelling of cigarettes, Rub-A535, and cat piss. Gerry scans the crusty black carpet, Folger's can ashtray, yellowed couch missing a cushion, and black mould running down the far wall from the only window. The bathroom is straight ahead of him, the toilet dead-tooth brown. The bedroom is off to the right, door almost shut but for an old shirt hung on the doorknob and stuck in the jamb.

You can leave your shoes on, Rod says as he limps to the kitchen counter and clinks two mugs out of the sink of slimy dishes. Gerry watches him run them under cold water, rinse out old tea stains, scrub them with his pinky finger, then dry them on his pant leg before pouring a glub of rum into each. Then Rod puts the kettle on to boil and pulls a bag of brown sugar down from his doorless cupboard.

What are you at, Rod?

Toddies. Make the rum stretch a bit. Cold night, you know.

Rod ladles a heaping soup spoon of brown sugar into each mug. Then he tells Gerry to go on and sit down. Reaching for

the kettle, he says, Always meant to have you over for a drink.

No worries, Gerry whispers on his way to the couch, his shoes crunching on the carpet beneath him. You lived here long, Rod?

Oh, five or seven years.

Rod puts the toddy into Gerry's hands, pulls the middle cushion to the other end of the soiled couch and sits down, kicking his sore foot out in front of him.

That toe bother you much? Gerry asks.

Oh yeah.

The sweetness of the drink and the liquor's lingering burn settles Gerry into his corner of the couch. He looks about the room, seeing it as much by scent as sight. *How does he live like this?* he wonders, glancing at Rod, who looks up from blowing on his mug, his glasses steamed and him smiling.

Need windshield wipers, he says, laughing.

Looks like.

You got a dog?

No.

Oh. I got a hambone in the freezer. Boiled it last week. Thought a dog might like it.

Rod looks down at the toddy steaming between his two big brown hands, half shaking, ripples catching the yellow light. Gerry glances from Rod to the door window and jumps when he sees a gaunt, bearded face staring in at them from the dark.

Rod! Someone's at your door.

Rod looks over his shoulder at the window and says, Oh that's Mick, my drinkin buddy. He waves and Mick comes through the door, says hi and pulls out a half-full whiskey bottle from the front pocket of his hooded sweater. Rod leans into Gerry: Good he brought some this time, 'cause he usually drinks me dry.

Rod straightens and says: Hi, Mick.

Roddy, you got a guest. Who's he?

My neighbour. Gary.

Gerry.

He helped me out with the cart today.

You do well?

Enough, Rod says, letting his hand fall on his pants pocket, over the hidden wad of bills tied together with an elastic band.

Sociable then, Mick says, holding up his glass half full of rye and clinking it with Rod's and Gerry's mugs. Sociable, they all say before taking a drink.

The night comes on like heartburn, drink after drink making Mick louder, Rod giggly, and Gerry mellow until Mick announces he needs to piss and stumbles around the corner. Rod's continued ha ha ha sounds to Gerry like an outboard putting and his own thoughts unreel again into the dark of the early-edition news, his right fist jigging his empty mug up and down, imagining smashing it in that archbishop's face, which becomes his father's face, and he thinks his dad looks a bit clownish in priestly garb. The thought vaporizes in a loud belch that brings a gulp of rum back up his throat and makes him cough, his eyes watering.

Mick trips back into the room, a thumb to his nostril as he sniffs loudly. His mouth looks like it's puckered around a crabapple and there's white powder on his lip. He sneezes and then smiles and Gerry can see that half his teeth are rotted away.

Roddy, I lost my keel.

Wha—?

There's piss on the floor.

Least it isn't shit, hey! Rod says, raising his empty mug to Gerry, who's not sure that what was said was worthy of a toast, but he clinks his mug anyway.

Mick mumbles something about his daughter as he laughs and coughs, something about her being home alone now and the weather getting nasty. He says he should go check and see that she hasn't lit the cat on fire. Little pyro, that one, Mick says sniffing, tipping the last of his bottle into his cup, his hand trembling. Learned it from that psycho kid, used to live up 'round the corner with his mother. She'll burn me alive one night, I swear.

He pulls out a lighter and a bent cigarette.

Best go check on her, I guess, he mumbles around the cigarette in his pursed lips, drawing between words as he holds the flame cupped to the hand-rolled tobacco tube.

Looks like a limp dick, Mick.

Mick stares at Rod, his eyes bugging out of his head. He draws long, and then spins the cigarette in his mouth so it's bent up.

How do ya like me now? he says, jittering, the bent cigarette scrawling his words in smoke. A trickle of blood runs out of his nose and down his whiskered, white-powdered lip, but he doesn't notice until he sees it on his cigarette.

Go see about that girl, Rod says as Mick reaches for the door, wiping his nose with his palm—the skin of his hand cracked and caked with grease. Mick exits with Rod's cup in his hand but leaves the empty bottle on the counter. The door slam breaks Rod's stare, his eyes swampy and witchlit, and he hauls himself off the greasy couch to get some more rum. Gerry hears Rod unscrew the bottle, the clink and *glub* as he empties the forty-ouncer, his swill and swallow, his long, liquidy burp.

Oh, well ....

What's that? Gerry asks, blinking.

Mick, he ....

Gerry peers across the room at Rod, who's leaning against the counter, holding his mug to his chest, staring at the door. The room seems hazy to Gerry, the air thick. His stomach is turning so he looks for something closer to concentrate on, to steady himself. A lamp with a duct-taped cord but no shade stands on the crusty carpet three feet from his shoe. A plastic rosary hangs from the switch. And he thinks of his dad's necklace, his Tigger tattoo.

You Catholic, Rod?

I used to work security for this wharf.

Gerry keeps staring at the lamp's darkened bulb, thinks *What?* He nods but doesn't look up as Rod keeps talking, not facing him but still staring out the window after Mick. Gerry

can hear wet snow pecking the windowpane.

There were these cats come around our lunch room each day in the warehouse, Rod says, his voice phlegmy. So I dipped my sandwich in rum and fed it to the cats. Seen them stumble and stagger. Geez, I tell ya. You should've seen them. When I told my boss for a laugh he said he'd have to let me go for drinking on the job and I said, No fuckin way. I quit.

So, Gerry drones, dropping his chin to his chest, keeping his eyes on the burned-out lamp, where'd you get the rosary?

Oh, well ... you don't have cats, do ya?

No. No cats.

He feeds it to her.

Who? Gerry asks, his twelve-year-old fingers fisted in his dad's necklace in a drunken memory and his dad saying *Easy there, my son.* He wants his father's necklace and his dad is saying he needs the beads so that God knows he's sorry. He faintly hears Rod say, Micky's girl.

Gerry looks up and Buckmaster's Circle fades into Rod's apartment. He sees Rod drain his glass and lick the rim, cluck his nicotine-stained tongue. The older man leans on the counter and lifts his sore foot.

Used to live up on Signal Hill, Rod says, checking his hand. There is a ketchup stain on the counter now squished between Rod's fingers. He licks his hand as he goes on with his random story: Went sledding down into Quidi Vidi. Fought with the Protestant kids after school. I could take on three at a time. Pussies. Drank once with this buddy who said he used to talk baymen into burning their neighbours' houses. For cash or something. Government cheque.

Rod makes a spinning motion with his finger and then stops: Did I cash my cheque this week? Yeah, he says inhaling. Yeah, I did. I remembers now.

Cash it or bank it?

Oh well. Yeah. My family moved out to Bay Roberts, hey.

When?

While back. I stayed 'cause I was fourteen and working.

Cleaning the church on Patrick Street. That's how it happened. Eventually. Only the once.

What's that? Gerry burps, watching Rod swipe his finger through the ketchup and stick his finger between his lips.

Oh well. You know. It's gettin late, hey.

Gerry looks up to see Rod biting his fingernail. Yeah, he says, watching Rod spit in the sink, she's gone, b'y. Gone. He says this but he's thinking *I'm gonna write about him. I'm gonna put Rod in a fuckin story.*

Rod looks at the empty bottle he's holding by its neck. Come on over anytime, he says. We'll do some more drinkin, you and me.

Sure, Gerry says, moving to the door.

Maybe Mick'll stay away, hey.

He's a joker, that one.

Yes, b'y, he's that.

See ya round, Rod.

It's screamin like cats out there, Rod says as Gerry opens the door and a gust of wind blows wet snow in his face. The wind whistles in the power lines, and the lamppost down the street is creaking and shivering its light. Gerry tramps through the snow, his cheeks hot and his hands cold, his mind spinning a story about Rod already and he knows he's got to see the guy's apartment again. Sober this time, so he can take it all in. Get it right. He looks back and sees Rod peering out at him: the old drunk's hands cupped around big pop-bottle glasses, peering through his window. Rod's breath fogs the glass and obscures his wrinkled face.

Natalie heard Gerry come in last night, late. He banged from wall to wall while staggering down the hall, singing and drumming the doors as he passed by.

I'm a Newfoundlander born and bled and I'll be one till I'm dry.

I'd even be an Icelander for sixteen bottles of rye.
I'm sure to heave with me head stuck in the can.
There's no place I'd rather be, except maybe in Japan.

She waited until she heard him snoring and then slipped into his room, untied his boots and placed them back by the door. He smelled of cigarette smoke and rum, and she told herself she'd give him hell in the morning for traipsing slush through the apartment.

But she forgot about that and now Gerry is on the couch by the window, cradling a cup of coffee, his eyes bloodshot.

Rough night? she asks, picking up her novel.

Gerry doesn't move, only wriggles his toes further under the couch cushions. His fingers flex on his mug and he farts.

A writing day then? Natalie asks, flipping a page and finding her spot, right after those two idiots accidentally shot the head off the one guy's son.

Natalie knows Gerry's patterns by now: during a hangover his mind percolates. Only the thoughts you have to force yourself to think through a ripping headache are worth writing down, he'd told her once, chewing on a whole roll of antacids.

So you're like a drunken Jedi? Lisette had asked.

Gerry would have told her to fuck off but his mouth was foaming.

Natalie watches him over the edge of her book: his fingers tapping his coffee stein like he's typing away at his laptop.

Yep, definitely a writing day.

Through the window Gerry is watching Rod rattle down the newly snow-ploughed street. Mick's daughter is in Rod's shopping cart. Gerry had watched the girl come out of Rod's apartment with him. She was wearing his pop-bottle glasses, and he was pretending to feel around blindly for her, throwing up handfuls of wet snow until he caught her in his big hands and hoisted her into his cart. At which point he took his glasses back from her dirty, bruised face.

Gerry didn't see the girl come to Rod's apartment and he has no idea how long she has been there, but now he has more than just creative reasons to break in. And he's wondering if Rod locks his door.

When Rod and the girl are finally out of sight, Gerry steps down off the couch and crosses the living room to kick on his boots.

Where are you going? Natalie asks, chucking her book angrily to where Gerry had been sitting below the window.

What's wrong with the book? Gerry asks.

He died. The David guy.

You knew that from page one.

It's how he died that pisses me off.

That's life, though, hey. Shit happens.

And where are you off to?

See if I can't make some shit happen.

Gerry grips the rusty dog chain that runs from a hole in Rod's door, where his deadlock should be, up over the support beam of the green, cracked plastic awning, where two links are hitched together with a combination lock. But the lock is un-clicked and the dial is missing. *Nice home security, Roddy*, Gerry thinks as he undoes the chain and creaks the door open, his hand on the word RAT spray-painted across the door's windowpane.

Stupid punks.

He steps inside and lets the chain chink into a pile at his feet. The apartment is in the same condition as the night before, except the dirty dishes that clogged the sink are piled on the counter now. Mick's empty whiskey bottle is sitting upside down in a glass tumbler and there's a brown skim of liquor in the cup. *Good to the last drop, hey Rod*, Gerry thinks as he opens the bedroom door.

The smell of body odour and piss makes him gag. A faint bleach smell wafts from a red mop bucket that has a straightened length of coat-hanger wire set across it, pierced through a Pepsi can half coated in peanut butter. Gerry looks in the bucket and sees three dead mice, clumps of their grey fur floating around their tiny bodies. He hears a purr and feels Snuggles rub up against his leg. The cat doesn't even glance at the peanut-buttered Pepsi can. There's an angry hiss and he looks down. Snuggles hisses again, shows her teeth. He gives her a kick, making her jump and dart through the doorway.

Gerry's family never had a cat when he was growing up, though there were lots that roamed the neighbourhood—wasted, feral things with half-chewed ears and matted fur. His dad thought they were filthy and shed too much, that dogs were better. But they never had a dog, either. Dogs cost too much to feed and in town you had to pick up their crap.

You'll never find me stooping to pick up an animal's shit, his dad had said, reaching for another beer out of a case he was splitting with his neighbour, Trudy's dad.

But you picked up people's shit and had me haul the bags, Gerry thinks as he crunches across the carpet to Rod's closet. The sliding door has come off its runner and is leaning against the wall, a cracked bootprint near the bottom. He searches the bizarre contents of the closet: items Rod must have picked up on his rounds. A naked Barbie doll minus a leg, the top half of it dipped in purple paint. An extendable grappling hook beside a broken toilet seat.

Frayed jumper cables.

Buddy doesn't even have a car, Gerry thinks as he moves the cables and finds a rusty old tire iron. He picks it up and reaches across to the bed, using the iron to lift Rod's blankets. The mattress sags in the middle and curls at the corners. Gerry looks under it and sees that the wire mesh of the bedsprings is held together with black zip ties. The mattress has a faint, brown body print on it: Rod's sweaty ghost from hot summer nights or three-day drunks or whatever he does with the smoky-voiced prostitute.

Looking at the body print, Gerry can almost feel his dad's thick fingers on the back of his neck, telling him that if he pissed the bed he'd rub his fucking face in it 'cause he wasn't getting a new mattress.

You're sixteen, dammit!

Gerry flexes his fingers around the tire iron, wishing he'd had something like it handy that day, something to swing at his father's head.

He snorts and scuffs toward the living room, trying to take in the whole space, the whole filthy apartment, so that he can recreate it on the page. He passes by the washroom and sees the yellowed linoleum peeling around the base of the brown toilet sweating with moisture from the bowl. And he sees there's water in the kitchen sink. Material: pink fabric. He flips the one couch cushion and sees cigarette burns on the underside. *Pink?* The plastic rosary is gone from the lamp now and ... *pink?* Gerry glances at the sink, takes three steps back, and looks in. He hooks the curved end of the tire iron into the brownish water and fishes out a small set of girl's panties. Pink and crotch stained.

He can't tell if the stain is a skid mark or blood. He drops the tire iron, and it shatters the mug he drank out of last night. He picks up the panties and holds them up to the weak afternoon light coming through the window.

What in the ...

And then he hears it: the cart clattering back down the street. Speculation ignites adrenaline and Gerry grabs the tire iron, scraping his knuckles on broken ceramic. He can hear Rod hauling his cart up over the snow bank.

He is shaking.

All he can think about is Trudy being hauled up onto his dad's lap and Rod hugging Mick's daughter and scooping her up in his shopping cart. Rod's whistling stops at the door and Gerry crouches by the sink. He can see Rod's shadow on the blackened carpet coming through the spray-painted window, can see there's no trace of the little girl with him now.

You're the same as him.

Rod calls, Hello? Who's in there?

You sick mother—

Hello?

The door creaks and cold winter air surges in around Gerry, who is crouched just out of Rod's sight. He shivers as Rod takes another step. He hooks the collar of his T-shirt on his nose, to hide his face. Then he swings around and cracks the iron across Rod's knees. The old drunk comes crashing to the floor.

Rod looks up at his attacker. His glasses are crooked on his nose, one eye magnified and the other minuscule, fear wet in both.

Gerry sees himself for an instant reflected in Rod's misty lenses. He sees his father's pitiful face pressed against the hood of a patrol car. He sees Trudy, Mick, Mick's little girl. He sees a scumbag in bright orange coveralls wearing a black plastic rosary.

And he starts swinging.

Natalie finds Gerry sitting on the couch late the next morning, rubbing his bruised knuckles and fingering a cheap plastic necklace with a little cross on it. She can't imagine him being religious—*superstitious maybe, but Catholic?* She laughs to herself and looks outside, seeing that more snow has fallen overnight. *The Telegram* lies spread open on the coffee table, and Gerry's stein rests on the opening story. Natalie says good morning but Gerry walks out of the living room and down the hall, clicking the necklace as he goes. He's left his coffee behind, the milk skim congealing in the cold.

Untouched.

Natalie hears a door close. Then she sees Snuggles dart from the kitchen down the hall and disappear into the bathroom.

Odd.

She moves Gerry's mug and sees a story about a man who's been beaten nearly to death in his apartment. It speculates that the man is known to police and was singled out as a police informant concerning a thug living in Rabbittown.

The article says the man was found half frozen at 4:00 a.m. by his friend who had just come up from downtown. The door to the victim's apartment had been left open by his assailant. He'd been struck repeatedly with a tire iron and half strangled with the cord from his own lamp.

A suspect has been arrested, Natalie reads, flipping to the end of the section to pick up the rest of the story, *but the RNC are still investigating.*

She hears the quick *glip* of a police siren just in time to look up through the window and see a cruiser pulling away from the neighbouring house.

Rod's place.

She gets up and kneels on the chair in front of the window, looking out.

A broken window. Police tape. A gull perched on an old shopping cart half buried in a drift. Blood on new snow.

The weatherman's hand sweeps from Labrador down Newfoundland's fanged north coast to St. John's, his finger squiggling from there down to Renews on the southern edge of the peninsula: the sea white against green land. He's talking about winds *rifling* in from the north. The pack ice circling the island on the TV map feels like a tight collar to Patrick, choking him. This is the first time he has felt this hemmed in, this claustrophobic, in his own home.

It was a heart attack, that's what Gerta said over the phone, and that was enough for Anne to call Porter Airlines and book her ticket back to Ontario. Her whirling about the house Patrick took as worry for her father Gurney, but since Hab showed him Anne's Facebook file he knows she has other reasons to get out the house that was once *their* house.

Patrick is alone, and a shot of the pack ice jammed into Middle Cove on the TV makes him feel that much more isolated from the world. Funny, because as a kid he would hop the ice pans and copy quick-like from one to the next. But he's spent enough time away from the sea that the idea of venturing out onto the slob ice now is terrifying—almost as much as admitting to his new congregation that his wife has left him.

He has long since sewn up his tongue to keep from swearing and save face as the new Pentecostal pastor in town, but *fuck*, he thinks. How did he not know his wife was having an online affair after months of listless sex, silent dinners, her pillow damp to his touch some mornings, though she always flipped it before heading to the shower before him?

He had thought she was just missing home and would eventually come around, once things were more settled.

But no, more was going on than that. *Obviously.*

And Hab knew about the affair. Knew for months and said *nothing* to him, not until the day they came back from the airport.

Dad, I think you need to see something.

He said it gently, like the voice Patrick used when Hab was seven with a scraped knee, sitting on his dad's lap on the concrete step outside their red brick house back in Peterborough, long before they moved to St. John's.

Patrick had kept the Promised Land clichés to himself when speaking of the move, but the thought of partridgeberry jam in late fall, showing Hab his old home in Fawkes Cove along the Killick Coast, and driving the Irish Loop in summer—brushing his fingers over those fossils at Mistaken Point—those thoughts married like milk and honey in him.

That dream of coming home seems like a farce now: treacherous, slick as black ice underfoot. *Home.* Thinking of it is as painful as the time he slipped on the slob ice and broke his front teeth. He was thirteen: strings of blood blowing across the ice like splashed ink on one of those weird paintings Hab likes so much.

Patrick has no idea why.

But when he thinks now of his hope for happiness then, he remembers his broken teeth—the briny taste of blood, Anne's betrayal like a sucker punch. He imagines a headline for this week's church bulletin: *Today's message is on the wiles of Jezebel.* It's a weak mental jab. And he keeps imagining her plane going down and her screaming and wishing she'd never left. He imagines dipping his finger in her blood and, with his eyes closed, painting her name on the oval of an airplane window, longingly, his hand conducting emptiness as he sits on the couch here in the dark. Motionless. The room silent. Stern. Because there had been the writing on the wall, all that time she spent in the computer room.

Why didn't Hab say anything?

Patrick feels like David betrayed by Absalom, but he also feels like Absalom, hanging from his long hair tangled up in the tree. Clumps of knotted hair ripping from his skull as he swings, feeling ungrounded in his thoughts, helpless against grief: that stabbing pain, like a sword between his ribs. But Absalom was the traitor, the backstabber. *My companion*, David had raged in one of his psalms, *my companion stretched out his hand against me.* Anne is the one Patrick would like to see swinging from that tree. *She has broken her covenant.* She is the one who ran away—the one who pierced him—not Hab. But why, he keeps asking himself, why didn't his son say anything?

And why didn't I see?

Patrick had taken Hab out for a hike at Flatrock just after Anne had left. The last big snowstorm of the season hit them hard and unexpectedly while they were out on the point and had to take shelter in an old army bunker—holed up with some punk kid from around the bay who was already huddled in the bunker when he and Hab had staggered in, snow-covered and half-frozen. They all sat in silence for hours, waiting for the storm to die down enough to make it back to the car—the kid in jackshirt, jeans, and ice-coated workboots. Patrick had wondered, as he sat there watching the kid spin a silver skull ring on his bruised knuckles, if the lad had been out on the sea ice before the storm struck. Thinking back on that day, Patrick remembers longing to be out on the ice himself, leaping from pan to pan.

When he thinks of the bunker he feels trapped, like David huddled in his cave, hiding from Saul who wanted him dead. He knows this is a silly comparison. No one is hurling spears at his head. But he feels hunted, betrayed, deserted.

He had offered the kid in the bunker a ride after the storm died down, but the punk had *hmphed* and walked off into the dark, hands deep in his pockets—didn't say a simple thank you for the shell of Patrick's coat thrown over him while he slept in the cold.

As thankless as Saul after David spared his life, Patrick thinks, though he knows he's being self-righteous in comparing himself to the Hebrew king. But he can't help it. He can't make sense of his life without seeing it enmeshed in the biblical story. The problem is that he'll slip into David's skin, see himself as a man after God's own heart. But then he'll remember how much of a bastard David was at times, and he finds himself more convicted than comforted. He'll picture what Anne has done as Michal's betrayal of David, when the shepherd king danced before the Ark of the Covenant. He has preached on the passage many times: David stripping down to his linen ephod—what Patrick liked to call his priestly Fruit-of-the-Looms—and dancing furiously before the Lord. Laughing, singing, sweating, foaming at the mouth, praising God and doing what he felt in his heart he should do—just as Patrick had done in moving here and starting the church. He had danced, preached, worked long hours, sacrificed ... and Anne had left him. He thinks of Michal's barrenness after she ridiculed her husband for dancing half naked before the servant girls. Patrick had always told his congregations that this was not a curse from God but occurred because David had never slept with her again. And Patrick wants to punish Anne in this way, deprive her of his love, but it was *she* who left him. Yet he feels as if *he* is being judged, like David for lusting after Bathsheba: his child, his church, stillborn.

What was it that he wanted so badly? Was it souls, converts, miracles? *Is it wrong to want these things?* Was it the church itself that was his Bathsheba? He smirks at this because when he thinks of the church he thinks of old Mildred Hallett, his first member, and the idea of lusting after Mildred's wrinkly, eighty-seven-year-old body sets him laughing until he can barely breathe.

But his laughter is nervous and joyless. His thoughts choke him: like thick mud around his limbs, his neck—he is Jeremiah in the cistern, Absalom tangled up in the tree, David hiding in his cave, Saul alone in his tower. He is Peter drowning, waiting for the hand of Christ. He is all of them and none of them. He's confused and alone——as alone as he felt the day Hab had showed him the traces of Anne's infidelity.

What stung most is that Hab had said that Anne's password was *Patrick*.

How'd you figure that out? he'd asked his son.

I just guessed.

You knew?

I thought she'd tell you. I wanted her to tell you herself. It shouldn't have been me.

And then Hab had gone upstairs to his room, leaving his dad transfixed in the monitor's cold blue glow.

Clicking her message box, Patrick had begun scrolling through. He was shocked to find out how long it had been going on: for almost a year, starting just two months after they moved in. *Has she been thinking of him while kissing me this whole time?* He kept reading and trying to imagine *Dave*. Had he seen him before? Had he ever met him? Did this Dave guy find Anne online, or did she find him? Pictures: he needed to see a picture of the bastard.

So he'd clicked on Dave's icon and brought up his page, opened his album, but there was only a fuzzy yearbook picture from high school and his profile pic. He noticed that Dave was broader in the shoulders than he was. But he was going bald. Hair shaved close to hide it. *Anne, for frig's sake, he's going bald! And he's ... pasty.*

Patrick had been flipping out in his head when Hab came down with a large duffel bag, packed. He handed his dad a folded piece of paper. Said he could call him there, indicating a number scrawled in red ink. *Natalie's number*, it said. And there was an address for Merrymeeting Road below.

Get some sleep, Dad.

And he was gone before Patrick could resent his son for sounding like his father.

Dear Patrick,

I hope this finds you well. (And I hope you can read the writing.) Gerta tells me she phoned you and Anne shortly after I was taken into the hospital. It wasn't a full heart attack but I am still interned here until they can perform an angiogram on me. That is to get things cleared up.

I'm writing (actually it is me, Gerta, writing for Gurney) because I don't feel well enough to talk long on the phone and you know I've always hated talking to disembodied voices. I know, funny for a man who has spent a lifetime talking to God. But the thing I've always loved about being an evangelist was talking to people, seeing their faces. And reading someone's handwriting is in a way like seeing his face. This is how it is when I read the Bible, though I haven't the strength to read it now. And Gerta hates reading aloud. (He thinks I won't put that in the letter but I've told him I'll write whatever he wants said.)

My reason for writing is to see how you and Anne are doing. Gerta tells me Anne came to see me but I was asleep and she didn't want to wake me. I wished she had. She came all that way. This question may be answered before you get this, but is she staying with friends or family here or in St. Lola? I would like to see her before she flies back to Newfoundland. But maybe she is visiting. I only ask because it's been a week and no sign of her yet. But I'm sure she is fine and tells you each night on the phone not to worry. That is Anne for you.

Tell me how the church is going and how many have been saved. Newfoundland was once the Pentecostal capital of Canada, you know. And I preached there many times in the early seventies. Once I prayed for a man missing three fingers and two of them grew back. I always thought it was strange of God to only do half a miracle. (Actually it was two-thirds of a miracle.) But the man said that God kept a

finger to make sure he'd come collect it some bright
morning. That memory is still clear as a photo now,
almost forty years later.

When you get this, send us word of where Anne is staying.

She told Gerta she had come to stay for a while. But Gerta
hasn't seen her since and I haven't seen her at all. Also, tell
us how Hab is doing in his new home. That's all for now.
I'm tired and should sleep. (The doctors say he's doing better
but he looks grey as a sheet.)

Yours,
Gurney (and Gerta too!)

Patrick sees a letter from Gurney in the mix of mail but he
doesn't open it, only tosses the whole wad in the recycling bin
with all the rest of the mail for the past week. He keeps telling
himself that he will go back through it all and pull out the bills
and the church-related letters. But for now the fact that the
latest letter from the Pentecostal Assemblies of Newfoundland
is wrapped in a McDonald's flyer eases something in him: a
guttural groan, almost a growl.

Deep down.

Official church business taken so lightly, treated with such
disrespect, is a small, affordable rebellion. He can always repent,
pull the envelope marked PAON out of the trash, and re-enter
the world.

Or can he? Sometimes he is not so sure.

He assumes Gurney and Gerta know now of their daughter's
choice. The letter probably says as much. Maybe they've sent
some words of comfort for him. That thought is almost enough
to get him off this couch where he's been sleeping for the past
week.

There were mornings this past winter when he would get up
late—with Hab gone to school and Anne in the basement on the
computer—and he'd come out to the couch to watch some

morning news. The couch would be warm as if a body had been curled there for hours. He always thought it was Hab who'd slept out in front of the TV all night, watching God knows what. But now he wonders—if he could go back to one of those mornings and feel Anne's side of the bed when he woke—he wonders if he would find it cold, sheets crisp. Was it her warmth he settled into on those winter mornings while she sat in the basement, typing with numb fingers to that man?

He sleeps with the phone on his chest. It shocks him awake each time it rings. But the call display never says *Anne cell*, it never comes up as the number Hab scrawled for him in red ink before his son left. So he lets it ring, lets it go to the answering service, which he doesn't check because the recording is Anne's voice.

He wants to hear her and he doesn't. He wants her to miss him and come back. He wants her to be hit by a car or assaulted. But he doesn't really want that to happen. Or does he? He feels guilty for thinking such things, wishing such things on her. He prays for her to come back, and in the same breath he prays for God to punish her—to make her feel guilty, plague her with insomnia, night terrors, voices in her head. Call her to repentance in a dream, like he called so many in the Bible. But more often than not he asks himself why in hell he is even talking to God. He knows the answer: because there is no one else. But for the first time in his life, he catches himself wondering if God even hears him.

Father, he whispers, lying on the couch, the phone on his chest, *if that's you—if you're here, in this room—tell me to come to you.*

The phone rings and his heart jumps. The number looks familiar for some reason, so he answers it and hears Hab's voice asking him how he is, telling him he should come for a visit— get out of the house.

I will, he says, I will soon. I wasn't expecting to hear your voice just now. But I'm glad you called. I'm really glad you called.

Dear Patrick,

I've just received a letter from Anne. In it she says she has left you. She says she is not going back to Newfoundland. She says she is going to London, Ontario to be with a man she calls Dave. (Who is this Dave, Patrick? Do you know him?)

She gave a Hamilton number for us to call her at, but I won't call her if what she says is true. (He won't call but I want so badly to. To hear from my own daughter's lips why she is doing what she is doing.) Patrick, you are like a son to me. You always have been, ever since you travelled with me the summer after you finished Bible College and we went to the Arctic together. You saw so much that summer. People healed in Rankin Inlet, set free from addictions in Iqaluit, baptized by the native pastors there in the frigid rivers of Frobisher Bay, the air swarming with flies and blood running down our faces because there were so many. And we didn't care, didn't feel it. Because of God's glory and joy.

To me that memory is more real than the memory of my daughter's birth. (He can say that because he wasn't there. He was out getting a sandwich! But I will write what he says.) You are the son of my choice, and the bottle of olive oil I poured over your head to anoint you on the shores of Lemming's Lake on that summer evening long ago stands out in my mind more clearly than your wedding day. (He is shaking now and crying. I asked him if he wants me to stop but he says no. Patrick, he is trying to touch you now. Feel that in his words.)

Patrick, I don't know why she has gone. I don't know where she has gone. If she was here I would not raise a hand to her either for comfort or rebuke. (I would slap her, stupid girl). She has done you a grievous wrong and my prayers are that she will see this and that God will

*help you forgive and that Hab will not be without his
mother.*

*But she is strong willed, Patrick. She's the only one I know
who can stand against the force of my prayers. (This has
always troubled him, since she was a girl.) Talk to me, my
son (our son).*

*I need to hear from you now. (You can phone our
home number or the Bancroft hospital and ask for
Gurney Gunther's room. Please call, Patrick.)*

*With Love,
Gurney (and Gerta)*

It's the third Sunday since Anne left. Patrick cancelled the
service on the first Sunday and sent everyone to Elim Tabernacle
on the second. He has no idea how he could possibly stand up
and preach. He remembers Gurney's words to him when he was
to preach in Rankin Inlet, and confessing that sometimes he
felt there was nothing to say, that he had no deep spiritual
vision to impart. *That's when you feel the cross*, Gurney had said,
placing his two heavy hands on Patrick's shoulders. And he feels
them now, their same weight—like a rough-cut cedar beam—
but he can hardly bring himself to get up off the couch. How
could he possibly stand up and say anything? But he knows he
cannot cancel a month of services without questions.

So this Sunday he called in a favour and asked Fred Archer,
a youth pastor from Mount Pearl who he knows from his
Eastern days, to preach at *New Life*. The name seems like a joke
now to him, only nobody is laughing. Or they would be, if they
knew that Pastor Wiseman's wife was off on some cyber-fling,
using her dad's heart attack as an excuse to get off the island.

Patrick knows he romanced the ocean in his descriptions of
it to Anne. But he wanted her to want to come here. Once here,
however, she must have seen through his stories: seen the
truth—that the North Atlantic is terrifying, frothing where it

gnaws at the jagged shoreline. Patrick came face to face with the beast the March day he and Hab went on that strange trek out onto the barren point at Flatrock—after seeing the grotto by the Catholic church and telling Hab about his grandfather's obsession with the Virgin. The sea was a heaving grey Leviathan that day, spewing the snow that drove them into that old bunker for shelter.

Sheilagh's Brush, Patrick's dad called it when Dale and he were kids and the March winds would spatter salt on their windows, all the way up Noseworthy Drive at the top of the hill overlooking the harbour. He remembers the taste of salt on the wind when he was a boy: the same as when Hab and he huddled together in that memory—that kid not saying a word but watching them until he fell asleep. It seems to Patrick like another world now: a brine-flavoured recollection. And he thinks of himself in that bunker as Jonah in the belly of the whale, rank with longing for Mildred Hallett's pease pudding and boiled potatoes—a big slab of stringy salt beef and that same saltiness the first time he kissed his way from Anne's toes to her centre, her long fingers tangled in his hair, drawing him down and him wondering if this was okay and half not caring.

When they first got to Newfoundland, all Anne wanted to do was get out on an iceberg tour and see puffins and whales and smell the salt air Patrick had talked so much about. It was so foggy they saw nothing and Anne puked all over the deck, her stomach no match for the swells, especially with no steady landmark to concentrate on in the distance. Patrick fared better only because he insisted on taking a Gravol before boarding the boat, knowing his sea legs wouldn't hold. They never had.

He wore his good Sunday shoes on the boat. He thought he was silly for doing so, until he saw that a lady across from him was wearing flip flops, and it cold enough he could see her breath. *Mainlander.* That was his last time on the water, though he remembers as a kid how they would dare each other to jump from ice pan to ice pan—*running the whale's back*, they called it. Crisscrossing the bay before their mums would yell and tell them to get the hell off the slobby ice.

But that was a long time ago. Before Patrick started wearing Sunday shoes everywhere. And before he began punctuating his sentences with Mainlanderisms like *eh*.

How are you doing, eh?

Yeah, eh?

Crazy cold weather, eh?

You've heard the one about the Newfie and the plane crash, eh?

He'd left Newfoundland behind him when he went to Bible College—left behind quirky relatives like his Great Uncle Gil and his father's unquestioned Roman religion, too. Now, having returned, he found it all different. As if the whole place had moved on and left him behind, in a past he remembered fondly but was unable to share with Anne or Hab—a past it seemed only he recalled.

He knows this out-of-joint feeling should not surprise him. He chose to leave the Catholic Church his parents had raised him in to go to a Pentecostal Bible College away on the mainland. The defiance, the righteous choice, being cast out— all that was once salt to him was now bland, a heap of white mineral no good for anything but being scattered over icy roads. That's why they moved to Paradise rather than nearby Fawkes Cove. His parents can smile at him at family dinners but being neighbours would be too much, he thinks, and worse with Dale living there now, since his divorce. Patrick hasn't talked to his brother in years. He doesn't even know Dale's son's name, only that he's been put in foster care temporarily since Dale and Rhianna's split.

Crazy arse. Maybe that was extreme, but then again Hab had never tried to blow up his shed. Patrick knows Rhianna hates his dad as much as she despises Dale, but he has no idea why. These are bits of news that have gotten to him like Yahoo updates in his inbox. Family spam. Delete delete delete. And now he wonders what all he's been told and has ignored, forgotten. All that has rushed by floods in on him now—all that he doesn't know. *They've gone on with their lives, and left me to mine, and mine has gone on without me. Whoosh.*

And here he is: left behind again, staring into the bathroom mirror, watching his hands tie a full Windsor around his neck as if the hands are somebody else's. He pulls the tie up taut with the top button of his shirt. But he has no idea why he is wearing a shirt and tie when he is simply going to see his son at his apartment. So he undoes the tie and casts it aside. Looks in the mirror. Undoes the top button. *There.* Dressed but not too dressy. Comfortable casual. *Anne's choice.* He places a hand on each collar, yanks outward suddenly, and pops a button off the shirt.

So much for that, he thinks.

Patrick untucks the shirt and pulls it over his head, leaving it on the bathroom floor as he goes to the bedroom to find another. He wants something he can wear untucked.

No, tucked is better. More comfortable.

He needs the proper outfit to show that he's coping—no messy hair hidden in a hoodie, no ripped jeans or T-shirts.

No camel skins, he tells himself. *You're no prophet and you're not homeless.*

He finds a green-and-beige checked shirt and cargo pants that are almost white. Then he fills the bathroom sink with water and carefully shaves his patchy beard, washing away the shaving cream and splashing on Old Spice.

He thinks, finally, he is ready. *At last.* He is just about to leave when he remembers that he hasn't brushed his teeth in sixteen days.

As he is leaving the house he notices another wad of paper in the mailbox: bills from Newfoundland Power, MasterCard, Rogers, Sears—and another letter from Gurney. He throws the bills on the desk and pockets his father-in-law's letter along with the last one Gurney sent, which had remained unopened in the recycling bin with all the junk mail and church business since it arrived.

Patrick thinks that today he may read the letters. He also thinks he might burn them. So he goes to the kitchen drawer, grabs the barbecue lighter and pockets it, too. When he steps outside he feels for a second like Moses leaving Egypt—excited and terrified. He drives slowly to the address on Merrymeeting Road, the one scribbled beneath Hab's contact number on that crumpled shred of paper. There is no driveway so he parks on the street. Every drive on the road is shovelled except the one at the neighbour's house, leading to the basement entrance. Patrick thinks the place looks abandoned.

Trashy.

He stamps the snow off his Sunday shoes before knocking, his fists gloved in leather. He smoothes out his coat, and knocks again.

A girl with her boots on answers the door. She's holding her jacket in one hand and a cigarette in the other. Can I help you? she asks, stepping out onto the stoop.

I came to see Hab, he says with less emotion than he's feeling.

He's in the tub now but you can sit on the couch and wait, if you want.

That would be great. Thanks.

You don't have a light, do you?

She's a little weirded-out when Patrick draws the barbecue lighter from his pocket. But she lets him awkwardly click and cup the flame, and hold it steady as she leans in and puffs. Nice, she says, and steps off the porch, looking down the street toward the Coleman's Grocery Store. Thanks for the light.

No problem, Patrick says as he watches her stroll away, wondering if she knows he's a pastor—or if that would matter to her.

He goes in, slips off his shoes and sets them neatly beside the random pile of other shoes, and then meanders over to the

green couch. There is a three-wick candle on the coffee table and a stack of novels on the lamp stand by authors he doesn't know. The novel on the top of the stack looks to be about alligators. The room smells of coffee and oranges. He couldn't drink a coffee now if he wanted to. His hands are shaking too much. He grips them tightly on his lap and tries to look at ease, sitting there surrounded by student messiness.

He hears the shower stop. A little while later the door opens down the hall and he hears Hab go into a bedroom. There is a girl's voice with his son's, and it is all he can do not to jump up and run down the hall to see what they're doing. But he reminds himself that Hab no longer lives in his house and perhaps no longer follows his rules. He wonders if he still goes to church. And if so, which one?

He hears the girl shriek and laugh.

Hab?

He starts but stops himself: *I have no control over him now.* He knows that his son has chosen to move out, to get away from their house, from him. And the shock of this hits him again like that belligerent gust of wind on Flatrock—that slap of cold air that nearly toppled him over the cliff and into the sea.

It was Hab's hand that stopped him from falling.

He remembers his own hands shaking for an hour after, like they are shaking now.

Patrick fingers the lighter in his pocket: grips it to keep his hand from vibrating, pulls it out, looks at it, pushes the safety with his thumb and clicks. The flame is the size of his pinky finger, which he passes through it twice before leaning over and lighting the candle in the centre of the coffee table, thinking of his duties as an altar boy during mass as a kid and of the lack of candles of any kind in the Pentecostal Church—no votive, Advent, or Christ candles at all.

He watches the three little wicks gutter, almost go out, and then begin to burn steadily. *A smouldering wick I will not extinguish. Pray for us now, and at the hour of our death.*

Wax pools as he puts his shoes back on and heads out the

front entrance, hearing a door down the hall open.

Footsteps.

His son's voice: Dad?

But he is running to his car now, flinging the door open and climbing in, turning it over and dropping it into gear. He pulls away from the curb without signalling and almost gets hit by a snow plough. The angry driver blasts his horn all the way to the light. But Patrick doesn't hear him. All he's thinking about, as he turns down Aldershot, is the quickest route to the boat launch in Fawkes Cove.

Dear Patrick,

I had a dream last night. The type of dream I've told you about: when I walk in the spirit and not in the flesh. You were in the dream and I saw a great seething gulf before you. It was dark. And there was smoke and snowflakes scattering like ash. (He woke up crying, Patrick.)

In the dream you were running, Patrick: running over the water with hail pouring down on you as you crossed the gulf.

I can't get you out of my head, son. (He speaks of you daily and when I come into his room while he is praying your name is on his lips.) Anne called Gerta and they spoke but I couldn't speak to her. I couldn't bring myself to say a word to my own daughter. She is strange to me now. (Anne told me she went to this Dave character and said she had left her husband and he panicked and turned her out. It appears he was married as well and he had never told her. She is living with friends in Hamilton, temporarily. Ruth and Christopher Rhynes, do you remember them? I mentioned her going home but she hung up.)

Patrick, be wary of this gulf ahead of you. Keep your footing. Trust in the Lord and not in yourself. The Psalmist says that God scatters his hoarfrost like ash, that he tosses hail like breadcrumbs. Who can stand against his cold?

I don't know why this storm has come to you but I see
you running. Finish, Patrick. Finish what you must.
But please write.

(Why haven't you answered our other letters?)

Sincerely,
Gurney (and Gerta)

Patrick can hear the pack ice grinding against the cliffs encompassing the bay, creaking and groaning against other ice pans. The seething white mass stretches almost out to the grey horizon. There is an iceberg out there—probably the size of the church down the street, but it looks no bigger than a fingernail from where he stands at the top of the boat launch on the south side of the bay, looking north to the other steeper launch.

In warmer weather boats dangle below where he stands on the ramp, ropes stretched from their bows to anchors by his feet, each vessel fastened tight against the fierce wind. An icy gale rips through his peacoat suddenly, freezing his ankles in thin socks.

Below him, the boat ramp is bare and ice slicked.

He reaches inside his coat and pulls out the two letters he has received from Gurney. He thinks for a second of opening them but he feels he needs to fall out of contact for a while: to think of something other than Anne's father, or mother, or Anne herself with that other man.

He rolls the two letters together into a tube and sticks the end of the barbecue lighter inside and clicks, his back to the wind, holding both the paper and the fire to his chest. It takes three tries for the letters to catch, but when they do he holds them flaming in a gloved hand, smelling the leather beginning to smoulder but knowing the paper will flame out before he gets burned. A few seconds in that wind and all the words are gone to ash, which blows away even as it begins to snow.

Anyone watching the bay from a darkened window would see a man in Sunday clothes taking hold of a ratty rope and

lowering himself down toward the heaving pans of ice crashing against each other, salt water sluicing over them, spewing between them.

Patrick is out of sight now, out of sight of everyone.

On the edge of the world.

No, Anne, I'll not be careful. If I can jump the pack ice from one side of the seething bay to the other, then it's not me who's sinned. But if I slip and drown, then so be it. You will have got what you wanted.

He lets out a whoop and leaps from the shore onto the slob ice, slips, scrambles, gets splashed by frigid salt water, finds his footing and begins to run. The pan he's on jars and rises, like a whale cresting, and he claws up it, toes the edge and leaps to the next pan that tips till he's up to his crotch in slushy sea water—the cold sharking as he lunges forward and uses the tilt to propel himself to the next pan. And the next. The sea heaving slob ice all around him. Eon-old ice is cracking like bones on rock. One slip and he's dead. But he's running, running like he's fourteen and devil-may-care. *My God!* he thinks, *this is it!*

Wooo!

II

Ruth told Anne that Hamilton is shaped like a horseshoe around the Niagara Escarpment, the city's industrial backside to Lake Ontario. *It must be a lucky town then*, she had thought. But that's not how she feels, sitting in Christopher and Ruth's Charlton Avenue apartment at their computer, in a dark backroom with sloped ceilings, looking up divorce lawyers online.

It's a half-hearted search: names, fees, hours of business.

Ruth is away at work at a retirement home up on the mountain, which is what Hamiltonians call their little rib of the Escarpment. The night Anne got there, she walked up the stairs to the cliff edge of Garth Street and looked back over the city lights. There were so many shades of purple glittering below the wind-whipped mauve skyline, and the steel mill's stack flame was a distant torch. In some ways it was like the cliffs by the sea when Patrick and Hab and Anne hiked from Signal Hill down into Quidi Vidi. Dramatic, but in a different way. Hamilton does not have the sea. It doesn't have water the colour of volcanic glass crashing against rocky headlands, shattering any semblance of silence. The sound of the waves now seems little more than a dream to Anne, her head full of the sirens that shrill constantly in this part of town.

She had thought the crow's view of the city at night would give her some perspective, but standing on those steel stairs only made her recall driving her rental car past Dave's door in that London subdivision—a green door badly in need of new paint.

Rusty Italian wrought-iron fencework had been bolted around the front patio, shrivelled boxwood lined the broken asphalt walkway. Anne had nervously hop-scotched the path, skipping over the frosted, grass-lined cracks. *Step on a crack and break your mother's back.* That was exactly what she was doing there: breaking everything she knew. But though she felt something gutting her, like a fillet knife in a fish's underbelly, she wanted to knock on that door more than anything.

Then what were you expecting? she asks herself, clicking her thumbnail against the beach stone in her pocket. *I'll figure it out,* she remembers thinking.

Click.

She wanted to fly the words like a jitterbug skimming, like fly fishing with her father in Beaver Creek, standing in the shade of the St. Olga Bridge, watching mice scurry after the cheese crumbs that fell from her sandwich, hearing her dad tell her that mice made good muskie bait if you hooked them right.

Click-click.

Nonchalant as skipping stones; squashing a mouse underfoot. She wondered if her father would ever speak to her again.

She kept her hands in her pockets, pressed flat against her thighs so they couldn't talk, but she could not stop her fingers from squirming, as if she had pockets full of worms—she was that nervous. She could not see straight until she hit the first step, when everything began to clear like river water three days after rain. *I'm doing this,* she thought. *This is it.*

Rubber scraped against granite as she dragged her heels.

What if he doesn't recognize me?

He said he wanted to see me.

Her hand was on the doorbell, eyes on the small bicycle chained to the patio porch. The small red bike flashed in her blinking even as her knuckles came down on the door with the chipped green paint. A child's bike.

She knocked again. She could feel the roll of skin just under her bra, beneath the rustling fabric of her jacket, which she had left undone. She felt every extra roll in that tight shirt with its

swooping neckline.

A camisole: she was going to wear a camisole underneath. But she had wanted him to see ... *what?* She hiked the neckline, knocked again.

Why isn't anyone answering? She thought the camisole would have held in her flab. *Come on, Dave,* answer the door. Her new jeans were too tight and she was breathing hard and trying to hold her stomach in.

She rapped harder, this time on the windowpane.

Stand straight.

Dave?

She tapped her finger on the glass three times, barely loud enough to hear. *Stop shifting,* she told herself. Then she heard steps coming toward the door and she tugged her shirt down to reveal some cleavage. She could see his silhouette through the sheer curtain. *Shoulders back, don't slouch.* The doorknob turned. *Can he see my bra lines through this shirt?*

Dave! she squeaked. She distinctly remembers squeaking.

And the shock in his eyes made her belly sag and her shoulders ache. His eyes frisked her, coldly—shoulders to shoes.

Anne?

Surprise!

What are you doing here?

Suddenly she wanted him to stop looking at her. She wanted to tug her neckline up. *Why didn't I wear that stupid camisole? Or a sweater? A friggin hoodie.* She wanted to be a snail and crawl inside herself, inside her crinkly jacket. She wanted to run: wanted to know in that second whether she had thrown away her life for nothing. The stone in her pocket carved into her leg.

Anne, he said, his voice rough, his words like slivers in her skin. You *have* to go. My daughter will be home soon. You can't be here.

Daughter? He had never mentioned a daughter on Facebook. *You're married?* Then she heard a bus coming down the street. She felt like a fish hooked through the gills as she clenched her fists to keep from slapping him. The bus stopped six houses down and three kids got off. She turned and walked away from him, tripping on a crack in the asphalt, feeling so tight in her clothes that she thought everything would split down the middle of her back—bra, shirt, jeans, jacket.

Skin.

She felt she was going to explode. Tears burned like birch smoke in her eyes, and she couldn't find her keys. *Just get the car started! Come on, come on!* And she jerked it into gear, wheeled out of her spot and screamed as a horn blared and the bus swerved past.

And then she saw Dave, with his daughter walking toward him. He yelled something Anne didn't hear, his hands on his daughter's arms. Anne shoulder-checked and drove on, crying—trying to find her way out of the stupid subdivision. Panicking when she drove past his house again, searching for the main road.

The highway, the highway: the mind-numbing 401.

She kept herself together until she saw a gas station with a McDonald's. She ordered four cheeseburgers at the drive-through, parked, and began eating. Pushing the greasy burgers into her mouth half a patty at a time, until she choked and threw up into the bag with the rest of the burgers and the paper split and her upchuck ran over the seat—the smell of vomit stinging her eyes until she let go and cried, coughing and spitting and trying to wipe up her mess. But the more she rubbed, the darker the stain in the seat became.

The smell lingered all the way to Hamilton, where she knew people who would take her in—she hoped. The cold wind gave her a headache, but she had to keep her window open to vent the nauseating stink.

By the time she found Ruth and Christopher's, her eyes were bloodshot and her throat burned. She could feel the stone in her pocket dig into her hip with each step up the fire escape that led to their third-floor apartment: same as it did on her walk later that night, when that wretched day played itself out in her head again and again.

Anne tries to stop revisiting that day.

She attempts to focus her thoughts elsewhere, but she has only a computer to distract her. And she is sick of spider solitaire because she has been playing it since before sunrise.

She couldn't sleep last night.

Ruth is at work and Christopher is in his art studio, one of the front rooms of the apartment, off the tiny kitchenette. Ruth had shown Anne the strange little paint-splattered room when she arrived weeks ago. Canvases and boards stacked in all corners, bleeding deep reds, flowing blues, blistered yellows. As if Christopher had cherry-bombed his paint cans, holding his canvases over the explosions. Like the painting hanging in Anne's room that Ruth has told her is an icon of the Virgin Mary but which looks to her like thick yellow paint shot at a dark blue background.

Weird, she thinks, looking at it, her back curled against the sloping wall and her feet drawn up on the bed. She holds her knees like this when she is tired of trying to beat Ruth's high score on the computer, and she stares at Christopher's icon of Mary. She feels afraid sometimes, sitting in this dark room, looking at the painting and seeing no discernible face, yet, strangely, feeling as if she is the one being watched. Her eyes follow the strings of splashed blue veining the yellow *face*, if it can be called that—the deep cobalt circulating through sunlight yellow, leaving traces of algae green, submerged life in an orbed blaze.

She is afraid of what she has done. She doesn't understand her actions, the blood running through her veins—only that this is her life, in this small room, feeling fat and ugly and alone. She feels judged by the fog-burning yellow of Mary's face, by the eyes of God that animate her conscience—by her father and mother. And yet Ruth and Christopher are rivulets of rainwater, their care for her as relieving as tears. She cries when the door is closed and Christopher is in his studio.

As sorrow courses through her, submerged memories bloom like an algae cloud in a slow-moving, sunlit riverbed—Kyle holding up his ling and laughing; Hab hovering his hand above the board game's buzzer; Patrick tickling her stomach and sliding his fingers along the frill of her underwear.

This is as close to peace as she comes.

Sometimes she stands in her jacket out on the fire escape, looking through a line of blue bottles on the neighbour's windowsill. Some bottles are filled with glass shards and some with pebbles, and some are empty yet ripple with glass-swirled light.

Anne prefers the fire escape to the living room because she finds it hard to talk to Christopher, who often passes through that part of the apartment to get to the bathroom. He has started to bring her strong cups of French-pressed coffee whenever he makes a new pot, which feels to Anne like every hour or so. She tiptoed the first few cups to the bathroom and flushed them down the toilet, but she recently found an old pack of paper filters in the kitchen cupboard, which she snuck to her room along with a spare mug. Now, when Christopher brings her coffee she waits until she hears his studio door click and then gingerly filters the black tar into the other mug, removing the dark froth and grit.

Still, the coffee is thick enough to stand a spoon up in. *Intense*, which she thinks fits Christopher to a T. *Blazing blue eyes* she had thought was a description found only in the Christian romances she used to read, but his eyes really do blaze, especially when he looks at Ruth. *More alarming than alluring*, Anne thinks. *Like he's going to combust.*

She does not see what goes on in that front room, but occasionally she hears an electric saw or a drill. At other times she hears thrashing, like whipping: sharp strikes, strange noises, panting, sandpaper scraping.

Then silence.

Not like the silence in her house back in Newfoundland, where she could not see the ocean though she felt surrounded by it. *Isolated.* This is an expectant calm, unlike the dead stillness she has fled.

Miracles have been on her mind since her Facebook chat with Hab last week. He had reminded her again of her name's history—Anne the mother of Mary the mother of God, trivia that troubles Anne because of her son's growing fascination with Catholicism. And Hab reminded her also of the fact—which she doesn't remember occurring—that her father had raised her from the dead.

The story has been told in pulpits from Windsor to Iqaluit, Red Deer to Halifax, by her father. Growing up, she had thought everyone knew of her dad, the miracle worker. But in high school she began to realize that not only had many people not heard of her dad, but among the ones who had, he was often considered a bombastic charlatan. *Bombastic* Anne understood—her dad once walked up to her and Billy, her boyfriend at the time, when they were seated in the back row of the church, and said Anne was ready but Billy was not. He didn't say what Anne was ready for, but Billy was so embarrassed to be singled out in the middle of the service that he stormed out of the church and never came back. Anne's mom scolded her dad that night while Anne hid in her room down the hallway.

This isn't like the time you snipped that preacher's silk tie on the platform and called it a lesson in humility! Anne remembers her mom yelling. The boy might never darken a church door again. And he certainly won't be calling Anne anytime soon. What did it accomplish?

Anne heard the TV volume go up. WWF. Her father loved wrestling and would watch taped hours of it after Sunday service, especially bouts with his favourite wrestler, Macho Man Randy Savage.

When Hab was a kid he would beg to go to his grandpa's house to watch wrestling. He would say *please please please*, and when Anne finally said yes he would crawl onto the arm of the couch—so long as Patrick wasn't in the room—and body slam the couch cushions.

And it was between reruns of that old taped match with

Andre the Giant and Hulk Hogan that her father told Hab stories of miracles. Stories about severed fingers growing back, withered limbs waxing strong, cancerous lumps shrinking away—all beneath her father's soft hand—even that story of Anne being raised from the dead with a single word.

She has heard people talk of miracles like sharp knives, as things that mark or wound in that spiritual sense where to hurt is to be happy. But Anne doesn't know how she can be marked by something she cannot remember, can't verify, can't click her thumbnail against like the smooth sea stone she carries in her pocket from that beach near Port aux Basques.

When Patrick gave her the stone, he had said, Rub it when you're frustrated and think of all the hard edges smoothed away deep in the sea. She kept it secreted in her pocket like she kept Dave's name secret, though she thinks Hab discovered her that one day she left her browser open. She never rubbed the stone as Patrick had told her to, as if it were some magic lamp found among coloured shells—copper-swirled and purple. But she took to clicking the stone twice for the two syllables of Dave's full name, which he never used and which Anne never said aloud but only in her head: *David.*

She wanted to hurl the stone through Dave's window when she showed up at his house after leaving her family, after kissing her father goodbye in that hospital bed so few days after his heart attack, knowing that he would never speak to her again when he found out she had left Patrick, who was more son to him than she ever was daughter.

She still has the stone in her pocket, though she does not rub or click it now. Only thinks about it constantly. The pressure of it against her thigh, pressed into her skin through a thin denim layer by the tight jeans she bought at a mall on her way to London to see Dave. Nice jeans, Ruth had said innocently, the night Anne came to their door and asked if she could stay a few days. She knew them from summer camp meetings back on Lemming's Lake when Ruth would watch Hab while Anne went to the front with Patrick. They had always seemed like an easy-going, soft-spoken couple—a little eccentric but kind. That's why Anne sought them out. And instead of judging Anne that day she showed up on their fire escape, Ruth had hugged her and complimented her on her jeans and showed her to the bed in the back room where she and Christopher kept their computer. Ruth is nearly fifteen years younger than Anne but her tone was motherly, and Anne had hated Ruth's hand on her back then, the day she arrived, though she longs for it now.

It has been more than *a few days* that she has spent here, but she doesn't know where else to go. She called her mom and dad the other day at the hospital, but her dad—as she had known—would not talk to her. Her mom was polite, though Anne could feel the edge in her voice, like that sharp shell she slit her finger on while skipping clams in Lemming's Lake.

The sun is setting and would already be set in Newfoundland. Anne Googles the St. John's *Telegram*, as she has done every evening since running off Dave's front lawn. She does it to feel some cold connection to what she has left: to punish herself for being stupid; to see what the news is back ... *there*.

God, she thinks, *I almost said home.*

And now that she thinks it, she wants to say it but she feels sick and thinks it might be from too much coffee, but she knows it isn't. It's deeper than heartburn or indigestion.

The page comes up and the main story posted is about a car that was found earlier last evening crashed in the harbour at Fawkes Cove, just north of St. John's past Torbay. *The driver of the car, a 2004 Chevrolet Malibu, is missing from the wreck. The RNC are still in search of the owner, a Mr. Patrick Wiseman, of Paradise.*

Anne's face feels blistered. Tears suddenly well up in her eyes and her stomach knots. She scrambles for the phone and dials the number of the Royal Newfoundland Constabulary posted with the article.

Hello? Yes, hello, I'm calling about the car that was found in Fawkes Cove. No. No. I don't have any information. No. I'm

his... his wife. *I am his wife!* I don't care. No. Where is he? No. No! *Yes*, I can be there in the morning. I'll call you with the flight number. No. Yes.

Click.

Anne searches WestJet flights out of Hamilton as fast as she can type, calling out to Christopher and reaching for her wallet. What's the date? What's my credit card number? Come on: now, now, now! I don't care what seat. Just get me on a flight that leaves tonight!

Anne?

Yes, she almost yells.

What's wrong?

Can you drive me to the airport?

When?

She looks at the screen, clicks *Accept*: Now. My flight leaves in just over an hour.

But——

I'll explain, Chris. But I need to be on that flight now!

His blue eyes blaze with questions, but he only nods and reaches for the phone to dial Ruth at work. Yeah, Ruth, this is Chris. I'm fine. I'm taking Anne to the airport. Where? I don't know. I dunno.

He looks at Anne and mouths *Where are you going?*

To St. John's, she says.

She's going home.

The word stings like a treble hook snagged in her ear. She closes the windows on the computer and sets about throwing clothes into her suitcase. Christopher hangs up the phone as she crouches to pick up her underwear from the foot of the bed, that smooth stone digging sharply into her thigh.

N ails are driven through the man's hands and into the codfish he's cradling. He is cast in bronze and pinned on a plain white wall like a maritime crucifix. Hab is leaning in so close to the icon's feet that Natalie thinks he might kiss the crossed toes. She tugs on his hand to pull him back so that the people milling about in the gallery will stop staring at them. But Hab is insistent on the spindly legs, the vacant stare of the figure. So intent that Natalie is sure he has no idea how close his lips are to the statue's limp cock.

It's some time before she can manage to pull him away from his ogling veneration of the Jim Maunder bronze—his eyes swallowing it whole. He sees something more than she does in the art here in the gallery of The Rooms, the monolithic museum that shares shadow space with the Basilica next door. She does not know that to him the figure is his cousin Kyle nailed to that ugly freshwater cod he once caught. All Natalie knows is that Hab gets quiet around certain pieces. He stares at them with such intensity that she imagines he is seeing *through* the art, as if it were less a mirror to this world than a window elsewhere. Leaving the gallery, she thinks of telling him that his obsessive stare at the Maunder piece came dangerously close to fellatio. But she just giggles until he asks her what she's thinking, and she suggests going to the café on the third floor.

Natalie tells him that she will snag them a seat by the windows overlooking the harbour while he orders black coffee for her and hot chocolate for him. She has teased him about being a bit of a pansy when it comes to coffee, which he hates and calls *the black death.*

I'll take a medium bubonic, please, she says as she heads toward the window seats, her eyes buzzing around metallic bumble bees strung between silver lights, her backpack slung over her shoulder. She finds them a seat away from the cream and sugar station, hoping it will be a little quieter, more out of the way. So she can take a sip of Grand Marnier from her pink Nalgene bottle without anyone noticing. *A view like this*, she thinks, *even half obscured by fog, deserves something a little stronger.* The liqueur is also to wash down one of the four Ativan tablets in her coat pocket.

Sherl, a co-worker at the group home where Natalie works part-time overnights, gave Natalie a handful to try after she had complained about one of the kids stressing her out. She had fallen asleep on the couch the one night—which they are not allowed to do—and awoke to feel someone's breath on her eyes.

She was too warm in her sleep and tossing. Dreaming of a green door down a long pink hallway that closed when she reached it, and through the door a hall with gaudy silver wallpaper peeling and a dark wood door embossed with a yawning whale's mouth, and through that another hallway with warped floorboards and pieces of raw meat spiked to the walls and a door made of metal dented as if someone had tried to hammer it down with an axe—and another and another, on and on, until she opened a cardboard door with the word RAT spray-painted in dripping black across its creased surface and a rush of hot air blasted her face. Again and again, like someone breathing. Someone breathing on her face: standing over her. Another door clicked and the rotting floorboards fell away—jolting her awake. This psychotic kid, River, was leaning over the arm of the couch: his inverted face hovering an inch above hers. Their lips almost touching. His mouth open and reeking of Doritos. He had a perverse smile on his lips, and Natalie thought for a second he was trying to kiss her, or worse. His voice was unnervingly calm when he told her the phone was across the room. Imagine what I could've done to you before you got to it. Bitch. Think about that before you fall asleep again. Think real fuckin hard.

River straightened and Natalie bolted off the couch like a torched cat. He held up a pen with the end chewed off and pulled the ink tube out, mimed snorting a line with the hollow casing, laughed hysterically, and then, straight-faced, pretended to jam the pen case into his eye. He licked the plastic shell and then held it against the roof of his mouth, the other end pressed into his palm. Eyes wild and daring, daring Natalie—*come on*—to ram the pen up through the top of his mouth into his skull. Then he dropped it and laughed again, and Nat tried to laugh confidently with him, like it was all some big joke. But she knows she sounded unhinged. And River knew it too; he heard the rusty squeak in her voice. He snapped the red ink capsule and let it bleed across the coffee table, leaving it for Natalie to clean up, knowing she wouldn't say anything because she was sleeping on the job and that was grounds for being fired. He pressed a thumb into the red ink, reached over and printed her forehead, smirked when she flinched. A little Paki dot for you, he said. Then he turned and went to bed while Natalie smiled through gritted teeth, her heart cinching like a tourniquet.

She rubbed her forehead raw trying to wash off River's insolent inked thumbprint.

In the morning she told Sherl about the run-in, trying to make light of it, but Sherl said it was real: River had sociopathic tendencies. That one has got no ability to empathize, she said. A chip on his shoulder the size of a cinderblock. Pay attention to him, he's nuts, but don't let him get to you.

So this kid could jam a broken pen in my eye while I'm dozing off and I'm not supposed to let that get to me?

Hence these, Sherl said, pouring her a fistful of Ativan.

Are these …?

Prescription? Yeah. Try them. If they work, I'll set you up with a doctor who'll write you a script. Okay?

With a shift coming on at midnight, Natalie thinks she may

as well loosen up a bit. *Just one.* For now, that is. To keep her from the edge, like the precipice out this window: a steep drop into the hunkered shadows of row houses far below. She tries to concentrate on the faint city lights bleeding down beaded raindrops as she slips the Nalgene of Grand Marnier back into her bag.

When Hab comes back with their hot drinks he asks her about work and she tells him about River and his psychotic threats. The kid dissected a live hamster with a jackknife yesterday, recorded the whole thing on his cell phone and posted it to YouTube, she tells him. Working with that kid kind of freaks me out.

The liquid courage helps then? Hab asks, looking into his mug.

You saw the Nalgene?

You have some on your lip. Yeah, there.

She licks her lips, tastes the sugary orange, and forces a smile.

Just bracing myself. You don't know what this kid is like. He scares me. But I can't let that show.

So why do you stick with it? The job, I mean.

Maybe I'm making a difference. You know he sometimes calls me Mainland Burger 'cause we made burgers one day and didn't have buns. So I told him to put the patty on bread and he said only a mainlander would think of that. The nickname makes me smile. Some days. It's those times that make me think maybe I might be making a difference. Keeping him from jumping off the deep end. Really hurting someone.

Just make sure he doesn't pull you over the edge, eh?

I won't, she says, sitting back and slipping her hand into the pocket of her oversized army coat, fingering the three remaining pills. *Not as long as I have these,* she thinks. But says: Not as long as I have you.

She thinks that Hab sometimes has a weird way of responding to her cutesy talk. Most often he changes the subject—after going cherry red—which makes Natalie giggle. This time he doesn't really blush, just starts telling her this story

of him and his dad going to visit the Our Lady of Lourdes grotto out in Flatrock. Nat is getting used to Hab's storytelling. This is their first date night since he started crashing on Natalie's couch, their first real conversation, if it can be called that. She knows it is his way of having a conversation.

Or the result of being a preacher's kid.

The monologues she can get used to, but she is starting to notice how when Hab speaks he seems to look over her shoulder or at her chest. So she leans forward in her chair, both hands around her mug, to see if she can catch him at it. But his eyes are beyond her as he goes on about this time a month ago when his dad took him to see a statue of the Virgin and to stand on a stone where Pope John Paul II kneeled to pray.

Natalie is starting to think that she will never know what goes on in Hab's head, why he is always seeing something beyond her but not her.

He says that it was around the time he was thinking about moving out of his parents' house. After he'd got up the guff to come and talk to Natalie again. After the whole sweater incident had been ironed out.

Just after his mom left.

That's when his dad said, You need to know where you've come from to know where you stand. Apparently when he says stuff like that it means he wants to go for a drive and have some father-son time, pass on a bit of wisdom. Hab tells her it is something his Grandpa Gurney did with his dad when his father was being mentored in ministry, back in Ontario.

He tells Natalie about getting into the Malibu and heading off along the Outer Ring and then north toward Flatrock and Fawkes Cove. His dad started talking about this grotto—a Catholic shrine—overlooking the sea.

Hab says, You have to understand how weird it was to hear my dad, a Pentecostal pastor, talk about visiting a Catholic grotto.

He tells Natalie that his dad had started talking about *his* father, Pop, who Hab has only met a few times, even though they now live a half hour away instead of five provinces. He tells her that his dad grew up Catholic: confession, the Eucharist, serving as an altar boy—all the holy bells and whistles, until sometime in his teens when he rebelled. Hab rubs his knuckles over his bottom lip as he tells her about most kids his dad's age drinking their faces off or sniffing gas or trying weed when they could get it. But he says his dad's rebellion was to sneak out to Pentecostal revival meetings here in St. John's.

As far as his Nan was concerned, Hab's voice lilts, he'd gone beyond the pale, been faerie led.

Natalie has no idea what that means but she tastes the coffee and the liqueur in a hiccup as Hab goes on about his dad sneaking out to these meetings and getting drunk on the Holy Spirit. Church-lingo, he tells her, for being a Bible-thumping badass.

Getting laid out for some carpet time with the Creator.

That was his dad's way of spiting his parents, especially Pop, who apparently turned really religious around the time his son started high school. He stopped drinking and carousing and spent most weekends in his cabin up in the woods behind Fawkes Cove, where he saw visions of the Virgin Mary.

Hab whispers this as he pours some salt out on the table, shapes it into a swirl with his pinky before telling Natalie that his dad had said their trip to Flatrock was an effort to explain his grandfather to him. But I don't know, Hab says, licking his finger and dabbing the salt. I think it was more Dad trying to backpaddle his own life—trying to figure out his connection with this place now that Mom's gone back to the mainland.

He has drained the dregs of his hot chocolate, and Natalie offers him some liqueur.

It's Grand Marnier. Orange-flavoured.

No, I'm good.

You'll like it. Promise.

I'm fine, he says, his eyes strangely cold.

Diddly then.

Wha—?

Okay. Okay.

But Natalie feels the need to take a stiff swig or two to keep her mind off the three pills in the pocket of her coat, off her cold fingers pulled up inside the sleeves of her jacket—her hands numb at the thought of being locked in the house with River for another overnight shift.

I'll just be a sec, she says, getting up.

But she needs a minute hanging onto the counter edge in the washroom to convince herself to take only one more of the Ativans instead of all three, though it feels like River is squeezing her neck and kneeling on her chest. She cannot breathe until thirty seconds after swallowing the pill with a swig from the Nalgene, knowing it can't have kicked in yet but that it soon will.

That door in my dream—

She remembers the dream: sparks and strange calm. *Like stepping into a warm bath with Hab.* Something she thinks they should do. *He would like that.* But he is too much of a prude, she thinks, which is what she kind of likes about him. He is slower than most guys: a strange mix of gentleness and passion, like crème de cacao and vodka swirled together in a shot glass.

Natalie inhales and tastes her alcoholic afterbreath. She runs her fingers over her buzzed hair and tiptoes, a little high, back into the café. Hab smiles at her from their table. She notices that he has moved his chair closer to hers.

It was a few days after St. Paddy's Day, he says as she scooches in beside him, picking up his story where he left off. Calm as anything. Only grey. A wet-woollen day, Dad said. Barely any wind and only a few snowflakes. So we thought nothing of walking down from the grotto to the beach and out onto the rocky point that slopes up from the harbour. The point out there is like a fang. Dad wanted to show me the breakers out at the furthest tip.

Forget Cape Spear, Hab says, dropping his voice an octave to imitate his father, I'll take you right to edge of the world! You know, he says, his voice rising to his own range, I'd never seen a grin on his face like that day. He was nearly bouncing. Ready to run. Not slump-shouldered, like he'd been around the house since Mom took off. Or sullen and quiet like he was up at the grotto, standing in the Virgin's shadow.

Hab goes on about his dad leading him up what he said was a path but what looked more like ice-covered bedrock—windswept, so it was easy enough to walk if you could keep your feet under you. Which, Hab says, I had a harder time doing than Dad. I was surprised at how surefooted he was. And calm. Even with the swells blowing geysers sixty feet into the air below us.

Natalie follows Hab in his story like he followed his dad that day—out to these two massive boulders near the point.

Like in that Squires painting, Hab says looking past her. That big granite monolith stranded on that soapstone plain. I thought they looked like giants hauled up out of the sea and frozen in place. Like the legend of the dwarfs turned to stone in Norway, howling forever as the wind up the fjords. Only these stones were massive.

Hab tells her of ducking in behind them and his dad trying to yell something at him.

I couldn't hear him over the wind, he says. It'd picked up steadily on our hike out. He'd had all that time to talk to me at the grotto but he hadn't said much till then—when I couldn't hear a thing! Wind shrieking. Waves exploding like bombs on the shore. So I leaned in to hear him, and I looked up and saw a figure on the cliff edge above us. Like a ghost. Seen it crouch and vanish. That's when Sheilagh took her first swipe.

Around Paddy's Day, and a few times as late as the Feast of Saint John the Baptist, Sheilagh's Brush, the last big winter storm, blows in hard and sudden. Lisette told Natalie that on Old Christmas Day. *For a Prod like yourself, not being used to marking time with saints' days,* she said, blowing smoke out her nose and holding her cigarette aloft, *that would be somewhere between March and June.*

Natalie remembers that she was at the group home the night the storm hit. Hab was on her mind then—had been, all day. She had actually called his house in the afternoon, when she

should have been sleeping. But she hung up after three rings.

Have I told him that?

Should I?

There is a drop of coffee sliding down the side of her mug. It stops at the heavy thumbprint. Lip balm she dabbed on in the washroom after she wiped the liqueur off her mouth. Most girls use their pinkies. She uses her thumb. The amber drip splits and slides sluggishly around the oily print, drying out before rejoining, staining the mug with a brown horseshoe.

Lucky but not so lucky.

She has to go to work tonight. This thought stands huddled with Hab in his story, out of the wind behind that massive troll-like rock. *Did he say troll? Toll: like a fine. Would I get fined if I locked River in his room? Or would that go on my record? What if they found out about the Ativan? They wouldn't make me do rehab. It's not like I'm addicted. The pills are prescription. Not mine but somebody's. Just stress pills. To take the edge off. Cut the wind down. Like standing behind that big rock out on that point.*

Two pills left. Her thumb rubs over their scored surfaces. *One, two. One, two, one, two.* She is fingering pills like Gerry's black plastic rosary beads and wondering if she left her lip balm in the bathroom.

Hab is saying something about his dad pulling his head in close and yelling that they had to get out of there while they could still see the path. Hab tells Natalie they couldn't see anything but each other by that point. It had started to snow, and a few minutes later they lost sight of everything— the harbour, the path ... all gone in the shivering whiteout.

Hab was leading on the way back, though he doesn't remember why. And his dad was hanging onto the back of his coat—following.

I figured we were going up, he says, away from the water. It was hard going. And I'd slip and knock Dad down. Then we'd haul ourselves back up and keep going. Up. Away from the water. Away from the rogue waves that can pull you in sudden as anything and that's the last anyone sees of you.

Natalie thinks of those waves. Lisette has warned her many times about them: Don't be like the dumbass tourists at Cape Spear. Keep the hell away from the water!

Hab is telling her that he couldn't see his hand in front of his face for the blowing snow and that's why he didn't see the cliff edge until the wind took his hat and he reached out to grab it. And stepped right off into nothing.

Thank God Dad had a hold of my jacket, or I wouldn't be sitting here now.

Natalie toes his leg with her shoe and his hand squeezes her knee. She holds her empty mug to her chest: looks at him; wriggles her toes in her shoes to feel him; makes sure he has got the story right. That he is sitting here now. In this café on a clifftop overlooking the city lights swooping down from the Presbyterian Kirk into ink-black water. She touches him to know, really know, that it happened as he says it did, that he is here with her now. Hab came back into her life not a month ago and she loves that he came back, that he sought her out. She loves his hands and his laugh, where his eyes fall when he thinks she is not looking, his wonderful yabber about art and God, who he sees in paintings like the one in the stairwell, *Where Genesis Begins*. Natalie knows how they were both raised, in a church with bare walls and empty crosses, where God was a spirit and had no form, no body she could imagine, no hand she could touch, though she once thought she felt callused fingers take hold of hers in a service but when she looked it was only her own hands cupped before her in prayer.

She has a hard time picturing God now; it has become increasingly difficult to do so since the fire. Sometimes she even has trouble remembering Hab's face if she is away from him for any length of time. But she can always hear his voice, his tongue rolling R's when he's reading poems aloud. Or his eyes: she can always remember his eyes—the awe in them when he is blown over by a bronze sculpture, like the one of the man and the tree bending with the wind's rushing flow. When she can recall his face, it is always crumbling like crushed crackers into soup, like the day he broke down and told her about his mom having a Facebook affair. His arm over her in her bed and his body cupping hers like when he thinks she is asleep and he is staring at the curtained window in her room, tears running down his cheeks. Sometimes she asks him gently what he's thinking.

She wonders that now. *Why this story?* She wants to know how he will dovetail it to fit the one she has carved out of silence the past three days since she started taking Sherl's pills. Hab is a craftsman in thought and conversation. *Sometimes.* He can sand out silence with coarse patience, his body inquiring in cuddles and hugs, his arm around Natalie when they're watching *Bones*. His words seem to fit into her thoughts like no one else's, save maybe Biz's. But Biz is not here: she's gone, along with Toronto and the rest of Natalie's life before the fire. Her memories of conversations with Hab are a trunk filled with Russian nesting dolls—conversations inside memories inside conversations of memories told and retold.

So this one, this story, spun almost in answer to Natalie's confession that River genuinely terrifies her, seems like an attempt at empathy.

But Hab is real. He's here in this café in the clouds with her, fog shrouded so that the city lights glow dimly, wink and vanish like so many eyes in the dark. His presence is more calming to Natalie than the pills she takes. *Almost like Biz.* Or how she imagines a lover might be, though someday Hab and she may be lovers yet. *If he gets up the courage.* And Natalie is sure even then that they will not always fit smoothly together like both ends of those conversations that plane them late into the night, stained with several bottles of wine until she is lying with her head on Hab's lap and his hand is gently brushing over her buzzed hair.

Lulled. She swings inside that feeling like her tongue in that hammock-sounding word: *lulled.* So much so that she is finding it hard to focus. Hard to listen and to keep her mind off the likelihood of River strangling her with a lamp cord and the two pills remaining in her pocket and how she wants to slip into a warm bath with Hab: to have him look at her instead of past her into his own thoughts and worries. All clothes and distractions peeled away: nothing but water between them. She wants to ask him if he will take a bath with her when they're back at the apartment. Gerry's away at the library studying and Lisette's at work downtown for the night. But she asks him something else—after she puts down her mug and moves away from the table toward the stairs, pulling Hab along behind through rotating glass doors and into the icy rain—to show that she is trying to concentrate on what he is telling her.

So then what happened?

He tells her as they walk in the sleet—his head tilted down and toward her, his collar cupping his ears—that his dad pulled him up and somehow they managed to find an old World War II bunker on the ridge. Freezing rain is running down Natalie's face and in at the corners of her mouth. She can taste her own skin as Hab says: There was this kid sitting there when we stumbled in. Must have been the silhouette I saw on the ridge before the storm hit. We said hello but he didn't say a thing to us the whole time we were huddled there. Only looked at the ground, him holding one red fist inside the other, squeezing so hard there were white lines around his fingers.

Hab is saying something about their misty breath fogging them in while Natalie watches his words swirl and puff—he is walking fast, head down, not looking at her now. He tells her about sitting back to back with his dad to keep warm, and she can see the rain has soaked right through his jacket. She can see his shoulders and the curve of his slump inside his jacket. That kid, he mumbles. That kid in the bunker, he's only wearing a torn jackshirt; pulling his jean cuffs over the tongues of his boots; blowing into his fists. And he's just spinning his silver skull ring.

Hab tells her that even after hours of sitting there like that, his heart was still pounding from walking off that cliff edge. Eventually, he says, the rush left him drowsy; he was drifting off when he heard his dad's voice.

You know the song, *I'll Fly Away*?

Natalie thinks she knows it, as she turns her face up, letting the rain run down her neck. She knows the song and is singing it in her mind as Hab tells her that more than anything, at that moment, his dad wanted to do just that—fly away.

While the kid is hacking into his sleeve, scuffing his toes.

Hab: I began to think of the howling outside the concrete walls as silence. I asked Dad if he wanted to fly away because Mom was gone or because we were stuck in a blizzard. He said 'cause Mom was gone.

The pack on her back is keeping Natalie warm, but her legs are wet and freezing as Hab tells her about sitting in silence for hours, long into the night—the kid refusing to let them keep him warm as he's coughing into his coat.

I'd doze off mid-hack, Hab says spitting, and I'd jerk awake from falling. *I'll fly away, oh glory, I'll fly away. When I die, Hallelujah by and by, I'll fly away.* And I think now I know what Dad meant by that. *When I die ... I'll fly away.* He was telling me he wanted to give up. Like Kyle, who put the gun barrel in his mouth and toed the trigger. Like the look of that kid freezing there and refusing to share our body heat. He had copper-coloured eyes. Did I tell you that?

Natalie thinks of coppery eyes, rusted with frozen tears. *Just give up.* Natalie would like to give up sometimes. *But why? Why, really? Because everything is so retarded,* enough to send her over the edge. And she hears Hab say that instead of walking off a cliff his dad kept him from doing just that. And instead of letting that kid freeze, his dad waited until the kid fell asleep before peeling off the outer shell of his Columbia coat and slinging it over the kid's shaking body—the boy's knees poking through rips in his jeans.

Hab tells Natalie that this is what he wants to do for her, in whatever way he can: keep her from toeing the edge, or worse. Whatever that might look like, he says. The problem is that Natalie knows what it looks like: River's face an inch from hers, his threats hot on her eyes. His spit on her face—sick slurs—

stinging, like this ice rain needling her skin.

Hab has never seen the kid. He doesn't know what River is capable of. *Would his grip be strong enough to hold me*, Natalie wonders, *if it came to that?*

She doesn't let go of his hand, not all the way home. He has told her that he wants to hang on to her, but it is her hanging on to him. She feels his hand in hers: pulling her as she is pulling him so that he follows her into the apartment and down the hall with their wet coats still on, dripping everywhere.

Natalie?

She puts a finger to his lips and opens the bathroom door with her other hand. She switches on the lights, pulls him in and closes the door. She turns on the water and draws the curtain on the tub, turns and puts her hands in her pockets. Her right hand curls around the two small tablets. *Her lifeline*, she thinks, *until now*.

Nat—

I want you to take a bath with me, she says.

She can feel her face warming even as she says it. The water is hot and the steam is rising in the room. Her lips are salty from sweat and she tastes orange liqueur coffee on her tongue. She turns and slips her arms out of the sleeves of her big green jacket and lets it sop on the floor. She feels frowsy.

Nat—

She does not turn around because if she sees his face and his worry she might lose her nerve, and she wants him to follow her to this edge—to reach out and grab her. She wants him to see her, to really *see* her, like he did the bronze in the gallery tonight. She takes the bottom of her T-shirt and rolls it over her head, pulls it away and drops it to the floor, too.

Unclips her bra.

She can hear him turn around. She knows he is not looking; that he is afraid; that good church kids do not do this sort of thing, especially not a pastor's son. And she is starting to think this was not the outcome Hab had intended for his story. But she knows that you cannot always control how a story is heard

and it cannot always be understood the way the teller meant it.

This is my ending, Hab. Come on. I want you in it.

She reaches into her pocket and pulls out the two pills before sliding her pants off her hips—her purple underwear with the yellow trim. She opens the curtain and pulls the stopper to turn on the shower, but before she steps in she asks:

Are you coming?

There is no answer as she steps under the spray.

The pills are dissolving in her hand. She will count to ten. If he opens that curtain and steps in, she'll drop the pills down the drain. That will be it. No more pills, just her head against his shoulder and her arms around his waist, pulling him in.

One.

Two.

Three, four, five.

Six …

Hab?

The door clicks.

No answer.

Natalie opens her hand. The pills are smearing in a white paste. *Seven eight nine … ten.* She licks the palm of her hand, eases her cold face into the hot spray, and swallows.

Purple dye from the red cabbage is staining the wooden cutting board like wine, the colour of Hab's left eye this morning. Cubed moose meat sits bloody in a white bowl on the counter. His face still smarts. *Teach me to keep my hands up next time,* he thinks. He has spent the morning honing the dull butcher knife to a razor's edge with a whetstone given him by his Grandpa Wiseman on a visit to Fawkes Cove a few days ago: his first time in Pop's home.

It had been Hab's idea to call.

No, this isn't Mary Brown's in Torbay, the cranky voice on the other end had said, coughing into the receiver.

Is this Des Wiseman? Hab had asked.

Himself, if you're not a telemarketer.

This is Hab. Your grandson.

Where're you to?

Town. Can I—

I'm settin a plate for you. You need a ride?

And it was Pop's idea to drive into St. John's to pick him up in his S-10 Chevy. Pop was half the size of Hab's Grandpa Gunther, green work pants cinched over bony hips. Large veins on his arms, knuckles like jawbreakers under freckled skin. Big hands. But he had nothing to say to Hab on the long ride back to Fawkes Cove. It took Nan, dolled in an orange and pink flowered Florida shirt buttoned to her jowls, to melt the ice between them. She was like a great Gulf Stream of family stories and questions.

You seen a moose yet? she had asked. Or been out on the water?

Shagged a mermaid?

He means have you swum in the ocean?

No.

No, hey?

Well, come summer we'll take you to Northern Bay Sands.

Eastport's just as nice.

It doesn't have hot springs.

The creek only feels hot 'cause the sea's so friggin cold.

As I said, we'll take you to Northern Bay Sands.

You gonna gab or eat now? And who's sayin grace?

Dinner—potatoes mashed with kale, carrots and scruncheons—was swallowed up in a game of rummy and Pop had called Nan an old cheat and she'd said, He's sour 'cause he sucks at cards.

The mouth on you, woman.

Last card.

Joseph and Mary.

Don't think that by leavin Jesus out of it he don't know just exactly what you meant.

Hab thought that his grandparents were awkward and crass and wonderful. Nan had served blueberry wine that she had made in the fall, and Pop had said he might save his glass for paint thinner. Hab stayed for figgy duff drowned in caramel sauce and for the Habs game—*like your name, Lucky Charm*—which Montreal lost in overtime, and then Pop drove him home. But not before giving him the whetstone and a pound of moose from his freezer.

That was only a few days after Natalie had asked Hab to take a shower with her and he had run from the bathroom.

A week has gone by now since that night and she has barely spoken to him. She did not say a word to him last night at Sherl's party. Not even after he got punched in the eye trying to save Lisette from those two guys who stalked her from the Shamrock up the hill. *Good thing she carries mace and has no qualms about*

sacking guys, he thinks. He knows now that Lisette can hold her own and more. He also knows that he got his ass handed to him. And still not a word from Natalie all night long.

Nothing from her on the walk home either.

That's why he has decided to make her dinner. There is a bottle of Barefoot Merlot open and breathing on the counter.

The red cabbage slivers thinly under the sharp knife. Hab has a bowl of green cabbage to mix it with when he is done. A shaved carrot lies above the cutting board by the grater, an orange garnish in need of shredding. The idea is to make coleslaw but with an oriental twist. No mayonnaise for the sauce but a cup of olive oil in a glass jar with three tablespoons of soya sauce and two of white vinegar, shaken together with a Mr. Noodle flavour packet.

Gerry walks into the kitchen and opens the fridge as Hab is stretching to the top cupboard for a bigger bowl to mix all the ingredients in.

Republic of Newfoundland coleslaw, hey?

Hab looks down and sees it, the old flag in diced cabbage— the knife blade glistening whitely in the kitchen light.

Except without mayonnaise, Hab says.

What will you mainlanders think of next?

It gets worse.

Gerry pulls a beer from the fridge. He cranks the lid off with a hiss. Oh?

I'm making an un-boiled boiled dinner.

Gerry takes a sip and eyes Hab. If it's not boiled it isn't boiled dinner, is it?

I'm using all the ingredients but making them different. Mostly just not boiling them. Except the salt beef.

That's what's on the stove?

Yes.

But you're not boiling anything with it?

Only spinach and greens.

Gerry takes another deep swig, looks at Hab like he's apostate and says: I can't have any part of this. I'm going to Leo's.

He finishes his beer in an elongated chug as he watches Hab toss the two-toned cabbage together, tells him dressing and gravy can cover a multitude of sins and that he can pick him up an indulgence if he wants. Hab says no as Gerry dips a travel mug in the salt beef liquor.

You looking for a heart attack, Gerry?

Gotta prepare the arteries.

Hab glances at Gerry sipping the salty broth. He fakes a dry heave and Gerry snorts some of his cup and chokes a little as he says, Don't knock it till you've tried it. Then he drains the mug and tosses it in the sink before heading for the door.

Thanks for the dishes, arsehole, Hab calls after him.

I pay the rent, you do the dishes.

Hab thinks about telling him to fuck off but doesn't, and in the next second he hears the door slam.

He pulls the skillet out of the oven—where Lisette likes to store it—and puts it on a front burner with a splash of oil. When that begins to sizzle, he sprinkles in sliced almonds and sesame seeds, stirs, and watches them brown.

This whole cooking thing is not new to him. When he and his mom cooked together, she would show him different things, like how to brown mushrooms in butter and garlic before adding them to spaghetti sauce, or how a splash of lemon sharpens whitefish whether it's battered or not. His mom had taught him to measure tablespoons in a cupped palm, told him about shredded ginger.

But this is the first meal he has prepared on his own since she left—since their last Facebook chat weeks ago when Hab wanted to ask her why she'd gone but only managed to ask if she knew her name was the same as Jesus' grandmother, Saint Anne. He had forgotten that he had already told her this and she had confiscated his book of saints' names before they moved to Newfoundland. When he remembers it now, he thinks it was a stupid question, that what he meant to ask her was if she was coming home soon—that he missed preparing meals with her.

Like this one.

The idea for this meal came from Nan, who he doesn't think his mom has ever met, except at her and Dad's wedding, or so Hab has been told. He thinks about this a lot, that his father's parents have been kept from him, and he wonders how different his life would have been with them in it. He has heard his dad say things about Pop, something the old man did ages ago that most likely led to his mystic conversion. When he remembers these things, he wishes that the slash between Catholics and Protestants—between his father and grand-father—was not such a festering wound.

He knows that stabbing pain, though, being cut to the bone—when Natalie had told him to get the fuck out, when his mom left his dad, when the Pentecostal fire in his father hushed as cold as cinders after rainfall. He knows this feeling, when passion is doused leaving a worthless, charcoal existence. But he persists, not thinking of this meal as an act of faith, though it is. He thinks of the recipes given him by his nan, and he thinks that his mom would like her, even though Nan's got a thing for the Sacred Heart of Jesus, which his mom thinks is stupid.

He knows now that Nan thinks jigg's dinner is stupid, even though it's his father's favourite dish and he has more than once asked Mildred Hallett from the church to come over and make it. His nan told him when he was over that she would make boiled dinner and fried chicken if she was having a crowd over, but she couldn't stand the stuff herself. *All boiled together in a pot and the only thing you can taste is salt*, she had said and showed Hab a recipe book she had made up with every variation on cooking cabbage, carrots, turnips, potatoes, and split peas that did not involve boiling them altogether in a pot with a chunk of salt beef.

She prefers moose meat flash-fried with butter and onion.

Only thing salt beef's good for is flavouring spinach or making a pease pudding or figgy duff. Nan told him this in her kitchen that overlooks Fawkes Cove and the sea. I gives your pop his taste and throws the rest to the dog, but don't tell him that. It'd give him a stroke.

Pop and Gerry both, Hab thinks as he crunches the leftover Mr. Noodle over the cabbage before scraping the browned almonds and sesame seeds overtop. He gives the sauce jar a last shake and pours it out before sinking his hands into the oily mix and tossing the salad. The cool cabbage feels good on his knuckles, bruised from the one punch he was able to land last night. He loves putting his hands in food, licking his fingers afterward and trying to turn on the taps with his elbows.

The oil between his fingers makes him think of holding the bottle of baby oil for his dad as he used to pray for people at the front of the church during the altar call. There are kids in his classes at university who say they have come from Pentecostal upbringings out around the bay and they laugh off the oil and dancing and the speaking in tongues. They make jokes about their fathers and grandfathers casting demons out of vacuum cleaners, saying they are simple men with simple faith and the world is a much more complicated place now. Hab does not know these fathers and grandfathers or their world, but he cannot help thinking that his classmates are cowards—and that secretly they love these men they now mock and that the guilt of this is what makes them so sullen.

He does not even know what he believes anymore, but the oil on his hands and the memories it brings are not bad. He is trying to turn the taps on with his elbows and thinking his dad is a very different person to him now than when he carried that bottle of baby oil for him, pouring it out to be laid on people's foreheads and ears, as a cross over their lips. Hab is pouring out dish soap into his own hands, over his red raw knuckles, and remembering his dad painting old women's smiling faces with his oily hands—his painting prayer.

Not like an actual painting, Hab thinks, and yet, exactly like that. His dad's prayers, like Grandpa Gunther's, were thick, impasto-textured—brilliant. And full of boastfulness and show, sure, but also love. Whatever else he may doubt, Hab does not doubt that his dad loved everyone he prayed for, especially Anne.

Though Hab does wonder if his father could have loved her

more, enough to keep her around—to have kept her from wanting to leave.

If she still lived here, Hab knows he would not be living at Natalie's apartment or be going to parties on Carter's Hill where joints are being passed around. Like at that party where he saw Natalie being slipped a bottle of pills from her friend Sherl. Gerry had walked up with them from the Shamrock after some drinks. On the way they had passed a kid spray-painting the word RAT in neon green on the wall at the boot of Carter's Hill. Hab had thought he recognized the torn jackshirt and work boots—the kid from the bunker at Flatrock—but the kid caught him staring and told him to fucking well mind his own business. He remembers Gerry burping and saying *Carry on Pollack* as he pushed him up the stairs.

Kid's got a steel bar in the snow by his boots, Gerry had whispered at the top of the stairs. Best keep walkin, b'y. Hab had nodded and they did just that, carried on. And as they were making that steep climb from the staircase to Sherl's house, Gerry had looked up and said: I wonder which door's the dealer's.

Eh?

Dealer on this street.

How do you know?

Iced shoes strung over the hydro line.

That's not just some kid being an asshole?

Gerry had shrugged as Natalie knocked on the door, looked at her watch, and said hello when Sherl opened the door and ushered them in, saying: Welcome to the best view in St. John's —too bad it's dark out, hey!

Hab remembered looking out Sherl's front window onto the street, keeping an eye out for Lisette, who was supposed to walk up from the pub after she got off at 2:30 a.m.

Gerry, Natalie, and Hab had all gone down to hear Arthur and Con O'Brien on a Sunday night when Lisette was bartending. They had sat by the window nearest the door because Gerry said he liked the whiffs of smoke that ghosted in

whenever the door opened. Never catch me with a fag in my mouth, but gawd I loves the smell!

Natalie had snorted into her drink.

What?

Think about it, was all she had said over the crowd and the music.

Hab is grating the carrot over the cabbage salad now, wondering how it was that he ever heard the guys at the table behind him and why he was the only one that heard them talking about the bar girl with the sweet ass.

Lisette.

I'd take her bent over the counter there, the huskier one said as Hab took a sip of beer. While she's got my balls on her chin, hey! The other guy's voice was throaty and hoarse.

Coming back to the table with another beer, Hab had seen they were two cleancut guys, wearing dress shirts without ties, sleeves rolled up past their elbows: business class. Their table was full of empty Coors bottles and shot glasses.

It was when Hab had heard them getting up to take a leak that he ducked in front of them on the way to the washroom and hid in the stall. He heard them talking about Lisette again. Seemed they were Shamrock regulars and had been ogling her for a while. Had even followed her home once and knew her route up Carter's Hill.

Streetlight's out by those stairs, last I checked.

Stuff her mouth with it.

Fuckin right.

He heard all this while these guys were swaying in front of the urinals: pissing half their loads on the floor—breathing hard.

The water boiling in the pot is pea-coloured because of the spinach and salt. Hab tongs the steaming greens out onto a plate and turns the element off. He fishes out the salt beef onto the red-stained cutting board. A fork in the centre and he slices into it the way he wanted to cut into those guys when he saw them through Sherl's smoky window, waiting and shivering by the stairs at the bottom of the hill by the graffitied wall that kid must have abandoned. The salt beef pulls apart in strings and his bruised knuckles gripping the fork remind him of pulling open Sherl's door after he saw those two guys stamp out their cigarettes and head down the salted stairs. He had run down the hill, skidding on ice patches, and had jumped over the rail onto the one guy who had a hold of Lisette's arm, her hand dug deep into her purse. Hab had felt a rib snap beneath his knee and he heard a caustic *fuck* as he was hauled off the guy by his friend. Hab tried to roundhouse the other one but only grazed his chin.

The guy spit and socked Hab in the eye.

Hab pulls the potatoes wedges out of the oven, golden brown and glazed with olive oil and Montreal steak spice, along with the caramelized turnips and carrots, the sweet and salty smells marrying weirdly with the memory of waking up in the snow, his head next to a doorless microwave. Lisette is laughing and telling him he should have just let her mace the friggers and saved himself the black eye.

Too true, he thinks he said before she heaved him upright and they climbed the stairs and hill back to the party where Lisette told the story of his kung fu heroics and got a real laugh out of everyone but Natalie, who sat in the corner, eyes glazed, her drink untouched and her hands in the deep pockets of her coat.

Hab wants her to talk to him. He wants her to know he ran from the bathroom the other night not because he doesn't want her—*does she know how beautiful she is?*—but because … he doesn't know why. Fear, maybe. Preacher's kid syndrome. Her naked back braless like a sculpture—a photo. Her thumbs in her beltline, the curve of her hips, and he ran. Like a coward. A prude. The steam in the kitchen reminiscent of shower steam: his fogged glasses clearing in the hall. This girl he loves offering herself to him and—

What's cooking, doc?

Natalie leans in the doorway, her green jacket slung open, dark blue T-shirt over her striped pyjama bottoms—feet bare. Hab reaches for the bottle of Merlot. Barefoot, he says stupidly,

knowing this is the one she likes, the one she used to share with her friend Biz when she lived in Toronto. Before the fire that scarred her belly while she was crawling across the hot floor under a cloud of black smoke. He can feel his fingers on those scars under her blue shirt even as he pulls out the broken-stemmed wineglass from the cupboard, pours her a heaping cupful and eagerly hands it to her.

She takes the broken glass, licks the spill on the skin between her thumb and forefinger and smiles. What's all this? she asks.

For you.

Hab breaks off a chunk of fresh baguette from Georgetown Bakery and hands it to her. He knows she likes to dip bread in wine and slurp the crumbs off the surface; that it has nothing to do with taste but with texture, for she cannot smell or taste anything since the fire. She knows Hab knows this and her smile deepens and Hab says: The moose will only take ten minutes to fry up. Then supper's served.

Where'd you bag the moose?

Grandpa Wiseman's freezer. Should've seen the rack on his wall.

Antlers make me think of Pentecostals, eh.

What? Hab laughs, throwing the raw moose meat in the scorching pan and thumbing a spoonful of butter in that pops and sizzles and browns nicely with the onions.

Natalie holds her hands up in the air—one hand cupping her wine glass, its broken stem seeming to pierce her palm in the weak light—and she mouths a theatrical *Praise Jesus*. They laugh together as Hab continues cooking—grinding pepper, sprinkling salt. His laugh jars his ribs like a hiccup.

Fried butter and almonds, that's what his shirt smells of as they eat on the ratty green couch that is the colour of Natalie's jacket. They split an orange for dessert and Hab watches her lick the juice from her fingertips. There is sharpness to the moment, clarity sheer as a knife blade. Each detail honed like the edge of that butcher knife on his Grandpa Wiseman's whetstone. Smooth. The filings, her gestures: hand on stomach, a laugh, left ankle tucked under her right knee.

Chop chop, little man, he thinks, laughing at something Natalie has said and pulling a pillow over his lap to hide his hard-on.

Hab tells her about his nan and pop and his brief visit to Fawkes Cove. He tells her she should come for Sunday dinner. He says, Don't worry, Nan's a wicked cook.

She says it would be nice to get outside St. John's, that she is feeling strangled in the city lately; that her job is stressing her out, especially this River kid.

Hab remembers her telling him about the kid—how he threatened her. He thinks of introducing Natalie to his grandparents. And he wonders for a second if his dad will come. He suddenly feels the deepness of that old wound, the ache of it, and worries about how his father is doing, alone in that house in Paradise.

Natalie leans forward and lights the three-wick candle on the coffee table. Shadows rise up in the room like raised arms, like the caribou antlers in that birchbark lithograph Hab ran off on the colour printer at school and hung across the room from them in a cheap Walmart frame. Hab looks to Natalie, her cheeks flushed with wine. He feels the heat in his own face. Imagines her—curled in her coat—like the figure behind the caribou skull in the glassless square, dreaming him dreaming her. The shadows are splashes of burnt umber, strokes of rust, white flecks of light dancing.

I'm a liar, Gerry scribbles in red ink, *just like my father. I have a stack of stories two feet high and that's all they are. Lies.* He is sitting by the window of Erin's Pub on Water Street, the big pane of glass shivering when the snowy wind punches it. His toes are cold in his damp shoes and he is thinking of the story he wrote about Rod.

He'd put the story in the third person to distance himself from the events, from that day he can barely remember yet not forget. He had wanted to replay the events objectively, in slow motion—the tire iron, the black plastic rosary, the pink panties in the sink. He told himself that this evidence needs examining, which is partly why he wrote the story. But he knows—as surely as the heartburn he feels after only two beers—that he does not care about evidence or certainty, or even about self-justification.

He wrote the story to get a good, long look at Rod, his neighbour, the old cripple he brutalized, *the drunk who lives next door.*

Gerry crosses out the present tense and writes *lived.*

He had been in Rod's basement apartment only once as a guest, a friend. The next time, he had broken in. He had written about both, explaining that the break-in was done so that he could see Rod's place again, have a sense of where the old guy lived. So he could write about him with some authenticity.

That sour cat-piss smell.

And that is when he saw the pink panties soaking in the sink. Skid-marked or blood-stained, he couldn't tell. But he

126

could not, for the life of him, think of any good reason why Rod would have Mick's daughter's dirty underwear in his sink. He thought of Rod's crooked smile, his browning teeth, his scarred lip and innocent eyes magnified behind thick glasses. He thought he knew him, knew what kind of guy Rod was: a rough-cut old man with a penchant for rum and cheap whores, but not a bad man. When he thinks of those panties dripping in his hands, though, he thinks of Rod's goofy looks as a predator's mask, a distraction.

Gerry recalls the thumbnail crucifix on the plastic rosary he tore from Rod's neck after he'd shattered his glasses and cracked his skull. He can still feel Rod's skin hot under his fingers, slick with new blood. The old man's pulse weak as a distant echo. He had run from the apartment when he'd heard footsteps upstairs. Scrambled up over the icy snowbank and raced down the street to lose his tracks in the salty street slush. They had found fingerprints on Rod's neck afterwards, but they had not been Gerry's. They belonged to the upstairs tenant who had come down to see what all the racket was about and had found Rod's beaten body, checked his pulse, and then had *not* called the RNC for some reason. It was Mick who'd found Rod at 4:00 a.m. and called it in. When the RNC discovered that the prints on Rod's neck belonged to the guy who lived upstairs, they had the man arrested and, based on later evidence and his criminal history, he was convicted of the assault. Gerry thinks of all this, of how relieved he should feel, but he cannot think of anything but Rod's pockmarked face. And the broken rosary in his pocket is a constant reminder that he is more than a liar.

Worse.

It was the pink panties. Their presence, stained and soaking in the sink, kept Gerry from fully condemning himself. He keeps wondering if Rod was not just an old pervert and that his beating was more than deserved. But there is no way of knowing for certain. All he knows is that in a split second he imagined a whole sordid, secret life for Rod and his rage made swinging the tire iron easy—sickly satisfying as he felt Rod's jaw dislocate, heard his collar bone crunch. Gerry knows that he did not kill Rod, but he also knows he has not stopped butchering him in his mind, making him out to be some demented freak, someone other than just the recycling guy next door who cared for a scraggly cat and who would ask permission to warm cans of ravioli on Lisette's charcoal barbecue on hot summer nights.

Writing the story, Gerry knows, was a way of convincing himself that Rod was a pedophile, like so many of the Catholic priests he has been hearing about these days on the news. And the thought of Rod—of anyone—doing that to a kid made him smoulder.

He said as much in his story. He had written about feeling filthy, lurking in Rod's stinking bedroom.

But I'm not as innocent as I let on, he writes now on notepaper. As he writes he kicks his skates under the table—boiling inside.

He is four and a half pints in, and he cannot straighten things out in his head. He can't sort out what he's done to Rod from what he wishes he'd been able to do to his father. He thinks of his dad and his crazed rants about the long-lost nation of Newfoundland. He had not really understood them when he was a boy and, as he grew older, he wondered if his father had understood them. But his dad styled himself a patriot, a masterless man—a regular old garbage-picking Peter Easton, rebel with a red face and faded pirate Tigger tattoo.

Gerry's dad used to tell the story of when he supposedly snuck into John Crosbie's house when Crosbie was chancellor of Memorial University, shortly after he had retired as the Canadian fisheries minister in the early nineties. In some versions his father masqueraded as a plasterer; in others he was a painter or an electrician. If he was drunk when he told it, and unusually animated, he was a plumber, though he knew nothing of plumbing except how to back it up with his massive morning dumps. That, of course, just signalled his punch line: when his father dropped his drawers and *shat* right in John Crosbie's fancy shoes. For takin the fuckin heart out of this country, his father would rage, slapping the table and cursing the politician for spearheading the cod moratorium in 1992 instead of sending out an armed fleet to drive off the big international fishing trawlers like the Icelanders had done.

He knew his father hated telling the story with their neighbour Ted at the table, though, because Ted had apparently been there and had helped Gerry's dad get into Crosbie's house and he always said, Yes, but that's when the honourable JC caught you with your arse hanging out. The way Ted told it, Gerry's dad got whipped within an inch of his life with John Crosbie's belt and had his face ground in his own shit. That wasn't how it happened, Gerry's father would say, shaking his head and going red. It was the only time you've ever shaved that dirty moustache, Ted would chuckle back as he rolled another cigarette. And then they would fall to laughing or cursing and carrying on with each other, while Gerry and Trudy stole sips of beer from their fathers' sweating bottles.

Gerry wondered what Ted had done to his dad when he'd found out about what had happened to Trudy. His father was missing four teeth, the tip of his tongue had been bitten off, and he had a blackened necktie bruise, like he had been strangled, when the RNC came to arrest him. Gerry knows his dad must have been relieved to be arrested; he didn't fight them, though he always fought the cops. It had made no sense to Gerry then, and it was not until years later that he began to make sense of it, began to really hate his father for what he believed he'd done to Trudy, who had moved with her dad to Corner Brook so that she could grow up away from her abuser. But they didn't need to move, Gerry thought, because when his dad got out he moved to Renews.

Gerry has not seen him since. He has thought many times of renting a car, driving down the Southern Shore and finding the shack by the sea where his father now lives. But he has never gone through with it because he could never make his seething anger take the shape of what he actually wanted to do to the man. Now, though, now he knows what it is like to break open skin, crack bones—blind someone.

Yet, try as he might, he cannot twist Rod's face into his father's.

He orders another drink and as the bartender passes him back his change he remembers the strange letter his dad sent him a few years ago, postmarked Ferryland. It was pen scribbled on notepaper torn from a spiral-bound notebook and the corner was coffee stained: three circles overlaying each other. How long the letter had sat on his dad's table before it was sent he had no idea, but in it his dad apologized for all that he had done and not done. In broken English, rife with misspellings, he wrote that living in Renews had been fine until a young mother had recognized his face on a website listing the whereabouts of convicted sex offenders. Since then he'd had teens throw stones at him and call him a pervert; young mothers called their children inside when he walked down the road on his way to the store; and he had even had a man in the passenger seat of a pickup fire a rifle over his head during moose season. He said he was terrified and wanted to move but didn't know where to go. He slept with an old bayonet he'd found in a field outside Bay Bulls. He wanted to return to St. John's but wouldn't until his son asked him to. He had found God and knew the *relefe* of confession and hoped, one day, his son would forgive him and ask to see him again.

Gerry sits with his pen hovering over his own notebook and remembers crumpling the letter up and saying it would be a fucking hot day in hell when he asks to see his father again. But he also remembers the chill of the Basilica on a blustery Sunday morning early in October, the sulphur smell of struck matches and cigarette smoke wafting into the narthex from three old men taking quick puffs before mass. Even now he has no idea what he was expecting to find in that vaulted room illuminated by the bodies of stained-glass saints, that sanctuary that his father said had been stuccoed by a convict in the 19th century. *Us sinners are good for something, hey,* his dad had whispered, cuffing Gerry on the shoulder, but Gerry knew that his father had no art besides bottle picking. He had only been to the obligatory masses as a kid: those that his father was drunk enough to want to attend when he was swamped in bleary-eyed nostalgia—Christmas, Easter, All Souls Day.

But the day Gerry went alone had been the first time in a long while that he'd been back to the Basilica. During the mass he had heard nothing he remembered, but walking out the front door he'd looked up at the white marble statue of John the Baptist staring out through the Narrows to the open sea, holding a baptismal shell in his giant right hand, nothing in his left. And he remembered the night his father had him climb up to the statue and pry loose *Johnny-boy's* iron shepherd's crook. The thing must have weighed half as much as Gerry's ten-year-old body, but his dad had insisted on bolting it above their entrance. Keep the devil from the door, he had said, winking as he walked away. Gerry knew it was a trophy for his dad, a conversation piece to prove how daring he was, even though it had been his son who had retrieved it for him. But the wrought-iron crook had pulled loose of the water-stained, mouldy gyproc one night after a rainstorm and had come clanging down on his dad's drunken head, so his dad had thrown the *Goddamned* thing in the dumpster. *If Christ Almighty wants to club me again he'll have to do it with his own Jesus bloody hand!* Gerry had laughed bitterly at the memory, even as one of those same three men he had passed earlier offered him a smoke and asked him what the joke was.

Gerry liked that his dad was a pariah in Renews: that he was mocked, spit at, cursed, and even, in a way, hunted. But the idea that his dad had now found God irritated Gerry. Why should a church whose priests had buggered kids be able to absolve the old fucker and dare to say he was forgiven? Where was the bloody hand of Christ's judgement then? Where was the crook in his dad's conscience? How could his father possibly believe that a few Hail Marys did anything but waste time and callus the thumb that rolled the rosary beads?

He had not been back to the Basilica since that day. But he had watched from home, on cable spliced from his neighbour's line, as the media continued to flay the Irish Christian Brothers to the bone, as stories surfaced about priests involved in the abuses who had been shipped to mainland rehab centres and then given new religious postings elsewhere in Canada, bishops and priests constantly denying these accusations, and Gerry more and more imagining what it would feel like to smash those bishops' smug faces in——to claw his father's eyes out of his sunken sockets.

He thinks now that while his father must have been reacquainting himself with liturgy, he had been delving into contemporary literature and he had even begun to write a little—short stories that he would mail in each year to Arts and Letters competition and which, each year, were mailed back to him with nice, hand-written rejection slips and useless feedback. Why did he even take up trying to write? He has asked himself this more often lately. In his first years of university he had thought of himself as the original postmodern Romantic—— thinking he was the first to swim up that stream. But after thrashing about in the upper pool of higher education for a few years now, he hears the *Dead Poets Society* credo differently. Now the words *carpe diem* make him think of a bloated bottom feeder—his dad with dorsal fins and whiskers—rather than an injunction.

He is thinking about quitting school to try writing full time, but the thought of maybe living in poverty again scares him. He knows what it is like to eat dry Mr. Noodles every day for lunch and plain macaroni with ketchup every night for supper. He does not want to go back to that. University life has become comfortable for him. He has begun to think of student loans as a steady income, good grades as job security. He has, on occasion joked with Natalie about going for his PhD if the writing doesn't work out. The first time he had mentioned it was back when Natalie had moved here from the mainland and Gerry did not know what to make of her. *But she's cool*, he thinks now, sipping his beer, clicking his pen, *she fits with Lisette and me here. Even likes my taste in books.*

Though she dog-ears them, and that pisses him off.

He'd told her that once, out on a hike, but she had just laughed and told him to smile as she angled her camera up to get his face and the Canadian flag atop Cabot Tower. He'd stuck his tongue out like Gene Simmons and had given the Canadian flag the finger, all the time thinking the PhD idea was a lie because he had already pretty much decided to abandon academia, having found no more enlightenment there than in the Church.

The Church, once a magical, mysterious place full of glowing, stained-glass saints staring down on him at Christmas and Easter, now seemed hollow and gutted: as empty as the Irish Christian Brothers' orphanage before it was razed to the ground, the land sold to pay off victims, and a Sobeys built in its stead.

Gerry had tried to think of what he was doing with his writing as substantiating life to the page, making something that was more meaningful than anything he'd found in school or church. But as he reads over the story he has written about Rod—the story he has now received funding to turn into a novel—he feels sick because the story is both a condemnation of Rod and a love letter to him.

His ambivalence about what he's done often sours to guilt, try as he might to convince himself otherwise. That's why he wants to flesh out Rod's character, give him a history, a context, maybe even a reason for doing what he did to that girl. Hab had put Gerry in contact with his nan and pop, who live in Fawkes Cove, where Gerry has decided to locate Rod's home. Gerry has already been out there a few times to visit, and Hab's pop, Des, let Gerry nose around in his shed, which he said he was planning on renovating: Don't know that you'll find any story ideas in here, but you can look.

Gerry had found little of interest except a rusty old tobacco tin with some obscure letters rolled up inside. But he had decided that Rod's *home* would be in Fawkes Cove, and, if his novel follows the course he has outlined, he will return Rod to that quiet outport in the end, maybe for a peaceful death. Now, though, he cannot seem to get beyond the short story that started the whole thing: he cannot get past that day he waled on Rod's flinching body, unable to stop himself—not wanting to. He has not been able to see the events of that day objectively, no matter how hard he has tried to do so in writing them. He cannot forgive either himself or Rod, even though *he* knows he is the coward.

No, he thinks, *worse than that.*

The cold steel in his hand that day felt good, reassuring, just. Like a crisp close to a thriller, one that leaves a reader haunted. Like that novel he had read a month back—those last words of the serial killer X to the reader: *I know where you live.* Perfect. And terrifying. He remembers his pulse that day, feeling the blood throb in his neck as he crouched behind Rod's counter. He had been scared and livid enough to levitate, ready to explode. He had never felt like that before and he has not felt like that since. He'd been pissed off earlier tonight when he'd gone to Mile One Stadium for free skating and found it closed because they were setting up for a big magic show.. And he remembers thinking he wanted to slit David Copperfield's throat with his skate. But he hadn't meant it. He knows, though, that if he had had a skate in hand that day in Rod's apartment, he would have slit Rod's throat, or at least he'd have tried.

Gerry had run his thumb hard along his skate blade all the way down Water Street to Erin's Pub, thinking about this. The snow had started to slash down and he'd figured it was Sheilagh's Brush blowing in—again. The sting of his thumb's slit skin had been a strange relief to his remembrance of that day and his guilt over it. He had sucked on the wound, spit out the blood onto the newly white snow. And the salty taste had made him crave dark ale.

And to tell the truth.

Come clean. For once.

He no longer wants to be like some drunk mummer harassing an old woman for her rum because she can't see his face and he can be an arse and not be found out. Like when he was fourteen and he and his friends would dress up like they did in the old days and raise some hell around Christmastime: Gerry's step-mum's nylons over his face. He had once held up Queen's Convenience with a broken beer bottle, though he'd never been charged.

But mummers also scare the piss out of Gerry. *What a fucked-up tradition*, he thinks. A crowd of them had come over to his dad's house in Buckmaster's Circle when Gerry was thirteen. They had busted in and had started jannying about. One with pineapples for boobs and another in an RNC officer's uniform with a dildo strapped on backwards, and a third in longjohns, an old goalie mask and a purple wig. The one had gotten right up in Gerry's face and had said, *Gerry my son, I knows where you were last night.* So Gerry had punched the mummer in the throat and the guy had to rip off his mask to catch his breath. It had been Gerry's pop, who only had but one lung because of cancer. Gerry had felt genuinely bad.

But he'd been terrified.

Of what, exactly, he doesn't know. Something he cannot understand fully. Like those stained pink panties in Rod's sink and Mick's girl riding in Rod's cart down the slushy road. He had wondered why the panties were there, and why they were stained, and with what.

What did he make that girl do? What did he do to her?

This thought is as icy as the tire iron in Gerry's hand that day in Rod's apartment, hearing the old man suddenly at the door, blood rushing in his ears like so many roaring accusations: his anger frothing. He thinks of himself crouched there, fisting steel found in Rod's closet of random objects. The girl's underwear soaking in his sink.

Had Rod asked her to take them off or taken them off himself? Did he touch her?

What did he do to that little girl?

What?

Rod's footsteps on that day echo in Gerry's mind above the memory of Johnny Cash's quavering voice in the bar when he

first arrived, singing about how God was going to cut him down. Between the echo of the song's stomp and clap in his memory he hears those unsteady footsteps and then Rod's pathetic, cracked voice calling out: *Who's in there?* And then Rod scuffs into the apartment—*boom, clap, boom, clap*—the carpet crunching under his big green boots—*boom, clap, boom, clap*—his glasses cockeyed after Gerry takes out his kneecaps, before smashing the glasses from Rod's upturned face.

He remembers stepping over Rod's body, now huddled in a heap by the door.

He looks at the words he has written on notepaper stained with three pint-glass rings of beer: a page of his coil bound notebook, like that coffee-stained letter from his father. Red ink is scrawled from edge to edge. *His body heaped by the door.*

The word *blood* gashed everywhere.

Gerry knows it is Holy Thursday today because Hab had told him so and had invited him to an evening mass, but Gerry had said no and had taken his ice skates downtown to go to Mile One, thinking he would burn off some of his nervous energy. He is glad to be getting drunk instead of sitting in a service or even gliding around an indoor rink. And, really, he needs to be drunk to write about the truth of what happened when Rod came home and found him in his apartment: surprised him, scared the defensive street punk he once was back into full swing, made him hairup like a cornered cat. The notebook is soaking up spilled beer on the table in front of him. The pen in his hand is shaking.

This scrawled confession feels as lukewarm to him as the almost half pint of bitter he gulps. Coffee-coloured foam slides to the bottom of his empty glass. He folds up the notebook and wedges it into his back pocket, leaves his table in the corner by the window and heads for the bathroom in the back past the bar, past the slot machines.

The room is small and the trashcan in the corner is overflowing with damp paper towels. There are two urinals on the left with stuffed headrests nailed to the wall above them, green

A BLESSED SNARL

fabric split from so many drunken heads leaning there. Gerry stares at the one in front of him as he pisses and leans back to avoid the spatter.

There is a groan from the stall next to him and a wet heaving sound as someone vomits into the toilet. Gerry spits into the urinal, zips up, and goes to wash his hands, but there is no soap and the paper towel is all used up.

The sick man in the stall turns out to be a girl in the wrong washroom who heads out the door before Gerry, so he hangs back a bit in the shadows. *Don't need anyone getting the wrong idea.* The musician's Spanish-sounding guitar around the corner slips inside the body of an old Irish song and makes Gerry want to kiss someone. *Anyone.* Except maybe the girl who just heaved her guts out. *She should be to her table by now.* He rounds the corner and heads to the bar to ask for soap and paper towels.

But he stops short at the sight sitting there on a stool.

The same orange coveralls sooty with street grime from collecting recyclables. Scuffed green rubber boots up to his knees; knitted beanie cockeyed on his greying hair; a new cane hooked on the bar edge by his elbow. And Gerry sees the shopping cart out the big front window.

He has not seen Rod since he left the old drunk in his dingy apartment; since he saw the medics taking his body away on a stretcher. He had wondered then, feeling numb looking out his bedroom window, if that last blow to the head did more than knock Rod out cold.

That was months back now.

But here he is, in the flesh, sitting at the bar in front of the kid who almost killed him.

Gerry thinks Rod will see him as the old guy turns stiffly so he ducks in behind him but catches sight of an eye patch on Rod's right eye, under his thick glasses. Rod asks for more rum in a gurgling voice and holds out his glass to the bartender, and Gerry spies a wad of bills in Rod's other hand.

He's working again, he thinks, relieved for some reason.

Then Rod turns to the door to see a bouncer ushering the

sick girl through—her miniskirt tucked into the back of her red thong, bum cheeks pink in the cold—and Gerry dives back around the corner into the bathroom. He catches a glimpse of himself in the mirror over the sink: lines around his eyes red and cursive, like his father's eyes after a few drinks. The door opens behind him and he rushes into the single stall and locks the door, realizing too late that he is standing in puke.

He grabs for the loose roll of toilet paper but it flops and rolls under the stall door, unravelling as it goes, right up to that familiar set of scuffed rubber boots. Gerry can hear Rod pissing and then he sees the cane lift out of sight. He thinks Rod might know it's him, and the old guy is getting ready to kick open the door and cane him. But then Gerry sees the straight handle of Rod's cane slip into the toilet paper cylinder and roll it back under the stall door, against his vomit-slick shoe.

There ya are, Rod says, and Gerry tries to disguise his voice by making it deeper. But the suck of air and the sick stink underfoot turns his stomach, and he spins and upchucks five pints into the toilet.

Better out 'an in, Rod laughs and Gerry hears him leave.

Gerry is sick again and he is not thinking clearly, at least he doesn't think so, because he is trying to imagine a way out of the pub other than right past Rod at the bar, but he knows there isn't one.

Get out of the stall at least.

Frig.

He gently pushes open the door and peers out. Rod is still there, sitting at the bar, eye patch to Gerry and another drink in hand. Gerry thinks he can blindside Rod and slip out the door, collar up and head down. But Rod is looking toward the window, toward Gerry's now-empty seat. He wonders if Rod had seen him there from outside, across the snowy street, before he got up to take a leak.

Does he know I'm here at all?

Gerry still thinks he can sneak past him. So he steps softly until he is three feet away ... *now two, one.* He hears the bartender ask Rod how he's going to get his cart up the hill in the blizzard that's coming down now.

Rod: Chain it up in an alley. Get it in the morning, sure. I gots to be to the courthouse tomorrow either way, so I can pick it up after.

What they charge ya with this time?

Not me, Rod cackles. A guy I know. Hurt his little girl.

You defending or testifying against?

Against, b'y. Against.

Glad to hear it, the bartender says as Gerry passes behind Rod's back. We could do with a few more bastards behind bars, hey?

Gerry is trying to hold steady what he's hearing, trying to keep his thoughts from spinning with the crowded room.

Tell you what, the bartender says to Rod as he tops up two rum and Cokes, when you come for the cart, stop in and I'll buy you a drink.

Sounds good, b'y, sounds good, Rod slurs and coughs into his sleeve.

Gerry has inched his way to the door but he can still hear Rod's thick voice: *I'll take another now, though*. His fingers touch the brass handle and the door swings in suddenly and knocks him into the corner. Three big guys with goatees, earrings and leather jackets come in, smelling of cigarettes, stamping work boots and swearing about the cold. Gerry pegs them as being on shore-leave from the rigs.

Sorry, buddy, they're saying, Didn't see ya there.

But Gerry is trying to push past them without a word, wondering who it is that Rod is going to testify against, and that's when he glances and sees Rod looking up at him and then over to where he had been sitting by the window. Gerry sees the orange-clad old gimp start and he turns and runs out into the weather.

Snow lashes down on wind whipping up Water Street and drifts against shop doors and around car wheels. The snow is unploughed, wet, heavy and hard to walk through. It soaks

Gerry's ankles and shoes. *Stupid to wear shoes this time of year*, he thinks, cursing himself as he tries to run and slips.

He is pushing up Water toward George Street through the drifts, wondering if it is Mick who Rod is going to testify against tomorrow. His thoughts are racing from Mick to his daughter to the stained pink panties in Rod's sink when he sees lights coming down the road: snowmobiles racing illegally, taking advantage of an unploughed downtown after midnight—drunk or on a dare.

Two of them whiz by, and in the lull Gerry hears Rod's voice calling:

Hey!

And Gerry walks faster, kicking at the snow—wondering why Rod would take the stand against Mick—trying to move his body faster through the snow.

Hey buddy! You were sittin by the window!

Rod's slurred and phlegmy voice calls again but Gerry keeps his back turned, his thoughts pummelling his skull, beating him down. He is thinking now that Rod might have been doing something else with that girl than what he had imagined: maybe Rod really was nothing like his father. *Trying to help the girl, after Mick*—

Hey! He hears Rod yell again above the screeching wind and he looks back, thinking that if the old guy is walking with a cane now he won't be able to catch up with him in this heavy, wet snow.

Again Rod's voice calls above the gale and Gerry glances to see the old drunk coming after him with his own skates in his hands: waving them crazily, the blades flashing in the snow and dim streetlights.

Move faster, he pants in his mind.

The snow is up to his shins and the wind in the power lines is buzzing like those Ski-doos coming back and Rod's voice is yelling at Gerry, telling him he forgot his skates even as Gerry steps out onto the road, his thoughts wheeling and lurching. He hears a sudden roar, spins and sees a bright light flash.

The Ski-doo stops just shy of busting his kneecap.

What the——?

I need a ride, he tells the driver, who is cursing him through the muffle of his full-face helmet. The guy on the sled looks up and sees the girl in the miniskirt on the sidewalk—waiting for a bus not coming in this weather—recording him on her cell phone.

Come on, he says, thumbing Gerry to the seat behind him.

Rod is almost caught up to them, stumbling in the snow, trying to juggle two skates and a cane. Gerry tells the driver that Rod is a drunk after him with those friggin skates, *so hit it.* The guy does, and Gerry almost rolls off the back of the Ski-doo as it wakes Rod in a wave of wet slush.

Where to? the driver yells over the engine noise, dusting up to eighty klicks.

The Shamrock.

And that is where the guy drops Gerry before buzzing off at the sound of a siren from a cop car parked around the corner. Gerry slips off into the shadows between buildings, comes out into the neon lights of Mexicali Rosa's and heads down past the Cotton Club and the dancers smoking outdoors in flimsy robes. They are not smiling like they do onstage. *Why would they?* Gerry realizes. *It's miserable out tonight.* He recognizes one of them as a girl from his American Lit class and he waves, but she just blows smoke and seems to stare right through him into the stormy night.

Gerry moves on, hands deep in his pockets, his thoughts tangling his dad's stories with his own like his fingers cinched up in that black rosary—shitting in John Crosbie's shoes, sneaking into a drunk's apartment, stealing the sceptre of John the Baptist, splitting open a man's skull for something that maybe he didn't do. Had he been wrong? Was there no justification for what he did that day? *Was I that fucked up?*

All he can think about as he crosses over toward Mile One Stadium is that Rod is alive and okay and he is so relieved that he is crying and coughing at the same time, snow melting on his face—hot in this frigging cold. He had been digging in his thoughts through sharp, shale rock memories of his father, to unearth the truth of the day Rod caught him in that rundown apartment and he whacked the old man and left him for dead.

He'd told the cops, when they came to his door early the next morning, that he knew nothing. He had been surprised at how easily the lies came, as fluidly as writing about it, fictionalizing it. He lied but also told them the truth: that the guy who lived above Rod had been beating a buddy on his porch one night earlier in the winter, yelling: Do you know who I am? Do you fuckin know what I've done—what I can do? Did the little pissers tell you that in Whitbourne? Do you know who the fuck I am?

And that had moved the searchlight from Gerry to this guy— Troy Hopper—and, fortunately for Gerry, Troy had a history of violent domestic abuse *and* he had a meth lab in his closet.

The RNC took those things into account, along with the bloody tire iron they found wrapped in a cloth in Troy's drop ceiling. He claimed that he had lost it in the snow months before and that he thought Rod must have found it and stashed it in his apartment. *Whoever the fuck did this, they used that thing and I hid it 'cause I didn't want it coming back to me.* Gerry had sat in on the trial, out of curiosity, and when he heard this he remembered when they'd watched Troy beat a guy on his porch and drop something heavy into the snow bank— something Rod had scurried off with into his apartment.

Troy was asked why he didn't just call in to the RNC that he had found his neighbour beaten and half frozen. *Would you cunts have believed me if I had?* Gerry could not have planned a better cover-up or picked a better fall guy. He had listened to Troy tell the judge to go to hell, and he had watched him get convicted, handcuffed, and sent off to the penitentiary— knowing that it should have been himself in those irons, ducking his head and crawling into the back of a cruiser headed toward Her Majesty's Penitentiary.

Gerry had watched and said nothing, done nothing except, every day, peer out his window, looking for Rod to come back to that dirty apartment, which he figured would never happen.

That became a certainty the day when Gerry saw the next-door landlord throw Rod's stuff out onto the curb in garbage bags for pick-up: those pink, stained panties gone—a mystery. Like the drunk who was washing them for some reason in his sink. He does not know why he never imagined he would see Rod again; why he had thought Rod would go away, especially when the memory of him haunted Gerry as constantly as the memory of his father.

All he knows is that Natalie has seen a difference in him since that day. She has said as much. Gerry knows he has gone from outspoken to moody. He has stopped his inane rants about the Republic of Newfoundland and the motherfucking mainlander tourists—cheap echoes of his dad's ravings and rants. And he wonders if his father even cares about these things anymore or is now more concerned with surviving his neighbours.

Neither Natalie nor Lisette mention Rod, but Gerry thinks of him every time Snuggles purrs and rubs her face up under the cuff of his jeans. Nor have they asked Gerry about his taking Snuggles in after Rod was taken away in an ambulance. Gerry thinks they must wonder about him, though: his involvement, maybe.

Deep as the grave, Lisette has said when he is not in the room, when she and Natalie are talking on the couch over wine or splitting oranges with Hab.

The stairs behind Mile One rise up into the whorl of white in the night sky like the steps of an ancient ziggurat. As Gerry begins the long climb up to where he will meet Barter's Hill, he pulls away from the downtown craziness of Ski-doos on Water Street in this snowstorm and Rod flashing those skate blades like knives above his head, calling out and falling in the snow as Gerry sped away. He doesn't think Rod knew who he was at all: just wanted to give him his skates. But Rod's presence in the bar was a hand on Gerry's scalp, a blade slipped between bone and skin, flaying him open.

His lungs are raw and his Sunday clothes are salt-stained, soaked and half frozen with sea water from his mad run across the slob ice. But it is not the barbecue lighter in his hands that Patrick's thinking of, sitting in his father's cabin in the woods above Fawkes Cove. He's recalling how his father's uncle once told the story of a midnight mass in Flatrock when the priest asked those gathered if they wanted to renounce Satan and all his works, and a drunk called excitedly from the back door: *I do, the fugger!* Even half-hypothermic as he is, Patrick smiles, remembering his great uncle telling the story at that family reunion in 1994: Patrick's first time in his father's house since he'd left Newfoundland years before, around the time Dale and Rhianna split. But it's that odd story that sparks in him now—the lighter clicking away uselessly—the strange feeling that his life's a looping track and that, as fast as he's run, he's come right back to the beginning.

Patrick longs for the burn of hot tea on his tongue, in his throat, recalling the excessive drinking in his father's house. His childhood must have been as frigid as he is now because there was always a top-up of rum *to keep off the chill.*

He thinks of his great aunt Kate now, Gilbert's second wife, grabbing his great uncle between the legs, whispering something in the old man's ears, and laughing loudly as she leaned away for her gin—Great Uncle Gil's face flushed plum like their bathtub stained from sangria. The dirty mix of homemade wine, sugar, and crushed partridgeberries was a Christmas affair imported by Gilbert and Kate, who were the only Wisemans from Fawkes Cove to have been to Montreal, Spain and other places abroad.

Holding the dead lighter close to a crumpled newspaper, Patrick thinks of Gil, once a reporter for *The Telegram*, who covered several famous battles in the Second World War as a young correspondent—or so he said. He can hear his dad's voice in the cabin's deserted stillness, telling him it was the war drove his uncle to drink as much as he did, but Patrick knows his dad had not served in the army or been to war and could nearly match Great Uncle Gil drink for drink in his younger days, back when he worked for Smallwood's government and travelled a lot to the outports. Patrick remembers his dad drunk more often than not as he clicks the frozen lighter uselessly, hoping for even a tiny flame to ignite the kindling in the cold stove, recalling sleepily when he had tried the sangria once as a fourteen-year-old. He liked the fruity pungent kick of it, but was so sick that night that he vomited chunks of carrot out his nose.

Him being on his knees in front of the cold stove brings to his mind the many times he had testified in church services that this was his first and last night of drinking and the beginning of his search for God outside the candlelight and incense and imported statues of his family's Catholicism—gone beyond the beyond, his nan said of him years later. Confession that had once been such a relief to him became embarrassing, and because he was not going regularly to confession he denied himself the Eucharist by crossing his arms over his chest when he approached the priest, until his father asked him one Sunday what it was that he'd done and not confessed. He looked past his father in the pew to his Great Uncle Gilbert who was popping a breath mint before crossing himself and staggering bleary-eyed toward the aisle—the priest intoning *the body of Christ* each time a wafer was placed on a tongue. But he could not answer his father either that day or in the weeks that followed.

Just talk to the boy, Gil. Will ya? He looks up to you. Patrick had heard his father say this to his great uncle one day.

Click, click.

The lighter won't even spark in his fingers, and all he can see before him is not his blue, shaking hands but the dash of his great uncle's car on that day they drove down through St. John's, out past Kilbride to Bay Bulls. His Great Uncle Gil had driven straight up to the door of St. Peter and St. Paul Church, turned off the car, and reached over to the glove compartment by Patrick's knees to draw out a flask tucked under his car insurance.

This, my son, is where I met Christ.

Patrick thinks of that day and how he'd thought his great uncle was, for one moment in his life, going to be serious and solemn. But the old man took a swig and jerked his thumb out the rolled-down window: *And that's* him *right there!* He gestured to a statue of the saviour with arms raised on a pedestal about twenty yards away. He took another swig and then pointed out Patrick's window. *And that,* he said crossing himself as he touched the flask to his lips again, *is his mum.*

Can you believe—the old man began after a moment's silence, and Patrick thought Gil was going to chastise him about his lagging ability to believe in his family's religion. *Can you believe Joseph never once shagged her?*

Patrick remembers the old man looking down at his belly spilling over his belt and then staring out the front window for a long time before saying anything. *Patrick,* he said after a while, his voice low and guttural, *I'm old and I'm not a good man. So don't look up to me. Your father wants me to straighten you out, but you listen to me and you'll become crookeder than scoliosis. Faerie fucked.*

He giggled at his take on *faerie struck* and took another drink.

Your father sees visions, ya know.

The comment had come at Patrick like a feral thing in the

dark—like the shiver seizing him now—clawing at his questions, biting his lip to silence as he heard his uncle go on: He thinks I'm the more grounded man in the family, Patrick. And he likes me because I've seen the world and I still goes to church. Sign of strong faith for him, I suppose. Comforting habit for me. Nice to have the old boy in the big hat lie to you once in a while, tell you you're forgiven. Your dad wants you to take confession.

What kind of visions? Patrick remembers asking as his great uncle turned the car on and backed down toward the road and the gate.

Of *her*, Gil said braking and motioning out Patrick's window with his enormous chin at the Madonna standing on an orb and crushing a serpent.

Mary?

Yeah. Apparently her face is rusted into the flashing around the chimney at the cabin—or some such nonsense, Gilbert said as he pulled up by the gate of the church.

Does Mum know?

I know. And now you know. You also know I've nothing deep to tell you, right?

Patrick tries to focus on the lighter in his hands but he is back in that car years ago, watching his Great Uncle Gil take three long swigs, shake the hollow flask, and cluck his tongue. Ya know, he said with a hiccup, this whole bay was once ablaze. Every last house. And the old church sending sparks higher than the rest. It was Admiral Richery who started the fire back in seventeen-something-or-other.

The thought of fire smokes uselessly in Patrick's mind even as he hears his great uncle's voice, the elderly man telling him of Admiral Richery who tried to storm St. John's but, finding it too well defended, threw a tantrum and burned Bay Bulls to the ground instead.

That kept the old man laughing to himself all the way back through the Goulds and it makes Patrick grin coldly now as he remembers the guide on the boat tour out of Bay Bulls,

because the guide told the same story. That was a week after they'd moved to Newfoundland: a week of unpacking, microwave dinners and then the boat tour on that grey day when they saw no icebergs and Anne puked all over Patrick's Sunday shoes.

Patrick's run across the heaving sea ice in those same shoes had been two steps from a suicide attempt. It was something he had done as a boy but also something Anne would never approve of: leaping from pan to slick pan, tilting sometimes suddenly into the frigid water—the pain like a polar bear gnawing his legs. And running: like a child, dare-devil, mad man. Propelling his body forward, mind flailing. Half stunned, and frightened to death of drowning.

It was a crazed burst of desperate momentum after weeks of lying on the couch waiting for a phone call from Anne saying that she was sorry, that she was coming back. But the call never came, and there was no starter's pistol other than his fierce need to break free of her like she had broken free of him.

He had done it—made it across the bay from the south boat launch, where he left his Malibu unlocked and the keys under the mat, to the north launch where he stood, soaked and shivering, looking out at the cathedral-sized iceberg rising above the cliffs at the mouth of the cove—hearing it crack with a thunderous *boom* as it split down a deep blue freeze-line and calved, birthing a monstrous wave that swept over his running path. The sight of that newly split, eon-old ice made him think of that boat tour in Bay Bulls, Anne's disappointment at seeing no icebergs, the skipper's fiery story and the memory of the first time he had heard it in his uncle's car.

All this comes to Patrick—calling him away from his concern to light a fire into a false Darby warmth—as he sits in his dad's cabin, freezing. He's shivering and his mouth tastes of salt from his bloody chapped lips. His clothes are still damp, his peacoat and pants soaked through, and his socks frozen stiff. He cannot feel his toes, yet he cannot stop his mind from coiling back to Great Uncle Gil and these strange memories from his youth.

He is staring into the cold mouth of the old wood stove, thinking of his uncle weaving drunkenly around potholes on their way back through St. John's that day. Patrick's recollections careen from that drive to the last time he saw Great Uncle Gil in 1994, the old man's strong chin sagging into his sunken chest, his face sad, and Eliza, his fourth wife, always telling him to not look so down.

And then Gil had told them the story of the interrupted midnight mass to get people laughing. After that he headed off to the kitchen to top-up his glass of rum. That's when Eliza told them all that the story was not Gil's but had come from a new book of memoirs by an Irish writer she liked very much and that Gil had only passed it off as his own because he knew it would get a laugh. Patrick begrudged Eliza her truth—told only when her deaf husband was out of the room—and he hated the way the disclosure made his great uncle seem smaller when the old man stepped shakily back into the room, his tumbler brimmed brown and his eyes fierce and watering as he stared at his hand, willing the shaking to stop.

Patrick is willing his own hands to stop trembling. He holds them together, fingers locked around the barbecue lighter in his coat pocket. He had thought himself pretty smart for having the foresight to bring it along—though he had intended it only to burn the letters from Anne's father: a way of cutting himself free. Now he holds the lighter in his frozen fingers—his stiff leather gloves by his feet—trying to click the starter, but there is no spark, no flame.

No surprise, really, that the lighter would be frozen, since his peacoat is stiff with slushed sea water and freezing rain. When he arrived at the cabin his glasses were speckled with ice globulating the grey evening light as he tramped through crunchy snow, his ankles raw in thin socks from the hike through the bush. He had been carrying one plastic bag of groceries with him when he arrived and went straightaway to grab two junks of spruce from the woodpile. Then to the firebox in the shed to get some paper, as he and Dale did when they were boys. But the box was empty. He went around to the cabin door then, tried to feel out the key hidden in the gap between the warped window fitting and the wall, but it wasn't there.

Why isn't it in the old hiding spot?

By this time his legs were going rubbery and he knew he needed to get inside and get a fire lit. He tucked his blue fist in his coat sleeve and punched in the window by the door. He'd already ripped his coat on the jagged glass by the time he realized he had punched in the window furthest away from the doorknob he was trying to reach. So he smashed the other window, jimmied the lock, and finally got into the cabin.

That was how he came to be here, trying to defrost his lighter in clammy hands, wondering at the burning sensation in his feet, ankles, and calves. Wondering why he had been driven to jump from ice pan to ice pan across the heaving bay. Knowing it was to prove something, but what? To get away, okay, but to where? Or was it just to feel himself running, his pulse throbbing in his neck, legs going numb, lungs bursting—pitching his body forward?

He'd bought the groceries at the corner store: everything he'd thought necessary to survive up in his dad's cabin for a few days. To be alone and not in his house with her things still surrounding him: her Herbal Essence shampoo in the shower; satin soft floss on the counter; the smell of her clothes still dirty in the laundry hamper.

He left the car by the boat launch in Fawkes Cove, where he'd ventured out onto the crashing spring ice. As far as he remembered, cars parked alongside the road, as long as they weren't within city limits, were no problem in Newfoundland. Folks would probably think the owner of the Malibu was visiting relatives out around the bay and had parked there to avoid getting stuck on the icy hills.

Two or three days were all he needed, and he only had enough food for that long anyway. Two cans of tomato soup, a tin of creamed corn, four cans of ravioli, a box of Tetley's, and a Mr. Big candy bar. All in the plastic bag on the metal table with the one wooden leg across the room, behind Patrick's back.

He is still sporadically clicking the lighter each time he opens his eyes as his head nods and his body keeps jerking him from warm sleep. *Click.* Blink. *Click.* He slips from the chair to his knees, bent over the lighter like a supplicant, shaking. And then his eyes close and do not open. His body sways, jerks, and falls to the floor.

Smoke like cream swirling in stirred tea. A touch of rough heat, hand-like on his cheek. Burning. Cold fire. Knuckles kneading into ribs. *Sit up, ya sook.* Singing swallow's *hoo* in the hollow dark like a kettle whistling. Red glowing coals sparked. Scraping iron, creak and latch, *My son. Silly as all get out* this stuttering and trying to stop a word long enough to say it.

G-g-great-Uncle Gil.

Long dead, Patrick.

His name coming to him familiar as a spanking for sneaking the sangria: the voice, the swat, the swift kick.

Dad?

Yes, my son.

Patrick opens his eyes a slit. Glances about him. Candlelight coming in soft washes from the table. Jack-o'-lantern glow giving shape to the dark room. Night. He is wrapped in a greasy old sleeping bag where he had fallen on the floor by the stove. But the stove is glowing now, and throwing waves of smoky heat. He goes to move his arm up his body and realizes he is naked except for his feet in heavy woollen socks that are not his, his ankles itchy. Then he sees his clothes drooped over chairs seated about him and the stove, so many soggy skins steaming.

Faerie fucked. Great Uncle Gil's voice laughing in his head, but that is how he feels lying here—though he would never say so. Like he has been dragged through the woods and stuffed in a burrow or ditch. Kicked and slashed. Like the abduction stories of children by the little folk told by his nan to make him go to bed in her old saltbox that stood too near the sea to sleep soundly, the house alive with creaks and groans. He feels like King David at the end of his life, lying in bed, old and feeble, unable to keep himself warm, worrying about the future of his kingdom, his son.

See you brought supper, Pat.

His dad's voice is coming from behind him now, by the table.

There's not a can opener in this whole cabin, though. Guess you were just gonna gnaw into them, once you got hungry enough.

Right now Patrick wants the Mr. Big.

D-d-dad?

Yes.

C-c-can you pass me the chocolate bar?

I'm after eating it.

What? Patrick half rolls over to look at his dad cockeyed from the floor, his father in big green rubber boots up to his knees, blue jeans, grey sweater, red-checked jackshirt torn at the elbows—thick moustache, bony hips.

When you're this big, they call ya mister, his dad says, thumbing his chest and smiling crooked.

You ate it?

Patrick rolls back over as his dad says yes.

How was I supposed to know you'd pull through? I think a candy bar for your frostbitten arse is a fair trade. Speaking of frostbitten, what in hell are you doing up here, half soaked and my two windows busted in?

Holiday.

I told you he wasn't right in the head.

Patrick glances back at his dad still standing by the table.

SNARE

Who're you talking to?

Our mother.

Mum's here too?

Our mother. There, you can see her face in the creosote. By the stove pipe.

Patrick looks up at the flashing on the wall and the black stain dripping down from the old rusted pipe, above the list of names carved into the wooden wall below the flashing, almost out of sight behind the stove: Hawco, Murphy, Now, O'Leary, King, Johnston, and Hynes. *Whose names are those?* He once asked his father. *Folks I ... visited. Long ago,* his dad had answered him. But the names were never as strange to him as the inky creosote apparition, even after he found out who the names belonged to and what it was his father had done.

Patrick had come up to the cabin after that long ago drive with Great Uncle Gil to Bay Bulls, to see his father's *vision* firsthand. He had never heard his father talk to it before, did not know the stain was to him animate still.

Your mother, Dad. Mary's a cult figure.

I'd say he doesn't mean it but he does.

Don't talk to it, Dad. It's black ooze. Tree gunk.

Creosote from burning green wood. I know what it is, Patrick. I'm not some dumb git you need to patronize. I've also seen that stain take the shape of her face. And I've heard her speak. Least I can do is answer back when it happens.

Hail Mary, full of grace, Patrick mutters angrily.

Full of shit's what ya mean, isn't it?

I said *grace*.

I heard the word but your tone told me somethin else.

Patrick sucks in his lips. Puffs out his cheeks. Blows out slowly and asks: Is that what you get from her, Dad?

If I'd got it, I'd wash her away with bleach. Gives me the willies sometimes.

Patrick closes his eyes, curls up in the sleeping bag. His thighs are still burning and clammy to touch. He has never

spoken with his dad about his so-called visions before. Never wanted to. They had always seemed so pagan and medieval, like his nan's talk of faeries and fey folk. Not at all like the dreams and visions of Gurney, who raised his own daughter from the dead when she was only a girl and passed away in a freak fever. His wife Anne recalled to life by a word. There was something of the fearsome Old Testament prophet to his father-in-law, something laughably yokel about his own dad. His silence around his father was like the bread his nan told him to carry in his pockets when he'd go off to play in the woods—to protect him from the faeries, *little jeezlings* she'd call them as she cut a cross in a fresh loaf of Irish soda bread.

Don't get him going, he thinks. He feels safe in silence: clammy childhood hand around a lump of hardtack. Patrick stares under the woodstove at the chunks of crumbled bark, bits of ash, and burned-out matches. The cabin smells of wood smoke, damp wool, moss, and mould. His face lies against the rough-cut wood floor. He wraps his arms around his naked body in the sleeping bag, feeling the chill axe his will to move. It's more tumble-down timber shack than cabin, but here he lies on the floor of his father's retreat, his shrine, where his dad would up and disappear to, always, it seemed, in the worst weather. As a kid, he had thought his dad was off to town to do some drinking, which his mum has told him used to be the case in the sixties and seventies. After he had quit his government job and stopped travelling to the outports. But no more drinking now. Not after seeing *her*. This is what he has told everyone anyway, but Patrick knows of the hand-labelled wine bottle in an old sock under his dad's workbench in the shed out back of his place. *Bordeaux*. It was still there the day he left for the mainland. Patrick cannot imagine it's gone now.

Patrick?

He can hear his dad take a step closer and lean on the back of one of the chairs serving as a drying rack for his clothes. Yeah?

Why were you up here, passed out and soaked to the

bone when I came in? What were you thinking in that head of yours?

Patrick shrugs in the sleeping bag, his posture making him feel vulnerable, childlike. I needed to get away, he said.

From what?

The slow crackle, hiss and pop of igniting sap in the flicker seen through stove slats hypnotizes Patrick until his tongue forms her name: Anne.

You two havin problems?

She left me, Dad.

And it is as if the cabin is an airplane hull cracked in half midflight and he is sucked out of his numbness into a stinging vacuum, grief lacerating his face like alder branches across the eyes—like when he would run through the woods as a kid to get away from his dad's voice telling him to come help with the wood.

He winces and falls to weeping, trying to muffle his sobs by burying his mouth in the sleeping bag.

His mind pulsing against memories of Anne that billow out like a drag chute, slowing the pace of his panting—her quirky humour and talking hands, her shocked look the first time she saw her reflection after having her head shaved for a church fundraiser, the wrinkles around her eyes beginning to fade for lack of laughter, her resistance to his lung-burning longing to return home.

The memory of her leaving is a sudden ragged tear and he feels himself in freefall, choking, trying to catch his breath.

He wants his father to crouch over him, to feel those big hands press through the fabric—the weight of them on his shoulder. But his dad stands slumped over the chair, thinking maybe that the sleeping bag is arms enough around his adult son, staring all the while at the creosote Madonna.

Early the next morning, before sunrise, Patrick walks on alone through the woods in his Sunday shoes, thin socks, trousers,

collared shirt, and woollen peacoat. His hands are dug deep in his pockets and his tongue is still chalky from the scalding tea his dad gave him before he left the cabin.

He had not moved the whole night, not questioning the queer silence that settled after his dad told him about his psychotic grandson, Dale's boy, and his wingnut mother Rhianna who's accused him of drinking still and other crazy shit that has turned his own grandson against him.

Dale was some stunned, b'y—to marry that one, he said with his green boots crossed near the fire. Tryin to pull things together now and get his boy back. Bought the place at the top of the hill. The old bungalow. He's jackhammering bedrock in the basement. Hauling it out in ten-gallon pails, stone by stone. Said it helps keep his mind off things Crazy said before she took off. Stuff about *me* she said she could never tell him. *Me*. I don't even wanna know what she's said about me. I just hauls the buckets for him. Help make the basement a proper room for the kid, if they ever lets him out of foster care with all the shit he's after doing.

Patrick had never heard his dad say so much to him before. After the story he pulled silence tight about his ears—his dad settling in the creaking chair—hearing only the flames flicker. He had slept soundly on the floor. His dad was still on the chair, chin on chest, when Patrick stirred in the cool morning. He slipped out of the sleeping bag in the predawn dark and crouched naked and shivering in front of the stove to stir the coals and throw on another couple junks of spruce. He no longer felt feeble, as he had the night before; he felt invigorated, ready for a challenge, like a young man ready to take hold of a kingdom at war with itself and bring peace. He dressed with his back to his dad, the older man watching through barely opened eyes as Patrick pulled on immaculately white boxer briefs, then his trousers. *Left leg first, like when he was a boy and I'd take him and his brother swimming in the pond up in the hills.* Collared shirt buttoned from the bottom up and left untucked.

Dad?

Patrick's hand soft on his shoulder and him pretending to breathe evenly, feigning sleep. Yeah, wha—?

I'm heading out now.

Stay away from the water.

Patrick smiled, wondering if his dad knew of his foolish race across the pack ice the day before, when he was running like hell, half hoping to drown.

I will, he said.

We can gnaw into a can of ravioli, if you want.

Bring a can opener up with you next time.

Let me know beforehand next time you tries freezing yourself to death, okay?

I will.

I'll make some tea before you go.

After tea, Patrick walked out of the cabin and left his dad to his silence, a mysterious backwoods communion he would never have known about had it not been for his Great Uncle Gil. They would make quite the trinity were they all three still living: Pentecostal pastor, Catholic mystic, apostate drunk— all seeing the world slantwise. None of them any more at peace than the others.

He's following his dad's tracks out now, not sure of where his own go off to at times. He wonders what it was that brought his dad up to the cabin in the freezing rain. *What brought* me *besides hypothermic stupidity?*

When he breaks from the trees at the top of the hill over-looking the cove, every dogwood branch sticking out of the snow is iced clear and distorted as the lie that spring has come. Each glistening branch knifes the morning glow so that the new pale skin sunlight is slashed from forest to sea.

He breathes in the scene sharp, squints against the violent light.

The hills, houses, tendrils of wood smoke hanging in the frigid air. The stillness fierce as a runner's high: as euphoric as when he leapt from the last tilting ice pan and landed safe.

He moves on.

It is not until he reaches the boat launch that he realizes his car is gone. *Tell me it hasn't been towed,* he thinks, looking around. That's when he sees the RNC officer jogging across the road toward him, the patrol car idling in the early morning cold.

Patrick Wiseman? the constable asks.

Yeah. Where's my car?

Down in the bay. You're within a few hours of being reported a missing person. Come on now, I'll take you to the airport.

My car's where?

In the bay.

Where?

In the bay.

Patrick blinks: How did it get there?

We're investigating that.

Stunned, Patrick stares at the police officer. And you're taking me to the airport *why?*

Your wife's flight will be landing shortly. In the meantime I'd say you've got some explaining to do. Like where you were last night and why you left your car. And I got to call it in that I found you.

Patrick feels as dizzy and disoriented as he did the night he drank his fill of sangria. The unasked question surges in his throat: Anne's coming back?

The officer escorts him to the cruiser and they head off toward the airport. Patrick's mind is grinding——steel on steel—— questions sparking off.

Why is Anne coming back?

Who would have pushed the Malibu over the cliff?

Where did I put my keys?

A day ago he'd driven this road in the opposite direction, blind to everything except the need to get away from his deserted house. He had driven right to the edge of the world, the end of the road, climbed down an ice-slicked boat launch to where the sea was heaving three-ton pans of ice up against the rocky cliffs—the sound like breaking boulders.

And he had leapt onto the crashing slob ice hoping to die but scared enough of dying to run and leap, slip, stumble and run again, jumping from one rolling ice pan to the next. Desperate and utterly exhilarated—more alive than he'd felt in years. His chest pounding then as it is now, his breath ragged and eyes wild, remembering his race across the water—not certain of landing his next step, only knowing the thrill of his body pitching forward.

III

T he old guy in the aisle seat on the plane looks a little weirded-out, and Anne thinks it's probably because her hands are talking again. Her fingers started the conversation at about thirty thousand feet after taking off from Halifax, where she had missed her connection and had an overnight layover. She has tried to keep the volume at a minimum, but things did get a little carried away when Righty suggested that Patrick might be dead. That is when Anne noticed her elderly neighbour eyeing her and the call button above his head.

Patrick's my husband, she says to the man.

This doesn't seem to make things okay. He still looks at her and then down at her hands, which are facing each other, thumbs to middle fingers like duck bills. Anne's neighbour looks from her hands to her face.

They only talk when I'm nervous, she says.

The old man smiles suddenly, his eyes disappearing in wrinkles. I hates flying, he says grinning. Then, when Anne thinks he is going to look away and return to the weather channel he has been watching without earphones, he asks: So whereabouts on the mainland you from?

I'm actually headed home to Paradise, she lies, thinking the fib will require less explanation than saying that her husband's car was found in the ocean and she fears he may have killed himself because she left him for a guy she met on Facebook.

Paradise, the old man chuckles, Does it live up to the name?

It's ugly subdivisions mostly, Anne thinks. But she says: It does, 'cause my son lives there.

He smiles and they don't say anything for a while, until Anne's left hand quacks at the guy, asking him what time it is.

There is a ding and the seatbelt sign comes on. Time for us to be landing, looks like, the old man says, reaching for his belt. Anne's is already snug. She looks at her right hand and even though it is lying there on her knees, like hands normally do, she knows what it is saying: So, Anne, are you wearing black for the funeral?

Shut up!

They still talking? The old man asks, looking over at her hands. Anne notices the white band on the third finger of her left hand. Her wedding ring is in her checked luggage, rolled in a pair of brown ankle socks.

This one won't shut up, she says, shaking her right hand and then sitting on it, like she used to do when she was a kid and her father would ask her if her hands were talking to her again.

I fart when I'm nervous, the old man says suddenly.

I don't smell a thing, Anne laughs.

Flying don't make me nervous.

What does?

Lettin the missus drive.

Anne sees him glance her way to check if she's smiling before his eyes disappear in wrinkles again, chuckling away. Anne can imagine the man's wife waiting for him at the airport in St. John's and him letting wind loudly when he settles into the passenger seat beside her.

You hear about the mainlander who landed a plane in the fog?

No, Anne says.

He came in hot and had to jam on the brakes before he hit the trees.

Anne's left hand starts chattering: Serious?

Said to his co-pilot. Jeez, that runway's short. And his co-pilot looked out the window and said, Yes b'y, but it's wide enough to land a plane on!

The plane lurches and Anne's laugh lands on her lap like a heimliched scallop. She sits on her hands, tells them to keep quiet even though they are whispering in her mind.

It's okay, my love, says the old man. You can see Signal Hill through the window. Clear day to land on. Just have to line her up and touch down.

Anne knows that there is nothing to see outside the window, and she thinks this guy must know that she knows that, that she can see with her own eyes. But he keeps on talking about the sights clear as day out her window, even while his eyes focus on the front of the cabin as the plane banks and dips.

There's Confederation Building, peacock proud, he says.

Anne sees fog, rain beading up on her window, flashing wing lights. And then she feels the back end of the plane drop and the wing flaps go up and her body tries to fly forward as the plane brakes and slows to ground speed.

You made that alright, without a peep from your friends, the old man says, smiling over at Anne. She pulls her hands out and folds them on her lap, holds them still.

It is not until they are walking through the terminal toward the luggage carousel that Anne realizes that the fog outside is clearing and rays of sunshine are shattering against the large windowpanes pebbled with raindrops.

Her chatty seat neighbour has moved on ahead of her in the procession. Regardless of how he feels about his wife's driving, he is moving fast enough that Anne can tell he wants to see her again. *Hobble skip.* That's how he's walking. Looking over people's shoulders and trying to weave around them. Anne feels none of that urgency or desire—none of that impatience. Time could slow like syrup boiled too long and she would be okay with it.

A drop of care here, drop of regret there.

Her knees almost buckle when she thinks for the seventieth

SNARE

time this morning that Patrick might be dead. The reality of that drops heavily on her like a sand sack in an old theatre. But she doesn't bounce back like Wile E. Coyote or the Roadrunner. She thinks of Saturday mornings and Hab begging to watch Looney Tunes, saying that Mommy had to sit on one side and Daddy on the other. And they would watch anvils crush characters and some would run off cliff edges and fall. But the cartoons always bounced back. *Not me, not this time*, she thinks. As she stands in line waiting for the bags to start coming in, she wants to cry, to curl up in a quiet corner and let go.

While she is trying to get hold of herself she notices two cops come through the closest entrance. They are scanning the crowd, and then one of them points in her direction even as she feels a heavy hand settle on her shoulder. Anne spins around and she thinks she must be dreaming—must have passed out and whacked her head—because there is Patrick, grinning like an idiot.

She thinks she means to reach out and touch his face, to see if he is real, but the shock of him actually standing there alive throttles her nerves and she punches him in the eye. She doesn't know exactly what happens next, except that there are cops and she tells one of them to get her bag. It's green, she tells him, with a red ribbon tied to the handle. And then there is yelling and somebody saying *calm down* but Anne is hearing everything as if she's underwater and she doesn't surface until she hears her name on his lips:

Anne!

She turns and stares at Patrick holding his sore eye: What?

Where are you going?

Where am I going? she thinks. *Home.* The word revs in her head but she is grinding gears between wanting to sleep and wanting to run. *Where is home now?* she wonders. *Am I going with Patrick? In our car? His car. We don't have a car. It's in the ocean. And Patrick ... is alive.*

Where's the car, Patrick? She turns and spits the question at him. She can see the policemen have stopped several paces

back and look like they're trying to give them space, like they're waiting for a street fight or something.

Patrick: Some punk broke into it and rolled it over a cliff into the sea.

Did you renew the insurance?

What? No. I don't know. Weren't you supposed to do that?

So we have a wrecked car and no insurance?

We?

We needed that insurance.

I'm alive.

We still need that insurance.

Patrick is staring at Anne in disbelief and Anne cannot actually believe what she is saying. It's like her right hand is talking, saying something so purely rational it's irrational—fixating on one thing. *Why?* she wonders. *Why is insurance the most important thing to me right now?* She keeps reminding herself that her husband is alive. But is he still her husband? *Do I still get to call him that?* She decides that she needs a café mocha.

Do you have change? she asks Patrick.

Yes. He pulls out a handful of quarters and dimes and pours them into her cupped hands. Should be enough there to get me a coffee as well. Two cream—

One sugar, I know.

Anne heads toward the Tim Hortons and glances back to see Patrick staring at the floor, his hand on the back of his head, and then he looks up to see the cops still staring at him. That is when he comes after her, but she is already sandwiched in line between a fat lady in front and a young couple behind.

What are you doing? he asks.

Getting coffee.

Why are you here?

Heard you were dead.

But I'm not.

I see that.

It's Anne's turn, so she steps up to the sugar-covered counter and orders a medium café mocha, a medium coffee—*two cream,*

one sugar—and a honey cruller. The lady behind the counter rings it up. Anne is short fifty-six cents.

Patrick?

Yes.

The girl needs another sixty cents.

Oh, sorry, he says as he finds a few more coins in his pocket and pays the girl. Anne walks toward a table. Patrick follows and sits across from her. His eyes remind Anne of Christopher's, though they're a different colour. *Blazing.* But Patrick is older than Christopher or Ruth. *Same age as Dave.* Dave: who made her feel like an idiot—cheap and stupid. His emails made it seem to her as if she was the centre of his world. His words were like fingernails tearing at bland wallpaper, peeling back her boredom to reveal dark, intricate knots and grains of happiness she had forgotten. His questions about her like old ropes of a tree swing hugging her hips as she pumped higher and higher—autumn leaves in her hair, heels skimming mud. But she remembers the sickening freefall—seeing Dave with his daughter, the bus horn, shocking as a rope snap. *Stupid, stupid, stupid.*

And now she is back in St. John's just after sunrise with her cold hands quiet finally and cupped around a café mocha at the airport. Sitting across from the husband she abandoned, who is staring at her as if, *as if* ... She has never seen Patrick look at her like this—his one eye swelling and going purple—and it makes her feel like she is another woman; that even though he is looking at her he is looking at someone else, like Jacob gazing over Leah's shoulder at Rachel. She feels that Patrick is seeing her as Hosea the prophet must have viewed his whoring wife when she ran away to be with another man, as if *he* is in the right and *she* is worth less than a crippled slave, able to be bought back with silver, pity. She feels as if Patrick sees her now as a stranger, someone who *could* actually abandon him, lie to him—cheat on him. *Yes you, Gomer,* her right hand wants to say, but its mouth is full of paper cup.

I didn't come to stay, she says finally, looking away.

Just to bury me.

She stares back at him. Blows steam off her drink. Sips.

Sorry to disappoint you, but there won't be a funeral.

She sips again, looks around, thinking Patrick's words were too dramatic—more like something her father would say. She looks up and sees Patrick's eyes screwing into her. She is sinking into stillness, like a stone settling after a wave's withdrawal, like the way she would blow out all her air as she jumped from the cliffs on Little Salmon Lake as a girl and let her body sink through the green water to the algae-slick stones ten feet below the surface, watching the world wimple and flash and fade—going catatonic, she used to think later in their house in Paradise when her mind would be racing like mad and her body would begin to freeze, as it had when the thought of leaving Patrick for Dave first came into her head and she did not realize the potatoes were boiling over on the stove. She realizes she has not moved the cup from her lips, unsure of how many seconds have passed or if they have ceased to pass altogether and time has mercifully congealed.

Are you coming home? Patrick asks, wrinkling his brow and looking down at soot marks on his hands.

Coming or going? Anne doesn't know. She doesn't think she is speaking, only thinking: wondering if she *comes* home whether that means *with* Patrick and that they will try to work things out, or should she simply *go* home, see Hab, apologize, pack, and leave—this time without the lies?

Do you want me to come home? The question sounds outside of her. She can feel her fingers pressing with each syllable against the side of her coffee cup.

I can get you a taxi, Patrick says. I have to go to the police station to file a report on the car. They already called it into the papers that I'm alive and well. Should be in *The Telegram* by the time you get to the house.

He did not say *home* this time: when Anne gets to *the house*. The house she left, abandoned, fled—an empty house. Like all those months before she made the break and went after

Dave. She decides in that moment that she will not go back to that silence.

I won't. I can't.

She does not answer Patrick, only sets her cup down, slides out from the table and heads for the ticket counters. Patrick is behind her, calling her name. She does not look back but she imagines the policemen are slowly drifting after him. Them. *Watching. Listening. Nothing better to do than follow a crazy lady through the airport, her husband calling after her.*

Anne!

Anne! Wait a sec.

Anne! For frig's sake!

But his voice does not hook her like it once did, sending chills down her neck and bringing a smile to her face. He says her name again, calling. And she thinks of her dad—the miracle-worker evangelist—who told Hab of how she passed away in a fever as a child and he called her back to life with a word, *Anne*: her name that means *grace* and *favour* and so fascinates her son who has more interest in art and Catholicism than in the Pentecostal church she and Patrick raised him in. So much has been poured into her name and so many people seem to call to her—whispering about her, talking behind her back if she stays and tries to make a go of it—that suddenly she cannot bear to hear it even on Patrick's lips. So she quickens her step and heads straight to the WestJet counter and asks for a ticket on the next flight to Hamilton.

Patrick is beside her and talking loudly but not loudly enough to cause those policemen—*creepy stalkers, watchers*—to move in and silence him. But he is loud enough to unnerve the lady Anne is trying to talk into selling her a ticket.

Patrick: Where do you think you're going?

Away. Where I come from.

What's that supposed to mean?

Newfoundland is your home, Patrick. Your dream. I never asked for this. Any of this.

Anne takes a breath and realizes that she has not said any of

these words because she is biting her lips to keep from crying, her hand in her pocket fisted around the smooth sea stone. She is gripping the stone as if it is the talisman that will hold her together until she can get her ticket and get away from Patrick, and the eyes that will watch and the lips that will whisper, as she is sure they are, now that they know she has left her husband.

Anne, *what* is that supposed to mean? Patrick asks indignantly.

The saleswoman: I'm sorry, Miss. Your card has been declined: insufficient funds.

Anne looks at Patrick. I need your card, she says, trying to keep her voice steady.

Patrick is telling her that this running away is ridiculous, even as he digs out his MasterCard and hands it over. The lady swipes it, prints off the slip and passes it to Anne to sign. But it is Patrick's card, not hers. Her card is a VISA, which has been declined. She passes the slip and pen to Patrick.

I'm asking you to stay, Anne.

His voice is pleading. Anne pushes the pen and paper another inch toward his hand on the counter. He looks down at it. Anne wants him *not* to pick up the pen. She wants him to ask *her*, not tell her he is asking. She wants him to take her hand and pull her toward the door.

But he picks up the pen and scrawls his signature.

She realizes that her bag is at her leg now, though she did not carry it over. She sees a cop striding away, one hand on his belt and the other scratching his shaved neck. She puts the bag up on the scale and it is conveyed away, disappearing through rubber flaps. And Anne knows that her heart is in that bag, wrapped up in brown ankle socks.

She turns to Patrick and she does not know why, but she goes to hug him and he almost dodges her. Maybe because he thinks for a second that she will punch him again——*his eye looks so sore*——or because he does not want to touch her. She squeezes his neck so that he will feel her desperation, her uncertainty.

So that he will hug her back.

But he taps her shoulder twice. There, there. Tap-out. End of match. She can hear the sound of her dad turning off the television after Saturday night wrestling, the click and *hiz* as the screen cooled, her breath catching even as she pulls away from Patrick, takes her ticket and heads for Departures.

On the other side of security, Anne finds a seat at Gate 3 facing the big window overlooking the runway. A young Indian boy is sitting on the heating grate by the window, waving his hands madly like he's being tormented by bees that nobody else can see. Anne stares at him, her mind full of what she has just done, and soon she begins to see the patterns in his movements. His face is not panic-stricken but unusually expressive for somebody in an airport waiting lounge. The boy is looking up above Anne's head. When she looks behind her she sees an older Indian woman in a bright yellow dress, wearing a bulky brown coat, waving her arms behind the glass of the viewing deck.

She looks back at the boy and realizes he is shouting something at the woman in sign language.

She glances back again and sees Patrick, six feet to the woman's left, making emphatic motions with his fingers and staring down at her. He is saying something through the glass, but Anne cannot hear him or make out what he is trying to say.

Natalie thinks that River is the type of kid who would be better off if every one of his fingers was broken. Keep him out of trouble, at least until he learned how to flick a lighter with his toes. She is thinking about slipping the kid extra sleeping pills with his meds tonight, then pulling his hand out onto his bedside stand and bashing his dirty fingers with a hammer. Crushing that leering silver skull ring he bought with reward money for doing his chores. The ring has gone missing from his grubby fist since the weekend, but it is there when Natalie thinks of breaking his hands. She has been smoking this thought slowly—like Lisette drawing on the occasional wine-tipped Colt—ever since last night, when she followed River from the boy's home on Pennywell to his mom's house on the corner of Calver and Rankin.

And watched him set fire to it.

The fire was in the news today when she got back to the apartment: third page of *The Telegram*. She flipped through Gerry's paper, looking for it as soon as she got home. *No witnesses*, the article said, and Natalie thought *Okay*. She has been talking to cops already this morning. They showed up at 7:00 a.m., an hour before her shift ended, to question River, who has a history as an arsonist, mainly setting trashcans on fire. Natalie was told that he once blew up his dad's shed. She knows that he was charged this past November for setting fire to a dumpster outside Bishop Feild College on Guy Fawkes Night.

Nobody said he was smart, she thinks.

But Natalie knows that River can act, *that's for sure*. When the cops described the *event* to him he was the perfect mix of shocked, concerned, and angry. So far as Natalie knows, the cops bought his story. It sealed the deal when he said *she* was his alibi.

Ask Natalie. She knows I was in bed from eleven on. Right? She was sitting right there on the couch all night.

The cops looked at her and she said *that's true*, even though she had taken seven photos of last night. One with River's face half turned and illuminated by the blaze he set in his mom's back porch, his eyes alight—a slight smile on his lips. His grey hoodie momentarily pulled back from his greasy black hair. Natalie has hard photographic evidence that River tried to burn down his mom's house with her asleep inside. And she lied to the police.

Why? She keeps asking herself. *Panic?*

Or was it to protect River? But from whom: the cops or himself?

Natalie knows that nobody died. The police said River's mom got out alive.

No death, no foul. Right?

She did not think about the absurdity of that thought when it first came to her, but it snags her now. She did not think at all about what she said or how she said it. There was no effort to mask her voice or choose her words or think about where her eyes should rest. She looked the officers right in the eyes and lied as smoothly as she sips wine. She thinks of the lie like her body between the cops and River: shielding him, for the moment.

The police left eventually. But not before the taller cop knocked over one of Natalie's boots by the door, stooped to set it upright, and apologized before closing the door behind him.

River started playing *Grand Theft Auto* with the surround sound jacked. First-person shooter games are generally not allowed in the units, but the alternative, Natalie has discovered, is to have a sociopathic fifteen-year-old flipping out on her. She knows that the kid's parents are divorced, that his mom is a sushi chef at Sobeys and his dad's a townie lawyer who lives out

around the bay. Natalie has met both parents on home visits, but neither one explains River, who once carved a swastika in the hood of Sherl's car because she said he was slaughtering people like a friggin Nazi on that stupid video game.

Instead of nagging him this morning, Natalie sat at the table in the kitchen, watching the minute hand on the clock above the stove bisect her last hour, hearing a hail of machine gun fire as she scrolled through the photos from last night on her camera. Until she found the one with River's face, innocent and bright as a child saint. *It's not real.* That's what she thought, sitting there staring at it. *This River* is not the one butchering in the next room. The sounds are real—gun fire, the wet *thack* of a limb being hacked off, a shovel splitting a skull open. But the carnage is digital. Like the photo in front of her. Like the memory of following River at a distance, camera in hand, wanting to capture a trashcan blaze or dumpster inferno. Like the ones she used to set and photograph in Toronto before her apartment building burned. Like the house on the corner of Calver and Rankin that she photographed last night.

Natalie is in her room now, thoughts looping, doubling back on her. A dark blue sheet is pinned over her window so that she can sleep through the day after a night shift, but she is wide awake. Curled up on her side and facing the wall where her Dead Man's sweater hangs.

She looks at the broad shoulders stretched square. She stretched the shoulders further than she had the last time she pinned it up to cover old pinholes in plaster, after she took it down and pulled it over Hab's head the night before he became her boyfriend. It was nearly a month ago that he'd appeared with two blood oranges, an apology, and the story of his mom's affair. He'd cracked her open that night like the eggs they made next morning for breakfast, even though she tried to maintain a stoic look all evening as she got him drunk on cheap wine so that he would keep talking and maybe touch his feet to hers on the couch. He never did that night. And he tried to stagger home drunk but passed out on the sidewalk and Natalie and Lisette had to pull him out of a snow bank.

That is when Natalie wrapped him in her Dead Man's sweater. And it was okay that time because it was hers, her own skin she kept splayed out on the wall like a crucifix or cocoon, her own past that she wrapped him in the day he told her his story and she told him hers.

The sweater on the wall is a skin she wants to pull tight around her. In the way she pulled her big green jacket around herself as she walked through the early April slush on her way home from work this morning: climbing the hill from Pennywell toward Merrymeeting; her mind in flames writhing around River's face.

Her face is hot but she is shivering under her blankets.

Friggin kid is all she can think when she thinks of River. She doesn't loathe him. But he really doesn't do anything to help himself. *Choices.* That's the child-and-youth-care-worker liturgy: *Life is choices, and you can make good choices or bad ones—it's up to you.* River's habitual *fuck off* is *amen* to that exchange: Natalie's wake-up call that he does not care, even if he does hear.

So, she asks herself, *why do I protect him? Why did I lie for him?*

She pulls the blanket over her head and breathes into cold hands cupped by her lips, wriggles her frozen toes around the small electric heating pad at the foot of her bed. Closes her eyes and tries to shut out last night: the half-stupor startle of River opening the front door and slipping out. They are not allowed to doze on overnights but everyone does, to get through until dawn. River must have been counting on that last night. But he was not counting on Natalie waking up and following him rather than phoning in to the RNC that he had run off. Natalie had noticed a new Zippo in the pocket of his torn jackshirt earlier in the evening, after he had gone to bed. She figured he had probably stolen it on his home visit to his dad's place the night before. As a youth-care worker, she was expected to search everything.

Natalie knew River was planning something. He had been

civil all evening, according to Sherl, who was on shift before her. Nice as anything since his visit with his dad, Sherl had said, shaking her head. Natalie knows that River is never nice unless he is scheming. The thought of this had been like adrenaline needled into her all night, keeping her awake even though she pretended to doze on the couch when she heard River on the stairs.

She watched through thatched eyelashes as he checked in on her—her breathing measured and even. Then he slipped his jackshirt off the hook. Natalie heard a soft hiss—cooking spray on the hinges—and the turn and click of the doorknob. She counted to five before jumping up, the wireless house phone in her hand, and going to the door, running her fingers over the greased hinges, and deciding in that moment *not* to dial the police and to follow River. It was like an old addiction—alien fingers curling around rib bones, racing heart, clear eyes—that desire to see fire kindled: a need, for her, like breathing.

Now, looking through a thick lens of several hours, she knows she wanted to see how far River would go.

A trashcan?

Dumpster?

Shed?

Three Zippo clicks in Natalie's mind like three mouse clicks—*oral to anal*—and the shock an explosion in her skull: her first time seeing someone that hardcore, setting fire to his own mom's house.

She knew the address, had taken River there on home visits that always seemed to end with screaming. It was never River who screamed, though; never his dad, either. It was always his mother.

Natalie is trying to remember if she heard River's mom scream last night. She's not sure. She'd raced away in a mad effort to beat River back to the group home. She knows that the woman could have died, been trapped. And she ran away and left her to burn. She remembers her heart racing—all her energy sucked out like oxygen in a back draft. Her hands deep in the big pockets of her oversized jacket, wishing she had brought her toque or not buzzed her hair so short.

Running, she remembers running, and the memory of her panting like the hum of a DVD player spinning up.

Stop.

Main menu.

She skips past the cops and her cover-up to lying in bed, looking at her Dead Man's sweater stretched out on the wall. She is thinking of how she has knit meaning into it through stories, stitched memory. Gerry has said that everyone, in some way, circles meaningless objects like cupped hands around coals and breathes on them—this is his definition of faith. Was, she mouths, thinking of her own faith: past tense like a pulled stopper from a half-full bottle of wine in the fridge, drained into a glass and sipped dry after work. She is breathing into her hands curled as if in prayer but there is no warmth in that thought. No hope of response. She feels something—some lack—that she had not realized was there until Hab began talking to her about God speaking through art.

Not just churchy art—kitsch Christs listlessly crucified—but in dark pieces where all the colours are cold. Or in that series of illuminations and drawings that Hab had showed her online—the sea and the scroll rolling together with the story of Job. She remembers the title of the series, *I make a covenant with my eyes*, and she thinks of the sad joy in that old man's weathered face, remembering the wonderstruck teen in his jack-shirt shrugging—so unlike River. And the bell, she remembers that bell, tolling the words *the sea, the sea* in her mind. Hab tells her that looking at this art, contemplating it, is for him like speaking in tongues is to his father.

She had grown up in the same Pentecostal church back in Ontario where Hab's grandfather Gurney was a deacon and preacher. It is a connection they've just found out they had. Roots in the same soil, so to speak. That was before she'd moved to Toronto from St. Lola, before she knew Hab. Before Biz handed her that first glass of wine and introduced her to a world outside her childhood evangelicalism. Before the photography school and her obsession with flames.

Before her world went to ash.

She has not said a prayer since that day. Not really. She is not expecting any miracles, so she does not ask. She has heard of miracles all her life, and if anybody were to tell her that miracles do not happen anymore she would tell them they were full of shit. But this defiance does not outweigh measured belief. She wonders sometimes if someone can have faith and not believe—photograph fire and not believe in the divine spark.

Yes, she thinks, *you can be that stubborn. That insistent.* She thinks of that sermon Gurney preached about Jacob wrestling the angel and refusing to let go without a blessing, even as the angel kneed him in the back, fish-hooked his mouth, and ground his beard into river mud.

But, for Natalie, the thought of hanging onto something, wrestling something that is not there, scares her, even as her memory of last night terrifies her now. Her heart was racing as she rested her camera lens on the fencepost by the road, relying on the dim streetlight instead of using the flash that would have given her away.

Full zoom.

Ten megapixels.

Her pulse pounding like in that camp service at Lemming's Lake when she was thirteen and dancing at the front of the tabernacle, shouting out to God and trying to be sexy and free, wanting to not want Christopher Rhynes to touch her, wishing to be pushed over into his human arms by nonhuman hands.

Palpitating heart, sweaty hands, cold feet, mind on fire.

She needs an Ativan.

She gets up and pulls the unmarked bottle out of her coat pocket and heads to the kitchen for a glass of wine, wrapping the big green army jacket around her as she goes. The pills dissolve fine under her tongue without liquid to wash them down. That's how she takes them at work, usually. But the wine will put her to sleep. Give her a different texture on the tongue other than the pills' chalky grit, that medicinal pastiness she hates when she wakes late in the day to go back to work.

She swings her bedroom door open in time to see Snuggles dart down the hall and into Gerry's open room. Rod's cat. She's still not sure if Gerry has a connection to what happened to Rod, but he *did* adopt the cat after Rod was beaten.

And now Snuggles lives with them and uses Natalie's dirty clothes pile as a litterbox.

Gerry *says* he looks after the cat but he's been too distracted lately to pay attention to his own hygiene, let alone that of a cat. She thinks of Gerry and his peculiar silence, his brooding, the faint bruises on his neck. He has changed recently; she knows this. He has become a stranger to her and to Lisette and Hab.

Hab, she thinks: her boyfriend who seems to have moved in with them since his mom left his dad for some guy on Facebook. Hab has since told her that this did not work out so well for his mom. The story came out over a glass of wine.

Barefoot Merlot.

Like the bottle she is opening now. She loves that first relieving pop of the cork from the bottle. It brings to mind Biz's eyes next to hers in their kitchenette in that tiny Toronto apartment, the *glub* and *swish* of the wine in the glass, her first sip. *Try it*, Biz had said. She has tried it, tried it all—so many different wines since. And she still comes back to the cheap Barefoot Merlot. Lisette cannot understand why; she says she likes zinfandels and fruity wines and she asks Natalie why she always drinks red. And Natalie usually says something snooty and laughable about tannic savour and burgundy aromas— though she still cannot smell a thing and drinks only for the smooth burn and the numbness that follows the first bottle. In her talk of smells and tastes she says nothing of Biz, who she has not spoken of since moving to St. John's more than a year ago.

Biz's absence is strong wine gone down the wrong tube. Natalie chokes and above her sudden hack and cough she hears a door click open.

Hello? she calls.

She looks around the corner and sees that it is Hab. She waves, pops her head back in the kitchen and thumbs the pill into her mouth. She coughs, drains half her glass and wipes her lips before Hab enters. She is topping up her glass when she sees his face—hair parted in the middle, twin cowlicks adorable. His eyes are not smiling, though. He is looking worriedly at the glass and bottle in her hands. She wants to see him smile like he did on that night that he made her dinner and they split an orange and drank wine on the couch and she didn't even think about the pills in her pocket.

It's pretty early for that, isn't it? he asks.

Your a.m. is my p.m. now that I'm on night shift.

I suppose, he says, blinking. I was just down to the Needs for hot chocolate. He looks Natalie up and down: Rough shift?

She takes a sip in answer. Smiles and looks down at her plaid pyjama pants. Her big jacket is wrapped around her like a housecoat. And she is holding that broken glass filled with wine by its spear, thinking she's glad she doesn't have to worry about her hair being poofy since it's shaved so short.

You were asleep on the couch when I came in, she says.

Yeah. Phone call woke me up. Dad said he'd been to the airport.

Airport?

Hab looks around. Natalie knows there is something wrong when he cannot look at her. Hab? What happened? Why was your dad at the airport?

He looks up at her and she expects tears for some reason, but he looks bewildered. As if the telephone conversation with his dad was a welder's torch cutting steel and he's been blinded by the flash.

Apparently Mom flew in two days ago.

Your mom is back?

No.

Natalie wants to pull the whole thing out of Hab like a tapeworm. But she waits until he is ready.

She flew back to Hamilton after they had a fight or something. In the airport. And Dad—no. She flew in because she'd heard that Dad's Malibu was wrecked.

Wrecked?

Some kid pushed it over the cliff in Fawkes Cove.

When?

Like two days ago or something, I think. Dad was up in Grandpa Wiseman's cabin. Don't know why. They don't really talk. Apparently Dad left the keys in the car on the floor mat. At least he thinks so. He doesn't have any keys on him now. Somebody let him into the church office yesterday and he slept there last night. So he's catching a taxi over today to get my house keys. That's why he called. To say he was coming.

Oh.

I think I should go with him. Back to the house.

Whatever, Natalie says, trying to make it sound nonchalant, reassuring. She is still trying to wrap her head around the whole thing, but it's like trying to put an angry cat into a box for a stupid photo. She thinks of the scrapes all up and down her arms from Snuggles.

Soft name for a pissy cat.

She takes another sip of wine and feels calmed—the Ativan kicking in—her movements like hollandaise sauce poured over eggs Benedict, *smooth.* Thinking of this makes her hungry.

Have you had breakfast? she asks.

No.

Want some … toast?

I'm okay. Not really hungry.

Hab turns and heads into the living room and collapses on the ratty green couch. Natalie sees Snuggles come out from the hall and rub against Hab's leg. Then up she jumps onto his knees. The cat rests quietly on his lap, like Natalie's head when they were watching TV one night and she felt a stirring there. Hab has not kissed her yet. Says he's not ready. But he likes to sit on the toilet while she showers and he lies with her in bed, his arm under her head, the other one draped over her side, hand under her shirt fingering scar tissue on her belly. When they lie like that she feels that stirring against her back——Hab's breath on her neck.

He looks up and sees her smiling.

What's the grin for?

You're cute, she says, and winks and turns, suddenly realizing she's high.

Steady now, she thinks. *Toast. That's what I want. With butter and jam.* She is searching for a loaf of bread in the freezer when she hears a car horn and Hab jumps to his feet. Snuggles darts back down the hall.

That'll be Dad, he says heading to the front door.

Call me.

I will. Get some sleep, eh.

And then he is gone and Natalie is alone with her hand in the freezer and her cheeks burning. No bread, no toast. So she finishes her wine and pours herself another full glass, which she gulps down until she is gasping and giggly and about to cry. *For no good reason*, she thinks. Except, maybe, the look Hab gave her as he headed for the door.

A look that screamed: *Who are you?*

She has her hands inside her sleeves and her arms wrapped tightly around her torso like she is hanging on to someone else—rocking, crouched against the cupboards. She is unbelievably tired. She knows this. She feels exhausted and needs sleep. *I need to not think.* But her mind is a staticky radio trying to tune in; fragments of conversation flying out of the buzz——*get some sleep ... you stupid slut ... I'll slit your fucking throat ... you fall asleep ... you're so stressed ... tired ... so tired.*

Natalie spends the rest of the day in bed, following River in her mind over Merrymeeting and down Rankin to Calver. Going over her steps, his steps, and worrying if any of those will be visible to the cops. Did that cop *pretend* to knock over her boots to check the make and size on the sole? *Or is that me being overtired and paranoid?* No witnesses, the paper had said. So nobody saw them or nobody is talking. If that's the case, then they will need an admission from her to touch River. To take him away to lockup. She can keep him from there, Whitbourne's special kind of hell. If she keeps her mouth shut. She can save him from that—from that trauma. She wonders how much a kid like that can go through before he is unfixable.

A blast of heat shatters a window and Natalie is being pulled and pulling toward the fire escape, with River in tow and a girl in front of her saying, *Come on, Natalie! Run!* And she is pulling him through the choking heat. Up, she is pulling him up the ladder, skin sizzling, bare feet, sweat on cold skin, boiling, and his hand slips from hers and he falls—

Hah! She inhales sharply, hearing a shin crack as the dream is cut short. She is back in bed. It is dark outside. She had been plummeting in her sleep, reaching for River. Trying to save him: pull him up. It was a dream, though. She repeats this to herself until she is sitting up in bed.

It's over now.

It is a quarter to midnight and she needs to be heading to work.

She does not recall the whirlwind of pulling her stuff together and getting out the door, save that Gerry met her in the hall and said hi on his way to feed Snuggles. You look tired, he'd said, and she'd said *thanks* in a frig-off sort of tone. And then somehow she made it in time to the unit.

Sherl meets her at the door and tells her little Liam is back from a home visit in Shea Heights. Liam, the new ten-year-old intake. Abused by his father, who is out of the picture now. The mom is trying to pull a life together. For Liam, she says. And she is one of the rare ones Natalie can see doing it. She is strong and determined to get her boy back. Not for her sake but for his. In this way she's different from River's mom, who is afraid of her own son.

Natalie smiles at Liam's name, and her thoughts are gone from River and the feeling she gets when she is around him of being a flimsy hut at the base of a volcano. *Good morning ashes*

in my mouth, she sings in her head, rehearsing lyrics from a song Hab downloaded for her onto Lisette's laptop, which she uses sometimes—more than Lisette, who works long hours waitressing on Water Street, which is where Sherl says she is headed straight away because The Navigators are playing at The Dock.

Sherl is singing *If Venice is sinking then I'm going under* as she walks out the door, leaving Natalie alone. She suddenly feels as if a hand is on her face, holding her underwater. A *glass of water*, she thinks. *That's what I need.* Her hand is reaching for that unmarked pill bottle in her pocket.

I just need to calm down.

A sudden panic attack is a hand clawing for her eyeballs so she takes three or four Ativan. A handful, maybe. She doesn't remember. Enough to get high. Chill out. She tries to calm herself so that she can hear her own heartbeat. Her eyes dart at strange noises. *It's nothing*, she whispers, *nothing*. Liam and River are in their rooms. She reminds herself that she is alone and suddenly she feels as if she is floating—each step like swimming—*strange*, she thinks, feeling buoyant as she climbs the steps to the boys' rooms. She checks in on Liam, first.

Hi, Liam.

Hi, Natalie.

You have fun at your mum's?

I had macaroni and cheese.

What do you want for breakfast?

Can we have pancakes?

Yes.

And she closes the door, saying goodnight to him. *Cute arse.* His face in the nightlight was droopy-eyed and drowsy: like Natalie is feeling now, ready to veg on the couch for a few hours before doing chores and updating log books. She stops to listen and check in on River by pressing her ear against his door. She can hear his voice, which she thinks is strange because he is speaking and she can't tell to whom.

Yes, he is saying, *no fuckwit, no they didn't. It was fuckin sick.*

The whole thing, right up in flames. I know. Deadly. Whore deserved it. Teach her. Pop's next. And that stupid slut sleeping on the couch the whole time. Stick it to her one of these nights. Cops next morning. No, told it to 'em straight-faced. Fuckin right. Cocksuckers walked right out the door. Haven't been back. RNC are arseholes. No. Didn't leave no footprints. Nothin. Like when we pushed that car into the bay the other night. Sick fuckin right. Keys right on the floor and the door unlocked. Arsehole. No. Yeah. No. I'm too slick to get caught. You gotta plan these things out.

Natalie can hardly breathe. Her hand goes to her pocket, to her keys. Each movement is a whisper. She fingers the one to the deadbolt on River's door. In case of lockdown, she had been told. Like when River loses his shit. It was a safety measure to protect the likes of little Liam, to protect the workers themselves—from *him*. The kid Natalie lied to the cops to protect because——

Why?

Natalie slides the key into the slot and clicks it. River halts his phone conversation. *Who's there?* he yells, but Natalie is stepping back from the door. *Who is fuckin' there?* he calls louder. Then he tries the door and, finding it locked, looses a spray of heated language stinging Natalie's ears like sparks. She can hear him—*You slut! Open this door, you cunt*—as she checks in on Liam. She cannot see the boy at first in the half-lit room, but then she spies him in a dark corner holding a wooden sword high, in both hands. His eyes are shining in the shadows, but Natalie knows it's tears she's seeing.

It's okay Liam, she coos.

She says it calmly, so calmly it soothes *her*. She hears the echo of her voice in her own head, a mellow voice reassuring the little guy, telling him that River is locked up.

No, he can't hurt anyone anymore. I won't let him hurt anyone anymore. No, you can go back to bed. You'll hear him for a while, but I'm calling the cops.

Like I should've done last night.

Natalie decides to show the RNC the photos she took last

night and tell them about the conversation she had overheard, thinking it will all be fine. *Of course it will be fine*, she thinks, walking away from River's door, hearing him wale on it with a hockey stick, screaming, *YOU WHORE! I'LL SLIT YOUR THROAT YOU STUPID SLUT! OPEN THIS FUCKING DOOR!* And Natalie knows it will be fine and that she will not need to break River's fingers with a hammer because her own hands are not even shaking now, thanks to the pills, and she is not upset that she cannot find the phone right off, even when she realizes that it is locked away in River's room and that is how he was having that conversation—on the unit phone he stole.

That's okay.

It's all fine.

I'll go get the police myself.

Liam will be fine.

It's okay, Liam! Natalie calls on her way out the door, the cold air like a rush of water in her face. We'll have pancakes in the morning!

The skillet handle scalds Natalie's hand and she drops the skillet into the wet grass, where it hisses. The pain in her palm sears: shocking as when she opened the apartment door yesterday to find Biz standing on the stoop, a cab pulling away from the curb behind her. Natalie's memories of Toronto had burned in that instant when she saw her friend for the first time in over a year, like her hand on the hot cast-iron seconds ago. She tries to make a fist, but it feels as if she's holding red embers.

Her palm blisters quickly and she thinks of Biz, her friend, here in Newfoundland.

It all comes jolting back to her now, the last twenty-four hours: opening that door on her old friend, who had grown her hair out and died it burgundy.

Memories of cushions pulled out from the couch, candles, camera flashes, fleshed-out conversations late into the night. Wine. Their crazy waltzing-about to jazzy old records ripped to Biz's MP3 player—an earbud each, the white wire stretched between their faces. Ordering pizza without cheese because the melted mozza upset Natalie's stomach. Reading aloud to each other from *Where the Wild Things Are*, not caring a hoot that it was a kid's book but melding voice to mood and laughing, always laughing.

Natalie has a faint memory of Biz's fingers in her hair, her friend's voice soft and singing her to sleep.

She hears Biz's voice now: sing-songy and coming up the hill toward their campsite. Natalie holds her burned hand by the wrist, rocks and cradles it, cursing herself for being so stupid.

You should check out the old foundation down by the water, Biz calls. Can't believe anyone would build that close to the ocean.

Natalie does not answer but starts walking toward the pond that will soothe her seared palm.

Natalie?

I burned my hand! she snaps, sounding angrier than she means to. But she does not stop to say she's sorry. She hopes her tone will be indication enough for Biz to leave her be for a little while.

The grass is damp from midday rain and smells of earth and evening, pulpy wood, pine. Biz heads after Natalie, calling out to her. And Natalie thinks maybe she should have snapped with more anger than she did. Biz follows her to the edge of the pond, where Natalie is squatting with her hand in the dark water, a grimace on her face.

Biz squats down beside her, hugs her knees, pulls long purple hair back from her face and hooks it behind her ear. She does not say anything, knowing Natalie would not want her to. But Natalie, knowing this, wants nothing more than for her friend to say something. She is uncomfortable with Biz's ease with her, as if after so many months of separation and silence they can settle into their old friendship unsinged.

I burned my hand, she says again.

I see that.

The skillet and that stupid stove.

Natalie pulls her hand out of the water and looks at the deep red line. She stares at it like a palm reader, trying to discern her unease with Biz. Trying to imagine this moment as if the apartment fire in Toronto had never happened, as if nothing had changed between them.

But things have changed. She has changed. She's cut her hair and keeps an electric razor to buzz it down every few weeks when it begins to grow out wispy and curl. She's worked at a

group home and given up photography for good and got herself fired for locking a kid in his room while she was high on Ativan. And she is afraid that kid, River, will find out where she lives and burn their apartment down like he did his mom's place, while Natalie looked on in shadow and snapped pictures of his every move. Pictures she took—while strung out—to the police station, where charges were filed against River and she was asked for a urine sample.

Sure I'll pee in a cup, she had said too loudly, just as long as you keep that kid away from me. She was on the toilet with the cup between her legs when her cell phone rang—the director of the group home calling after he had spoken to the RNC, telling her she was fired. That is when she flushed her cell down the toilet and let the bowl overflow.

All this has happened in a Biz-less vacuum.

All this and more.

She has fallen in love with a preacher's kid from back home and their relationship is a young vine in rocky soil, springing both new shoots and twisted thorns. But she loves Hab.

Has she said that to him?

They seem to be going through a dry spell right now, over the past few months, since she lost her job and had to go to court for child neglect and drug use. After she tested positive for downers and they found the empty Ativan bottle with Sherl's name on it in her pocket. That had triggered a quick end to that friendship and her supply of depressants.

But she realizes, slipping her burned hand back into the water, that she wants Hab's haltingness, *his* fear and stutter, more than she wants Biz, who knows enough to give her space, who squats there quietly, letting her stew and deal with the pain instead of talking about it, which is usually exactly what she wants.

Lisette calls from the campsite: Hey Nat! You mean to leave the stove on?

Biz: She burned herself—

I burned my hand!

I got aloe.

Natalie looks at Biz staring back at her. They say nothing and climb back to the campsite, where Lisette is rooting in her backpack. Here it is, she says, pulling out a green bottle. She goes to pass it to Natalie, but Biz takes it and tells Natalie to sit on the rock wall that their tent is staked within.

Thanks, but I can put it on myself.

Biz blinks and hands her the bottle. She tucks a strand of dark hair behind her ear.

You not bring an elastic to keep your hair out of your eyes?

No, Biz says, looking around for something to do.

Natalie can feel Lisette cringe even though her back is to them, her hand in her bag looking for something she doesn't need.

Biz takes a towel and wraps it around the skillet handle, puts the pan back on the camp stove. Asks Lisette where the oil is.

The hot snap and sizzle of oil in the pan makes Natalie's hand burn even more beneath the aloe's gloss. She squeezes her wrist to stop the aching pulse in her palm as Biz dumps sliced peppers from a Tupperware dish into the pan and swirls them.

Biz was always the cook in their apartment. Natalie's own culinary talent reached its zenith in tuna casserole with frozen peas. Over in the grass the yellow plastic dish with a plate on top is the minute rice, she thinks, which is probably done now.

She tells Biz it's ready.

Biz looks up at her, nods, and goes back to swishing the veggies in the pan.

Lisette pops open a jar of korma. Too bad we forgot chicken, she says, handing the jar to Biz, who adds it to the stir fry. I could've called Hab and had him bike it in.

I thought he'd be here by now, Natalie whispers.

Biz says nothing, only stirs the coconut curry and peppers, unaware that Natalie can no longer smell the milky spice.

The burn line bisecting her palm is a livid thorax, her thumb a butterfly's clipped wing. The sun has just set behind them and Hab has yet to arrive. Natalie is worried about him biking in the dark. She has not said anything to the other two in an hour, not since supper. Lisette is doing up the dishes down by the pond and Biz has joined her.

Natalie has walked down to the old foundation by the sea that used to be a house, before the January storm in 1966 that washed away the old suspension bridge, fishing stages and houses like this one. There is a tree growing up within it, but the green in twilight registers grey and dusk seems muted and cold. Like that black and white photo of Resettlement she keeps under her bed—that saltbox house floating eerily on the water.

Earlier, Biz had slipped her arm around Natalie's waist up on the new suspension bridge as they looked down at thousands of sun-speckled jellyfish palming and fisting like Biz's hand on her side, caressing the water beneath the waves.

Natalie had smiled and pulled away, saying they should see the other side. Biz had grinned and followed her across. They had swung themselves under the bridge on the far side, seen the thickness of the cables anchored in the granite cliff face, felt precarious yet secure.

Biz said she'd gotten Natalie's address from her mom, who still lives in St. Lola, even though her father has gone back to trucking in the States.

She told Natalie that she didn't call first because she wanted to surprise her. *You certainly did that*, Nat thinks, remembering the shock she felt when she opened the door and saw Biz standing there, her face electric when she smiled and said *Surprise!*

Natalie grounds herself in the memory: Biz's purple hair, clear lip gloss, black nails—her body. There. On the step. On Merrymeeting Road. In St. John's. Wholly out of context. Fabulous. And looking so full of life. Just as she remembered her.

But the memory is painful as well.

Natalie cannot remember exactly whose idea this weekend trip to La Manche was. Somebody had suggested they camp here in this drowned ghost town on the East Coast Trail, and she had thought it was a good idea to get them out of the confined awkwardness of the apartment. They had rented bicycles in town, packed bags, borrowed gear from Lisette's friends downtown—a crowd of Bonavista boys living in a basement apartment near Buckmaster's Circle.

Gerry said he wouldn't be caught dead sleeping in a tent.

We've come a long way as a human race, he'd said. No need to regress to living like nomads. And then there's the dysentery. If I go camping I do it out of the back of a van.

So he said he would get a van off his buddy Pete and pick them up after they were done roughing it. He said he was going to road trip down to Renews, maybe meet up with someone he used to know, and find them on his drive back. Then they could throw their bikes in the rear of the van and he would ferry them into town.

Hab had said that he wanted to come along, but he had to get an overdue paper finished and handed in so he could get his grade before August. He'd said that he would bike in today. Natalie keeps looking up the hill to see if he is waving down at her.

Still not here.

And because of this she feels oddly alone, even though the girls are just over the hill. She thinks of Biz and Lisette as a weird pairing. Biz, a Toronto-born graphic designer. And Lisette, a bar girl from the Bonavista.

And I'm the broken hinge between.

She feels naked in the night chill and in need of a sweater. All tied up emotionally and floating like that house on the water, her fear like waves crashing through windows, her mind lurching as she sinks, submerging herself into those memories of her life with Biz before the tenement fire in Toronto. She thinks of those painful recollections: her burned stomach and the way she pulled away from Biz's hand wet with ointment.

A chill washes over her and she imagines that January night in 1966 when sea swells poured through the front door of this house and out the back door, until the family finally abandoned their home and climbed to safety. Looking back to see their fishing stages creak, crack, and crumble into the waves.

They had all been forced to resettle.

She thinks of this abandoned outport they're camping in and how Biz seems to walk through the ruins of their friendship and see a ghost moving past like the shades of the thirty-some-odd people who once lived here. Natalie sees no ghosts. She doesn't remember much before the fire. A few things. But these recollections shock her when they come—they sear and burn.

Biz's body in this place, her presence here, blisters any nostalgia Natalie has for their life together in Toronto. She has no idea why. To her, there are only ruins, overgrown foundation stones, cement steps leading into a thicket of balsam and tamarack.

She wants Biz to admit this.

That it is all gone.

Broken.

Burned.

She wants to see Biz with her purple hair ascending that escalator in the St. John's airport, rising toward Departures like the angels on Jacob's ladder, leaving her to wake and find her pillow a stone beneath her ear—this hard old rock she has come to call home.

Her head hurts. She winces, then she hears voices from above.

Hab must be here now, she thinks as she begins to run up the hill.

When she sees that it's him she slips her arms around his sweaty body and he doesn't exactly know what to do, except drop his backpack and pull her in. He had wondered whether the bike ride down would be worth the effort or if he'd only be a third wheel on an all-girls camping trip. And Nat and he have

not *exactly* been talking since she got fired from her job and he found his own apartment.

Of all the greetings he had envisioned, he did not expect this. Not her lunging at him and hugging him so tightly that he winces. He sees her friend Biz over her shoulder, hair dark as night and pulled back from her face full of water and fire: her eyes foggy and dim, looking away.

We saved you some supper, Natalie says cheerily.

Awesome.

And he is pulled along in the dark to a fire they have built in another old foundation. He is given a plate of fried peppers, korma and rice, and eats while Natalie throws an armful of green pine boughs on the fire. The branches smoke and bring tears, kindle and send up flankers—sharp snaps of sap igniting. Ash worms wither, swirl and fizz on the damp earth.

It is an awkward arrangement in the tent that night, trying to figure out where people will sleep and next to whom. Natalie winds up in the middle though she had wanted a side, and Hab is at the three girls' feet. There is little talk going to bed and almost no movement, until Lisette's breathing evens out and Hab begins to snore softly.

That is when Natalie hears Biz unzip her sleeping bag. She feels Biz's hand slide over her side and she is caught between bristling and melting. Biz's hand pulls away and she can feel her friend drawing in behind her, pressing warm midriff against her back.

There is nothing more than this, save the warmth of Biz's arm around her now, her friend's hand on the front of her shirt—fingers feathering and falling still.

Natalie?

Yeah.

The night fills up their silence with water running down the hill. Natalie can feel her friend's breath on her neck, on her shaved head.

SNARL

Biz: He's sweet.

Hab?

Yeah.

Yes, he is.

There is the smell of earth and breath and moss-covered stone. The crinkle and slide of nylon, plastic. Words like hot coals. Silence raw as scalded tongues.

Natalie's thin cotton shirt wrinkles between her scarred belly and Biz's soft hand.

Is this okay? Biz whispers.

Yes, Natalie says, knowing this closeness will not last past morning. But for now she settles into her friend's warmth.

She thinks of the full life she and Biz had together, though it lasted only a short while. She had left a broken home as cold as the concrete floor in her parents' basement, where she would go watch TV so that she wouldn't hear their fights. She had met Biz and they had gotten the apartment together in Chinatown, and she'd purchased that orange silk scarf from a vendor on Spadina and tried to hold it over Biz's head during a rainstorm as they ran down the sidewalk. But the raindrops had come right through the silk until they were both soaked to the bone. And they had run with the scarf stretched between their upraised hands, high above the heads of huddled pedestrians on the crowded market street that smelled of sweet chili sauce, wet bodies, fried egg noodles, hot concrete, and mangos.

She had thought as she sipped miso soup and tasted her first scallop—wearing that orange silk scarf and listening to Biz tell her about this group home for abused kids she wanted to volunteer at—that *this* must be what Jesus had meant when he said he had come to give life in abundance. Gurney Gunther's words from one of those stifling midsummer services in the log tabernacle up on Lemming's Lake had come alive for her that day on a patio in Toronto, the subway rumbling faintly beneath them. The saltiness of the miso soup, the sandy grit in her teeth from the pan-fried scallop, and Biz's joy at telling her about how she thought she could help those kids had thrilled Natalie.

She had pulled the scarf from her neck to feel it sift across her skin, raising the hair on her arms, as had happened years ago when she'd prayed for the Holy Spirit to fill her twelve-year-old body.

She has tried to find those memories inside bottle after bottle of Shiraz, Merlot, Cabernet, Bordeaux, and Burgundy, but has found only numbness and cold. *Until now.* She has found Hab. Actually, she is not sure if she found him or he found her, but she loves that he tears heels of bread for her to dip in her wine so that the crumbs give the tasteless wine a texture and soggy substance. She feels Biz's body against hers and she likes the warmth, but she wants *Hab's* hand on her stomach, *his* breath on her neck. Biz's embrace is gentle and sweet, like a fond memory, but Hab holds on to her when he has a nightmare; his arms lock around her as if her body were a buoy in the open sea.

Only with Hab has her body felt that necessary, that desired.

She feels him shift at her feet and wonders what it is he is dreaming, even as Biz's breathing drops into the steady rhythms of sleep. Natalie realizes she is alone with the sound of the ocean wind gusting in the gnarled limbs of balsam and pine, her blistered hand cupped by her lips so that her breath soothes its ache.

Come sunrise, Natalie and Biz curl out of their sleeping bags and wake the others. They pack the damp tent and eat breakfast in silence—the granola burnt and the powdered milk lumpy. Lisette makes coffee by pouring boiling water over two teaspoons of grounds in her tin mug. She strains the hot, bitter drink through her teeth to catch the grit, cursing herself for having forgotten the filters. Halfway through, she tosses the last steaming dregs into the trees and lights a cigarette.

You don't like your coffee crisp? Hab asks groggily.

I like to drink my coffee, not eat it, Lisette puffs and yawns, spitting out grounds.

While Hab and Lisette banter and ready themselves to go, Natalie and Biz head down to fill their bottles from the pool. The water along the rocky shoreline is foamy this morning and thick with silt, twigs, and tree needles. Biz kicks off her shoes and pulls her ankle socks from her feet, rolling up her pant cuffs as she steps barefoot into the water, onto a submerged rock ledge. As she reaches out past the scummy waters, Natalie sees that Biz has gotten a new tattoo on her calf. She peers closer as Biz bends to fill the second jug and sees that it's a list of names inked in green that stretches from the back of Biz's knee to her ankle. But she can't make out the names; half of them obscured in ripples and foam.

As Biz steps gingerly out of the water, Natalie asks her about the tattoo.

Names of people gone missing in the fire, Biz tells her as she tosses the full bottles up on the grass and bends to tug on her socks and shoes.

Natalie watches the silt clouds settle in the coppery water where Biz stood moments ago on the submerged rock ledge.

Why?

I had nightmares for months after you left.

Sunlight ripples on the water as Biz tells Natalie about crawling along that corridor to the fire-escape in her dreams, elbowing her way over bodies that wheezed under her weight, bodies that ignited behind her and began to burn, screams scraping her nerves like rocks dragged across glass shattering in the intense heat—shocking her awake.

Biz inches a sock up to her ankle before slipping on a shoe.

I needed to know their names, she says. The people I crawled over in my dreams. Six began with X. One was three and a half. Jin. I didn't know any of them.

I'm sorry.

Biz looks at the foam along the shoreline. It has drifted over the place she was standing and there is no evidence of her ever being there. Why are you sorry? she finally says, pulling up a fistful of moss and tossing it in the water where she'd stood. You lived.

SAMUEL THOMAS
MARTIN

Natalie remains silent, looking at the ripples that roll out from the floating clump of moss. Her friend turns back toward her.

Nat?

Yeah.

You don't need to be sorry for living.

They climb the hill together in silence, the sound of water falling away in the rush of wind off the sea. They help the others pack and then begin the bike ride back toward St. John's. On the highway Natalie keeps checking over her shoulder when she hears a vehicle approaching, wondering if it will be Gerry back from Renews.

She finds it difficult to ride with her burned hand, and soon falls behind the others.

By the time Natalie begins the curving descent into Mobile, the others are far ahead of her, in the village or through it already. She is flying one-handed around a bend, the road-bed dropping off into gnarled evergreens to her right, when a van honks behind her, scaring her off the concrete and onto the soft gravel shoulder where she fishtails and her wheels wonk out from under her. She slides to a stop, her leg suddenly in agony.

The van pulls roughly onto the shoulder in front of her, spraying rocks against the guardrail that it grinds its bumper against, forcing the van to halt.

Natalie kicks her bike off her and jumps shakily to her feet. Her jeans saved her leg from being shredded on gravel, but she still feels badly bruised beneath the frayed denim. She is hurt but she is also furious, so she bites the inside of her cheek and limps up to the passenger side door, wedging herself roughly between the white panelled van and the steel guardrail. She hauls open the door—ready to blast the driver who she thinks must be drunk or high. But she chokes when she sees Gerry in the driver's seat, resting his sweaty mop of hair on the steering wheel, his right hand holding a balled-up sweater to his side. Glancing at her, he drops the frayed sweater and Natalie sees that his shirt

A BLESSED SNARL

is slit and his side is dark red with blood.

Gerry?

Nat, he groans, did I dent the van?

She feels herself chill as her leg throbs and her stomach turns at the sight of Gerry's blood-soaked shirt. Gerry, she says again, what happened?

I hit the guardrail, I think.

Gerry takes a sharp, painful breath and more blood oozes out between his fingers. It's a rental, he says as he reaches down, unbuckles his belt, and spins his knees toward the centre console. The van scrapes forward and Gerry jams the gear shift into park.

Nat, the guardrail, is it ...

We need to call you an ambulance—

No! Gerry wheezes and coughs. He bends with the pain as he crawls into the empty back of the van, dragging his bloody sweater by a threadbare cuff. No paramedics, he says, his teeth beginning to chatter. And no hospital either.

Gerry, you look like—

He cut me.

What?

Do you have any water? Or peroxide?

You need—

Nat. You can't call the cops. The moose—those moms—with the stones—they'll kill him. You can't tell them he cut me. I'll deny it.

Gerry says this deliriously, holding the sweater to his bloody side as he collapses into laboured breathing. Natalie slams the door, rounds the van, throws her bicycle in the back, and limps up the driver's side. She hauls herself onto the vinyl seat that's slick with blood, puts the van in gear, and pulls onto the highway, glancing back at Gerry who is bleeding into the grooves of the floor mat in the back, his head resting on one of the rusted wheel wells.

She comes across the others soon enough and honks for each of them until they stop and throw their bikes in the back and

climb in. Each of them asks what happened to Gerry, and each of them says they should get him to a hospital. But Gerry keeps shaking his head until he passes out in Bay Bulls, which is when they decide he needs a doctor.

He said he was what? Hab asks Natalie. Stabbed?

Somebody cut him.

Who? Biz asks as she pulls a spare shirt out of her bag and holds it against Gerry's side to staunch the flow of blood.

He said he was going to visit his father, Lisette breathes, her hand on Gerry's forehead, feeling his body temperature dropping.

His father?

Do you think?

We have to call the RNC.

He said no hospitals.

Which means he's in trouble and we should call the cops, Biz interjects.

You don't know Gerry like I do! Natalie snaps. If he said no he had a reason.

Reason or not, Lisette whispers, he needs a doctor, Nat.

So they drive to the hospital on Prince Philip and unload Gerry onto a trolley, which is when the police show up and they tell the officers all they know: that Gerry had gone to Renews to visit his father and that he picked them up on the Southern Shore Highway just outside Mobile, faint from loss of blood because of a knife wound in his side.

You know it was a knife?

He said he was cut.

What kind of knife? Belonging to whom?

He just said he was cut. Didn't say by who or with what knife. That's all I know. That's all any of us knows.

Natalie hardly remembers saying any of this to the police. She told them that she was the one who Gerry almost ran into, the first to see that he was hurt. She limps painfully up and down the hallway—waiting for news. She has forgotten that her hand held Biz's shirt against Gerry's side after Hab took

SNARL

over driving and that her fingers are covered in blood, which she unknowingly smears across her face in blotchy prints and rubs over her dry eyes. She has no idea that she looks like car wreck victim in a daze until Biz tells her she should go to the washroom to wipe off the blood.

Natalie splashes water on her face, the coolness soothing on her burned hand. She sputters and looks into the mirror to see Biz staring back at her. Bloody water drips from her chin; she can taste it on her lips.

Does Gerry have anything? Biz asks, leaning against a stall door.

Natalie splashes more water on her face and reaches with her good hand for the paper towel.

Any what?

AIDS. Or anything.

Nat looks at her blistered hand catching the pink water running off her face. She blows air through her lips, misting the mirror. Then she turns on Biz.

What type of fuckin question is that?

Biz takes a step back into the stall. Natalie wipes her palms over her face—flings blood and water off her burned hand against the stall wall.

You have his blood all over you. In your eyes.

He's my friend!

Biz takes another step back. She feels cool, damp porcelain against her ankle. Natalie is at the door of the stall, a sticky line of red like an incision along her hairline, around her ear.

I didn't say he wasn't. I just said—

That he might have AIDS! Natalie screams, leaning further into the stall, spit flying off her lips and hitting Biz's face. So what? What does it matter? His blood is in my eyes now. What can I do about it? If he's sick, then I'm sick already. He was stabbed, Biz! My friend was fuckin stabbed and you want me to ask if he's got AIDS?

The backs of Biz's knees are bent over the rim, her hand on the toilet paper dispenser for balance. Natalie takes another step

forward and Biz sits on the cold, pee-spattered porcelain rim, the plastic feet of the seat digging into her back.

He could have died on that road! Nat shouts, her face a breath away from Biz's lips. Biz feels Nat's words hot on her face and then Natalie spins around and bangs out of the stall. Her sudden movement shocks Biz, who shifts, her elbow pressing the lever as she stands.

Natalie has her head back in the sink, the water running. But she can hear the toilet flush and the door slam shut. She washes off the rest of the blood, uses the foaming hand soap to scrub her hairline. As she turns to leave she catches a glimpse of brown stains on the back of her shirt and pants: Gerry's blood soaking in.

Swinging open the door, she runs into a man wearing a canvas work jacket.

Sorry, love, he says, placing a big, grease-blackened hand on the door to hold it open for her, and that is when she notices the little stick figure without the skirt that she had missed on her way in.

She scans the waiting area down the hall but sees only Lisette and Hab.

Know where Biz went? she asks.

Outside for a smoke, I think.

I just had one, Lisette says. She wasn't out there.

Natalie flops in the chair beside Hab and rests her head on his shoulder. Lisette? she whispers, looking down and seeing that she still has blood under her fingernails.

Yeah, Nat.

Do you think Gerry could have AIDS?

Not unless you gets it from whacking off in the shower.

Oh.

Have you ever cleaned that drain?

No, I—

I have.

Oh, I was—

Gerry's a virgin. Despite what he might tell ya.

Hab looks over at Lisette, who is writing something in the air with the toe of her shoe. And you know this how? he asks.

Lisette continues writing in the air, her foot pointed like a ballerina. I knows, Hab, because we made out once and he told me, after he jizzed in his pants.

Hab coughs and gags a little, eyes wide and staring at his feet.

Natalie doesn't hear Lisette's confession.

She is looking through the glass of the main doors into the parking lot, watching nurses and patients on oxygen puff on their cigarettes. She is looking for Biz and wondering where she ran off to when a frumpy nurse—with a shock of pink in her bleached blonde hair—walks over and asks if they are friends or family of Gerard Malone.

No, Hab says, not looking up.

That's Gerry's name, b'y, Lisette says, leaning forward in her seat. Yeah, she nods to the nurse, we're his friends. Housemates.

Okay. Well, your friend is fine. We're going to keep him overnight, though, to see if any infection sets in. But the cut wasn't too deep. More a gash along his side. The main thing was blood loss, but we have him on an IV and he should be good to go by morning.

Can we see him? Natalie asks.

Not right now. The police are in there asking him questions. They'll be out to talk to you again, soon. So I'd stay where you're to. Now, who of the three of ye is the best nurse?

They look at each other, a bit confused.

Which one can I show how to dress the wound and clean it?

Lisette goes to stand but Natalie says, You can show me. I'll do it.

Alright. I'll be back for you when it's clear in there.

Do they know what he was stabbed with? Hab asks as the nurse turns to go.

He says it was a French bayonet, but he's a bit drugged right now.

The nurse with the shock of pink in her hair moves on down

the corridor and Natalie rests her head again on Hab's shoulder, hooking her arm in his.

Only Gerry could get himself stabbed with a bayonet, Lisette says, patting her pockets for cigarettes.

Natalie had meant to ask the nurse about a blood test but she remembers what Lisette said. She sinks back into her own thoughts, thrumming like her blistered hand.

They return to the apartment late, after Natalie has learned to change the dressing on Gerry's stitched-up gash, and they find Biz sitting on the couch, her bag packed and serving as a footrest. She is reading one of Gerry's dog-eared novels when they come in.

Lisette and Hab head down the hall, leaving Natalie leaning against the wall, staring at Biz. Where were you? she asks.

I thought I'd give you some space.

I hate that you do that.

Do what?

Natalie doesn't answer but she thinks of the close quarters that she lives in now, how even when she wants her space she can never get it because the apartment is so small and even when she goes downtown or to the university she sees people she knows or who talk to her as if they know her.

My plane leaves at seven tomorrow morning.

Natalie looks up. She'd been thinking of Gerry's stitched wound and how he looked at her coldly and said *I didn't want you to bring me here because now they know and they're going to pick him up.* She had asked *who* but Gerry hadn't answered, even as the nurse guided her hand to the gash and showed her how to clean it—Gerry wincing and looking away.

Seven?

Tomorrow.

She is thinking of the pain in her hand and of how deep the wound in Gerry's side might be beneath the black stitches. *Deep enough to fit my fingers inside?* Natalie sees Biz flip a page in the

book. She had not wanted to take Gerry to the hospital, but what if an infection had set in? *Who are the cops going to pick up?* Biz closes the book and tucks her feet under a pillow on the couch, swivelling to face Natalie head on. *It looked so raw.*

Nat?

Yeah.

Is Gerry okay?

Yes. He's fine. And he doesn't have AIDS.

Biz looks at her like the last comment was a slap. Okay then, she says.

And those are the last words they ever say to each other.

Hab sleeps on the floor of Natalie's room and Biz curls up on the couch and shivers through the night. Natalie wakes early and calls a cab. She waits outside in the predawn gloom while Biz brushes her teeth and washes in the kitchen sink. She can smell fresh bread from the Coleman's bakery down the road—fluffy dinner rolls, round rye loaves, and garlicky cheese buns. The cab arrives and honks as it pulls in, and Biz comes out the door with her bag in tow.

Returning from the airport, Natalie will walk the bikes back down to the shop with Hab and Lisette and when they come back Gerry will be home and lying on the couch watching *Deadwood* on DVD, and he will only say to Natalie that his cut is *gooey* and needs to be changed and will she help him with that? And when they are standing alone in the bathroom, he will put his hand on her wrist and say, *You did the right thing getting me to the hospital. Thank you.* And that will be the first tenderness of Natalie's day. Because Biz says nothing to her on the trip to the airport and Natalie pays the cab fare while Biz drops off her luggage and gets her ticket.

When Natalie changes the fluid-soaked bandages on Gerry's side, she will not remember if she and Biz hugged or not. She'll only recall the frigid airport, ribbons rippling on the vents, and her arms covered in goosebumps, remembering the feel

of that orange silk scarf whispering over her skin, knowing that it burned in the fire along with the twisted branches of her childhood faith.

Among all that she will not recall, she will remember watching Biz's purple hair ascend the escalator, that soft white hand she has felt on her belly, her side. Her angel's hand, her saviour's, like a wound now. That hand slicing sharply down Biz's side and lifting a pant cuff so that Natalie will see the list of tattooed names descending to that ankle she held onto once, gripped, dug fingernails into as she was pulled through fire that blistered her belly, like the red skin around the last name, so small now that Natalie can't read it but only dimly perceive the inflamed, newly needled flesh. That name: written on skin raw as the burn on her hand that aches now in the airport's cold interior.

She squeezes a palm that is not there, pressing fisted fingers against the burn line wet with salve, not knowing that she will find in that novel Biz was reading—the one that Natalie took from Gerry's shelf of signed copies, the one she read and dog-eared and devoured—a receipt for a tattoo parlour on Ropewalk Lane dated yesterday and time-stamped midway through that hour that she had placed her hand on Gerry's stitched side for the first time, felt his pulse in the spaces between her fingers, as if her hand no longer existed and her body had disappeared, ghosted into that deep realm of regret where language breaks and words stutter still.

She squeezes the hand that is not there, again, and again—those soft white fingers that caressed her side on the La Manche Bridge—and she feels it then: the burn, the blistered skin, the wet, sticky aloe. She makes a final fist before letting go and feels her pulse throb through her fingertips.

Gerry is thinking about that morning in Renews when he leaned over to kiss his father and got stabbed with a bayonet. His hands are cold and he is writing nothing on the blank white paper in front of him, but in his mind he is not in Des' cabin—he is sneaking up those rickety stairs to the attic his father was renting. It was easy enough to find out where he was living, everyone knew. *That house at the end of the lane that looks like it has no business being there.* Flaking blue paint and shingles curled like sneering lips against the seaward wind. *He rents the attic. I barely sees him except for when he buys baloney and eggs.* Gerry's hand on the coarse wood of the cabin table evokes the memory of his fingers running up that unsanded banister to the landing, the sun just beginning to crest the rocks and pierce the harbour.

They put his dad in the Waterford after, in a secure psych ward for patients with violent tendencies.

The sound of Hab's sketching across the table from him brings Gerry back to the cabin and the old cigarette tin on the table. He has not told Hab what's in the tin, but when he looks at it now he thinks of Hab's grandfather Des and the shed he is renovating, and what he knows of Des' story is like that empty, unfinished outbuilding. Gyproc walls mudded but unsanded, unpainted. He has tried to write it but fears he's sealed the cracks in the telling. He knows whose names are behind the stove, over against the cabin's far wall, up here in the woods back of Fawkes Cove. He knows the names because he found the tobacco tin with those old letters in it—letters to men named Hawco, Murphy, Now, O'Leary, King, Johnston, and Hynes—written in faded ink. A scuffed skull ring cast in burnished silver clinking in the can. And a newer letter on lined notepaper addressed to no one, asking *Who the hell do you think I am that I'd do that to you? Do you know he hates me now! Because of your lies! Holy mother of God, woman! I haven't touched an ounce of liquor in twenty years.*

Gerry wonders as he sits in the cold of the unlit cabin who Des was writing to.

Hab has brought him up to this place for an afternoon of sketching and writing. Said his pop took him up here in the summer. Showed him that soot stain on the chimney flashing and told him how it had come alive as the Virgin's face to him one night many years ago.

It doesn't look like much to Gerry, the black creosote stain. He had thought the same thing when he had quietly opened his father's door and stepped over the old, mud-stained newspapers spread on the linoleum. He wonders why he went there. Since the stabbing he finds it hard to substantiate that day in his mind—his thoughts, fears, uncertainty, doubt. He had slept the night in the back of the van behind the convenience store and had woken before dawn to sneak into his father's apartment. *Why?* Standing there in the gloom, waiting for his eyes to adjust to the darkness of the shabby room with one window, an old microwave, and a tin sink bolted to the bare-boarded wall. Boots by the door, toes scuffed, leather cracked, frayed laces sprawling. And the shattered two-by-four gripped in his hand. *Yes.* He had picked it out of a pile beneath the stairs with the intention of beating his father awake, of doing to him what he had done to Rod and now regretted doing. But it is the sound of Rod's raspy breathing that comes to him in this dark room memory—his dad snoring loudly on the mattress by the window. Water stains dripping down the wall below the sill and disappearing behind yellowed sheets.

Gerry realizes that his eyes are on the soot stain in the cabin, even while his mind is in that tiny attic room in Renews. He looks over and sees that Hab's attention is on the creosote Madonna. He follows his friend's gaze back to the far wall, but his eyes drop to the list of names carved there, half-hidden behind the old stove. Hab barely gives them a wink.

My dad almost froze to death up here this winter. Hab says this as he gets up and walks across the dirty old cabin to the wood stove. It's chilly this late in September, and Gerry shivers in his seat, hunkers down in his jackshirt.

You cold? Hab asks.

I need to take a shit.

Hab tells Gerry where the outhouse is. His words mist, and Gerry can feel his hands numb in his pockets as he heads out the door—numb as they were that day in his dad's room, fisted around that broken two-by-four with the one sharp, slivered end. He cannot imagine being up at Des' cabin in the winter, like Hab's father was, any more than he can imagine his father huddled in that attic for God knows how many years. No insulation and the only apparent heat source a small electric block heater with its duct-taped cord plugged into the single socket below the dripping sink. As Gerry settles gingerly onto the coarse boards of the outhouse seat he thinks it a wonder that his father's apartment never caught fire and burned the whole house to the ground.

As he rocks back and forth—to keep himself warm and get things moving quicker—he remembers leaning over his dad's body, wrestling filthy sheets into knots around bony ribs. *When did he lose all that weight?* His dad had always been thin but thick with muscle. The man he breathes over nervously in his mind is all shoulder blades and collar bones. A loose tent of brown-spotted, wrinkled skin stretched over emaciated ribs. He is close enough to see his dad's breath wisp in the cool morning light. His own breath smokes against the outhouse wall.

So close I could have kissed him. And he had thought to do just that, the desire strange as frost in summer, ice melting on a hot August morning—his lips to his father's forehead.

But he stopped inching nearer when his dad coughed in his face, the older man's breath rank, his gums raw and bleeding around blackened teeth.

Gerry brings himself out of that sickening memory with a last long fart. He wipes himself with crumpled newspaper, thinking they were stunned not to have brought real toilet paper. But he remembers too that he had not heard of such a thing until he was in high school. You can wipe your arse with the newspaper, his father would say, About all it's good for, you ask me. Ever since Gerry moved out on his own he has bought triple-ply toilet paper, as satiny soft as he can afford. And he has gotten used to it. So wiping his arse now with old flyers chafes him.

But he reminds himself of why he is here, *roughing it*, as Hab would say. He is here to work on the novel about Rod, to fill in the history he does not know with a fictional backstory—maybe even a happy ending. Most of the time happy endings make Gerry gag, but he wants one for Rod: he wants to be able to take back what he did, or make up for it somehow.

Ever since his first visit to Des' house he has thought that Fawkes Cove would be a good home for Rod in his book. But he knows he needs to get the place right, which is why he is out to Hab's grandparents' place most weekends: doing interviews, reading old letters, newspaper clippings—always greeted at the door with a back slap.

Gerry, how're ya doin, my son? Don't mind the mutt. He don't bite. Come in, come in. The pope's in Rome and the Habs are winning!

It has felt good to be thus ushered in and welcomed.

Safe.

But the more Gerry has found out about Hab's grandfather, the more he finds the floor beneath him as grimy and half-rotted as the floor in his father's apartment. Grease-slick and covered with the debris of a life he knows nothing about. Des has told Gerry that it's good he's doing his *writing researchy thing* now because if he'd come in a month Des would have had his whole shed cleared out and half the papers Gerry has been rifling through would've been burned in an old oil drum cut with a welding torch.

As it is, half of what Gerry has documented *has* been burned. *It's like racing against a mechanical incinerator*, he sometimes thinks. What scraps he can squirrel away he stacks in wooden crates that Des has promised not to burn until Gerry is done with them—old photos, letters, half a dozen major receipts, and the tobacco can Gerry found and wrapped in an oil rag so Des won't see that he's cabbaged it.

Gerry has, however, seen Des rummaging around the cupboard he found the tin can in: the old man muttering to himself and shaking his head.

That's why Gerry has started carrying the tobacco can with him in his backpack—because he's scared Des will go through those wooden crates and see he's found those letters—that weird little ring—and that he *knows*. He wonders what knowing would mean to Hab or to Patrick, Des' son. He wonders often what knowing means to *him*, except that it's a small comfort that he's not the only one with a dirty secret.

Back in the cabin after his frigid dump, Gerry sees Hab lighting a fire in the rusted stove and he thinks, in that instant, that if it was gloomier in here he might believe the creosote stain to be a face. *Candlelight and alcohol could definitely set off revelation*, he thinks. *There's a condensed history of the Catholic Church I could write*. But as he watches Hab hack at a junk of spruce with a hatchet, feathering the damp wood so that it will catch better on the bed of kindling, he thinks it has been a long while since anything has sparked in him.

It used to be that he could rant and roar, mock a mock accent—*yes, b'y, no, b'y*—scoff at islanders and mainlanders alike. He would never have called himself a patriot like his dad claimed to be, but he thinks how much of his dad has rubbed off on him. He still smiles when he thinks of that impossible story of his father taking a dump in John Crosbie's shoes, even though he knows it was a lie. Most of the time when he thinks of his father's lies all those stories seem like tinder to him——his temper the flash. And suddenly all his fond memories ignite and rage smoulders in him until any fondness he had ever felt for his dad combusts, leaving an ash scar through greenwood, an ache in him like the bayonet scar below his ribs.

Foolishness, Gerry thinks as he leans against the sill of one of the cabin's two broken windows. The fractured glass shatters the peaceful scenery and breaks up Gerry's thoughts. He had been in Rod's apartment just then, in his mind, on the day he broke the skin on Rod's face with the tire iron. He'd beaten that face until it was ground-beef raw. And then he'd shattered the glasses underfoot as he ran out into the snow.

He had thought of doing the same thing to his father. His original plan had been to confront his dad, whose face had been haunting his thoughts along with Rod's ever since he ran into Rod downtown. He'd told Lisette that he was going to see his father in Renews, but he hadn't told her about Trudy, how she had been diddled by his father. He'd had enough of torturing himself in his room though, unable to write anything, drinking bottle after bottle of Old Sam rum, bought with grant money from the arts council. He had felt—more than thought—that facing his father would give him enough courage to face Rod: if he could tell his father what he really thought of him, then maybe he would be able to tell Rod what he had really done to him.

There is a crackle from the stove and Gerry can hear Hab blowing on the embers, but his mind is elsewhere: his elbow on the warped windowsill, his hand through the broken glass, feeling the rain starting to come down and thinking of the night he went to Mile One Stadium with Natalie and Lisette and he saw Rod again. On the bench next to them, bent over, pulling the same skates Gerry had left in the bar onto big feet in tattered wool socks. Gerry had ducked back into the bleachers to watch, expecting Rod to wipe out as soon as his skates hit the ice—he was so wobbly walking. But when the old guy stepped onto the ice, his cane left on the bench with his battered boots, he took off as if he was on a breakaway.

Gerry had watched him weave in and out and around folks on the ice, outskating the orange-jacketed rink guards who were trying to flag him down, his scraggly face split in a smile that popped his eye patch up over his eyebrow.

That is when Gerry realized he knew nothing about Rod, or about his father.

He has examined his own face reflected in new bottles of Old Sam, thinking that hatred does not come from actually knowing anything. *It crawls up out of fear fucked by ignorance.* He'd imagined he was running from ignorance by being as unlike his father as he could be. But he has come to see himself differently lately: in his reflection in the toilet bowl after flushing for the fifth time, trying to forget the day he saw himself in Rod's pop-bottle glasses. Much as he has hated his father for most of his life, he has come to see himself as no better.

He can hear rain hissing on the hot chimney overhead. Hab is throwing a few more junks of spruce on the smoky fire. Steam rises off the stovetop like incense uncoiling from an altar, and Gerry knows he is a coward: he did not have the courage to face Rod that night at the pub.

All he has done is write that story. And then try to unknot truth from fiction in the note he scribbled the night Rod stumbled back into his life. He thinks of the old words of scripture from the mass he went to on his own, when he had come out and seen the sceptre-less hand of John the Baptist. *Is it not better to confess our sins one to another?* But even though he had wanted to visit that small boxed room with the red light signalling the priest's presence, he had not. Because he could not bring himself to confess to a priest. Not after so many buggering priests were absolved and shipped away with no consequence. Not after sacraments had been used to seal up so much.

He wonders if torturing himself—drinking himself sick— is penance enough. It hurts him. He's been to the doctor recently and found he has ulcers. He eats rolls of Tums to keep his stomach acid from burning his throat. He has masturbated

furiously while hanging with his belt cinched around his neck in his closet. He carved a sliver from their porch with a kitchen knife, placed the pointed end under his thumbnail, and pressed until blood began to drip. But none of this numbs him for very long, nothing he has done to himself has brought him peace— no bleeding ulcer, bruised trachea, or slivered thumbnail can cause enough pain to satisfy Rod's bloody ghost in his mind or make thoughts of his father vanish.

He has the story he wrote about Rod in his backpack. He brought it along with the tobacco can that sits on the table. While Hab sketches, Gerry again wraps the tin in the oil rag and places it back in his bag. He thinks of the ring in it, duct-taped so it doesn't rattle—so he will not see the silver skull leering at him every time he opens the lid. He feels that the skull's blank stare sees through him. And even thinking of it reminds him of the two confessions now balled up together in his bag.

But for some reason his crime seems small in the blaze of Des'.

The older letters date from the sixties and seventies, when Des worked for Smallwood's government. Nothing but those letters speaks of that time. It has all found its way into the fire barrel over the years, except for this can of letters to men from Bonavista Bay, most from small coves and islands to the north.

Places once unreachable except by boat. But that is only another hammer stroke to Gerry's mind: *the sheer effort and will it took.*

He has been sure of many things in his life. He has until recently had absolute faith in his inner compass pointing true— that he is nothing like his father and never will be. But this tin disc in his bag, this old cigarette can, is a magnet. Gerry finds his thoughts so often now spinning like the loose hands on a broken clock face. *Did people actually do that sort of thing? To their neighbours? And not to have spoken of it for three decades ....*

Gerry has thought of this as sutured silence. He knows that some stitches dissolve in the bloodstream but this, these letters, are a festering gash. Maybe not in Des' mind—but then why would he be looking in that cupboard and cursing? Maybe he was looking for something else. Perhaps he has forgotten altogether. *Just a scar.* Numb now to the cold. But Gerry feels gutted, reading the letters.

And that feeling revives his memory of being back in his father's attic apartment. Everything is quiet except the faint sound of the sea outside, the wind in the storm-curled shingles, the dripping of the pipe beneath the sink plinking into a plastic bucket. He is bent over his father's frail body, shaking in restless sleep. He's feeling his dad's breath on his eyes, smelling his rank, rotting mouth, hearing him snore and gulp.

Seeing him blink and gasp.

And then the bayonet rips through the sweat-stained sheets and slits his side open and his dad squirms out from under him, like a rat under a boot, and pins him to the bed, screaming: *Who are you?* And suddenly the world has become skin-split pain, the smell of urine, a rusty blade pressed against his throat.

He feels those same things now, thinking of what he knows Des has done, forever replaying in his mind what *he* has done and not told anybody about.

Hab is off at the stove again, his hands dark with charcoal and soot. Smoke about his head, in his eyes—coughing. Gerry reaches into his bag and pulls out a letter and stares at Des' sloppy cursive.

Smoke fills the room and Gerry chokes on it as much as on what he is reading: the truth a blistering blaze behind the penned apology. He thinks of the can as a cup of cinders.

An urn.

But it is an unused instrument because the letters were unsent. They were stuffed in an old tobacco tin and are yellowed now with age and moisture. They smell of mouldy Export cigarettes. *Why write the letters if you're not going to send them, Des?* Gerry wonders, especially about the newer letter that was written in answer to some unnamed accusation. But he thinks also of his own story and why he wrote it, why he confessed in

fiction no one would ever read, least of all Rod.

Writers speak of being brave, but are they? Or should I only speak of myself?

That should keep off the chill till the rain lets out, Hab says. And his voice echoes in Gerry's hollow thoughts.

Yes, Gerry says, looking over at Hab dusting his knees, wiping his sooty hands on work pants borrowed from his grandfather. That'll do.

Gerry is wearing Des' torn jackshirt over the bloody sweater his dad had forced on him, trying to stop the bleeding once he realized that it was his son he had stabbed and not someone come to murder him in his sleep. Gerry has washed the sweater many times, and the blood stains have faded to sickly ochre splotches. He wears it now when he sits down to write, but he has not written a thing since that story of Rod won him the grant. He had hoped today would change that. But as he sits here now, the page blank before him, he is not so sure.

Hab had looked at him weirdly when he came out of the house with Des' red-checked jackshirt on. He said he thought he had seen it somewhere before, on someone different.

Your pop maybe? Gerry had scoffed.

No, Hab said seriously, someone else.

Gerry remembers Des saying his psychotic grandson——Hab's first cousin——stole it off him for a while and that it was returned when the kid was shipped off to Whitbourne. Some friggin idiocy, Des said when he handed Gerry the jackshirt in the porch while Hab was with his nan in the kitchen. He told Gerry about his grandson stealing the coat. I'm afraid of him—my own grandson. More of my spark in him than I care to admit.

And Gerry had not known what he meant by that, but it makes him think of the kid in his care at the group home on Pennywell.

River——the psycho Natalie had looked after until she got herself fired. Gerry hadn't realized he'd taken on her job when he'd dropped out of university, after getting the grant, and applied for a part-time overnights position. River terrifies him.

Gerry is reminded of that, wearing this jackshirt punked from an old man. He tries to think of the frayed coat as Des' and not his crazy grandson's. It seems odd to Gerry that these old men's clothes—the jackshirt and the stained sweater—are here, on him, but the men are absent.

He looks up and sees the creosote Madonna staring blankly from the stovepipe, and in the shadows he thinks for a second that he sees it shift and sneer. But when he stares at it there is no movement, and all he can imagine is his father's shocked eyes when his dad had gripped his chin and forced his face into the light—to see who he was—the bayonet feeling like the sharp edges of his belt cinched around his neck.

He swallows with difficulty and tries to force himself to write. He tries over the next few hours, but he cannot force words onto the page. He and Hab stay until dusk, when the rain lessens to drizzle and a fog sets in. Hab has been sketching furiously for hours like a monk at his table, gesture drawings thrashed out in dark and sanguine charcoal—crows on strings flapping madly. Gerry has doodled but barely written a thing.

Except his father's room number at the Waterford.

The fire is low and almost burned out. It has been difficult to keep it going because the wind has been slanting the rain sideways, making it run down the chimney and stove pipe, flooding the embers.

You'll be able to find our way back? Gerry asks Hab, as they gather their gear. He hopes that Hab has packed a light.

But Hab asks him if he has brought a flashlight.

No. Didn't you?

No, but we should be fine. Pop said he marked the trail with orange tape so we'd find it easy enough.

Gerry coughs: Lead on Cabot.

Don't jinx us now.

He follows Hab out into the dark and damp. Their feet squish in the mud and he is glad for the rubber boots Des lent him. He is glad for Des' jackshirt around his shoulders, over his father's sweater—the two garments keeping him from

shivering. The fog hushes everything except their footsteps—even Gerry's thoughts, so that his mind is only on putting one boot in front of the other and following Hab's ghostly form through the washed-out spruce and pine, the smell of trees more real than the trees themselves in the obscuring haze.

Orange tape spindling from overhead branches, girdled around thin trunks, guides them. Gerry picks his way behind Hab down the hill into the cove, eventually coming to the road and the sea silent on its far side.

Hab is a weird kid, Gerry muses. He is happy as anything not saying a word half the time, though Gerry never hears the end of him chatting with Natalie in the next room. Especially since Natalie's friend Biz came from Toronto for a few days in the summer. Gerry had not clued in that Biz had left the day he came home from the hospital, the day the RNC had phoned to say they had his dad in custody and Natalie had gently washed his wound with saline solution and re-bandaged it with gauze and surgical tape.

He had thought to ask Hab about Natalie and Biz up in the cabin but was thankful enough for Hab's silence that he dropped it and drifted off into memories of his dad's apartment. He is grateful Hab did not try to strike up a conversation with him today. And that Hab has been able to get them out of the woods. He would never say it to Hab, but the thought of sleeping in the forest on a wet night, any night, scares the piss out of him.

He knows he is a bit of pansy that way, but he is scared of hardship—of a difficult, impoverished life. Standing in his father's apartment, he could not name the chalky taste in his mouth—the feeling that his throat was closing or that he was being strangled—but, thinking back, he knows it was fear. He was frightened when he saw how his father had been living; terrified that he would wind up in such a place; hating the feeling knotting his stomach that he deserved such a fate. Yet in that strange morning light, filtered through that hand-splotched windowpane, his father's face seemed to glow, each wrinkle outlined by shadow and every liver spot a dark thumbprint.

That is when he had leaned over to kiss his father's face.

He likes to think of himself as being able to endure hardship, to survive in the wilderness if he needed to, but he knows that St. John's is wilderness enough for him. Loose foundation stones. Rust. Random jut of a house out over the sidewalk like a dislocated hip. Moose in Bannerman Park some mornings. George Street Festival. *What a rut fest that is on a hot summer's night.*

He fears the woods because he does not know them, and he fears himself, his own nature, for the same reason. When he examines himself, stares steadily with his mind's eye at what he has done—without glancing away into distracting thoughts— he sees his fear and the violence it has made him capable of. *Who in hell am I?*

He had tried to drown out Rod's screams by standing in front of the speakers during George Street Fest—to crowd out his loneliness by wrestling his way into the drunken fray—but the drummer's wailing on the bodhran beat into his mind again and again what he had done. He remembers the heat from all those bodies—the muggy summer air.

Unlike tonight's chill.

The glaring memory of stage lights dim and blur and then come back into focus as the lamps on the side of Des Wiseman's house up on Noseworthy Drive. The climb up the hill and the night hike leave Gerry damp and puffing. He has a midnight shift at the group home tonight.

River is back from Whitbourne.

Gerry has a plan to try to keep the kid on the straight and narrow by promising him a bonfire some night on Middle Cove Beach. Gerry knows River is a pyro so the kid should go for that, he hopes.

When they reach the driveway, Gerry tells Hab to go on into the house. He will be in shortly, and they can drive back to St. John's. Just gotta grab some stuff from your Pop's shed, he says.

Fine. Nan will ask if you want tea. You want it in a travel mug, or you thinking about sticking around a bit?

Travel mug, Gerry calls over his shoulder as he heads for the backyard.

Keep an eye out for the dog.

Gerry finds his way in the dark out to Des' shed. His rubber boots muck up the path to the door, which is new this week: solid brass handle, double-paned window with the Home Hardware sticker still on it.

You know that Pimp Your Shed competition on OZ.FM? Des had asked Gerry when he was over about a month back.

I've heard of it.

Well, that's what I'm settin out to do.

Gerry flicks on the light inside. The wash of white on plaster and new gyproc makes him squint. *Unfinished as yet.* The room is still in need of sanding and a few coats of paint. The old clapboard walls are covered over, the bare board floor sanded down and ready for varnish. The room is wired and there is a wall of hooks from which all of Des' power tools will someday hang. Des has a stash of old paint cans in the corner, leftovers from his time working as a drywaller and painter. *After the Smallwood days.* And, Hab has told Gerry, after Des' conversion involving that soot stain up at the cabin.

Gerry traipses to the workbench, notices the shelf built into the wall for the big flat-screen TV that Des bought from the Price Club and has stored in a closet in the house for the past year and a half.

To look at him, Gerry muses, *you'd think sixty-year-old Newfie fisherman.* But Gerry knows that Des hates seafood, that his wife detests cooking jigg's dinner, that he gets seasick in the boat, and that he'd rather be left alone to his high-def hockey games than tramp down the hill to a kitchen party.

Doesn't even drink, Gerry thinks, though two weeks ago he'd found an unopened wine bottle in a sock under the old workbench. An aged Bordeaux. *Probably vinegared.* The label was written in black ink but faded, as if the bottle had been in the dusty sock for years. Gerry has heard of recovered alcoholics keeping time bombs hidden like that. But the wine bottle has gone missing since the renovations.

And Gerry is happy for Des.

This old man who is proof again that he doesn't know this place himself, though he reads of it splintered down in fiction. There is something that always escapes him, slips out of his hands, stands just out of sight, but he can feel it. Like when he has been hag-ridden in the night, knowing something is there in the room but unable to wake fully and crane his neck to see it as it slips out of view. Like Rod's battered face, still smiling in Gerry's memory of the old drunk cutting across the ice, without his cane or limp, at full tilt.

The thought of Rod is heavy on Gerry as he pulls out that award-winning story and the tobacco can. He scrawls a note on the first page of the confession he penned down at Erin's Pub, which is stapled to a draft of the story about Rod. He writes with a dull carpenter's pencil, folds the notebook pages scribbled in red ink and slides them into the can of letters, circled within that newer letter answering some unnamed accusation—something Des supposedly did while drunk out of his mind. Gerry slips in Rod's black plastic rosary, remembering that one word in blocked capitals written in dull pencil by another hand at the end of a page of cursive denial: RAT. He pulls up the tape pasted over the silver skull ring: hears it clink as he closes the lid on its empty leering. He wonders who placed it in the can—Des or the author of that one word?

RAT.

He places the can on the workbench because the cupboard that once held it has been torn away from the wall where gleaming hooks now hang.

He peels off Des' soaked jackshirt and droops it over the back of the chair by the workbench. Then he pulls off his father's old blood-stained sweater and hangs it on the open door of the unfinished circuit box. It swings back and forth, dripping onto the floor, water beading up on the weathered wood.

Gerry's jacket is by the door where he left it, so he slings it

on and grabs his pack as he looks back, smelling cut wood and plaster.

He hopes Des can read his handwriting. He figures the old man will burn the letters after all those years, and he hopes that Des will burn his story as well. With it gone, maybe he can start again, like Des is doing here in this old renovated shed. And maybe Des knowing that Gerry knows, and Gerry knowing Des knows about him in turn, will cut them both loose like severed jig lines.

On his way out, Gerry reaches for the light and sees a tin cup screw-nailed to the wall beneath a thumb-sized, tarnished crucifix. There is a splash of scummy water in it—holy water. His fingers twitch over the cup a second and then he stretches beyond it to flick off the lights.

The click of the door is like the clink of glass on rock, as a bottle washes out from him in his mind. Like that bottle he once put his confession in as a little boy—of how he dropped a cinder block on that wriggling flour sack when he was ten after he'd found out Trudy was moving away. He dropped the cinder block on the sack until it stopped whimpering. And then he threw it in the dumpster behind their row of houses and tried to forget about it. He had cut the bloodstain out of his new jeans and had gotten cuffed for it.

Do you know how much clothes cost? his dad had yelled.

His father's harsh words could not drown out in his memory that sickening, squishing sound, the crunch of concrete on asphalt, those last, weak kicks. He couldn't forget what he had done, even as a boy, even after the garbage truck had come and taken away the evidence. That is when he'd written it down in crayon on a sheet of construction paper. *Green.* Its eyes were green. Like Rod's. Like his father's. *Dammit,* he whispers, remembering. He hadn't known what colour his father's eyes were until he saw them flash in the morning light coming through that single window.

When his father realized that it was his own son he'd stabbed.

Gerry remembers putting that note in a bottle, like they did in stories, and hurling it off a pier in the Battery by the Narrows. He had wanted it to smash on the rocks and sink, but it hit the water and floated away from him. Like a last prayer—like that old priest reading aloud from the Psalms when he went alone to that mass and passed the three men smoking on the steps in the shadow of the Virgin.

Put my tears in your bottle and do not forget them.

He wonders if perhaps this is what he has done.

He looks across the yard and sees Des' old dog Jesse sitting under the eave by the back door, his fur caked with wet mud. Back from running freely about the cove. The dog knows Gerry and does not bark, only sits there as the rain pours down on them. Gerry sees Jesse's tail wag and runs over to the mutt, kneels on the wet ground and lets him lick his whole face, thinking of the last words in his pencilled note—*I once crushed a pup's skull with a cinder block*—his fingers sinking deep into Jesse's wet, stinking fur, his father's grey, greasy hair, the bayonet dropping from his throat, tears filling those eyes, those sea-green eyes bloodshot and full of remorse.

Patrick thinks of Hab in the car beside him as both a comfort and a cut into his conscience, like the last unopened letter from Gurney he has folded in his pocket, which he thinks he might read on the ferry. Hab is riding with him down to the Argentia Ferry just past Placentia, where Patrick used to play hockey as a kid on the abandoned American military base. Hab is telling his dad about this old footage he saw, in a Newfoundland history course, of liquid fire being hauled out of the earth, streaming from molten buckets of great industrial backhoes. After the Americans had left Argentia and buried reservoirs of unused oil and jet fuel, something Patrick never knew about as a minor league goalie.

It was crazy, Dad. It looked like they were mining lava.

They buried jet fuel?

And grenades. They think.

They wha——?

Didn't find them, so they stopped digging.

So I played hockey on a time-bomb?

Hab nods and says *yeah*, inhaling. Patrick smiles: it's a Newfoundland tick, breathing in the *yes*, and he likes that his son has picked it up—that sigh of assent and resignation. He wonders what else his son has picked up since being here, how he's changed.

Hab has come along to see his dad off to the mainland, where Patrick hopes to begin making amends with Anne, somehow. He has packed a single bag, sold the house, and yard-saled the rest. Except Hab's stuff and the computer, which they moved into Hab's new apartment on Malta Street—around the corner from the house that burned down a few months back and was in the papers.

His one bag, a blue tarp, and a bottle of baby oil.

Hab had raised his eyes not so much at the tarp as at the baby oil, but Patrick didn't feel he could tell his son where he got the idea—that the night Hab was conceived Patrick had unrolled a big blue tarp across their new queen-sized bed and Anne and he had slicked themselves down and slid all over that thing, making a huge slippery mess.

You don't say things like that to your son, he thinks. *That he was conceived out of laughter.*

Patrick wonders why he hadn't noticed that Anne had stopped laughing. Was it because he wanted to believe she would adjust to life here? That she would come around and enter into his dreams? He would give anything to crawl up into her dreams now, just once.

His dreams are gone to ash like the two other letters from Gurney that he burned on the cliff edge of Fawkes Cove.

The heaving of the ice that day was like the motion of this car on these rolling roads. Its shocks are gone and the brakes are a bit squishy, but as far as Patrick is concerned it is not too bad for a beater—it should hold together until he gets to Ontario. The insurance on the Malibu was valid after all, but Patrick found out the hard way that *collision* does not necessarily cover a car rolling into the ocean. And there was no evidence that it was not his fault—that he had not left it in gear or not put the parking brake on.

Insurance did not cover the *possibility* that somebody pushed the car over the cliff. That is why Patrick had to buy Job, this rusted-out Tercel.

Job? Hab asked when Patrick had told him the car's name.

Battered but not broken.

Are you sure?

Sure I'm sure. Come on already. I have a ferry to catch.

And that had started their road trip inland, down through Placentia Junction. Hab brought along his MP3 player and a cassette adapter. He tells Patrick that the girl singing is Amelia Curran and that he should slow down and watch for moose.

Thanks, Nan, Patrick says as he gives Job a bit more gas and wonders at the closeness of the grey sky. He revs the engine and hears something rattle under the hood, which makes him think of that tobacco can his dad had shaken on his last trip to Fawkes Cove, before Patrick packed up and sold the house. His father had asked him if he knew what was in it.

Of course he did. Patrick remembers the shock in his dad's face when he said that. He told his father that he'd found it as a teenager, looking for wood stain in the shed so that he could finish a footstool for shop class.

His dad had walked out of the renovated shed, pushed past him, and mucked through the wet grass over to where he had half buried an old dory, its bottom rotted out and its gunwales in rough shape.

Patrick's mom had told him, when he'd asked what was with the old boat in the backyard, that his dad was going to plant a little flower garden in it.

Flowers?

I'm thinking of doing the B&B thing, and we thought sprucing the place up would help attract some guests.

That why Dad renovated the shed?

No, that's so when I watches reruns of *Coronation Street* he can still watch the hockey game in peace.

Patrick remembers his dad kicking a spade into the rocky soil and turning it over inside the boat that looked as if it was sinking into the earth. His dad was working hard, not looking up at Patrick, sweat beginning to run down his face though it was chilly that day, wind whipping between the buttons on Patrick's peacoat.

Dad?

I didn't think anyone knew.

Dad, Patrick said stepping into the buried boat, watching his father bail big stones over the backside to make room for the truckload of topsoil he'd brought back from St. John's.

Patrick could see water in his dad's eyes, the veins on his liver-spotted hands bulging, his old fingers shaking the shovel in his grip. Patrick had reached over and put his hand on the spade, stopping his father's digging.

Dad, what did you want to tell me?

You know already.

Dad—

I wrote them all new letters. Sent them off a month back.

The sky had seemed to Patrick's eyes like fog passing through his father's wiry frame. He had felt like they were spinning, standing inside that sunken boat—heaving.

You sent them?

Two are dead. One had his lawyer send me a reply. Waiting on the others now.

Patrick grips Job's steering wheel and it vibrates his arms up to his shoulders, making him recall his dad's shaking. His father had obviously wanted to tell him, confess to his son, the pastor. *What was he hoping for? Absolution?* Patrick had put his hands in his pockets. He knew what his dad was guilty of—inciting those baymen to burn out their neighbours so that the outports would be cleared and they could *all* get their government money for resettling. It was an all-or-nothing program in some places. The government wasn't going to dish out money to help people move if they were going to keep their old houses. Some held out, said they could do without roads, electricity, plumbing, schools. They were the ones who, in the end, lost everything.

A splash of diesel and a dropped cigarette in the night and we were boating out the bay before the flames hit the second storey of your house. The tobacco tin was the only remaining evidence of his father's habit.

Knowing his dad's secret had made it easy for him to doubt his father's visions, his weird faith. But he now knows what it is to believe and to have been brought low, weighed down. He had

felt that day—watching his dad lean shakily on the shovel—like one of Job's friends: as if he had a right to say something to his father; tell him that perhaps confessing would reawaken God in his life. And, somehow, guarantee God's blessing. *If you were pure and upright; surely now He would wake for you, and make your house prosper.* But for the first time in a long while he had felt God in his father's cabin—the warmth from the stove against his naked, shivering flesh in the early morning. He had felt loved then. And he'd remembered, climbing back into his salt-stiffened clothes, what it was to love this man he had spent so much of his life trying to forget.

He had even begun to long for Anne again, to see her as she had once been. And then he had seen her at the airport and everything had turned savage. Then she was gone again. She had not heard him yelling through the glass of the viewing deck, screaming and motioning like a crazy person, begging her to walk back through security and stay.

I don't know, he had heard his dad say as the wind picked up. They might even try to take the house. Lawyer said they were gonna sue. I haven't told your mum. Don't know how.

So are the paths of all that forget God. Patrick had thought this, mouthed these words from the Book of Job, but he kept silent and forced them from his mind, looking at how his dad shook. More than sixty now and scared of losing his house for something he did as a young man. He could not bring himself to tell his dad that things would be fine—that no lawsuit like that would stand up in court—but neither could he bring himself to tell his dad that this was the wages of sin, this worry that rots the bone.

He had thought it better to not say a word since he didn't know the right ones to say. He had always been so confident in prophesying—attributing his words to God, believing that God spoke through him. Looking at his dad leaning on that shovel, though, he did not say anything, only took the old man in his arms and felt, for the first time in too many years, his father's strong fingers clawing into his back, feeling his dad's lips move against his neck, asking him not to go.

Hab had said the same thing to him when Patrick had told his son he was selling the house and driving back to Ontario. You don't have to go, Hab had said, strangely serious. She should be the one to come back. Yes, Patrick has thought since, she should be the one to return. But he fears that if he waits he may lose her for good.

Driving on this empty highway, he hopes he is not too late. But because he fears he might be, he presses the gas pedal and feels Job's rusty frame shake and the wheels shimmy as the speedometer wavers toward 120.

Walking along the highway rimmed by scrub brush and spruce, Hab recalls his half-conscious dozing in the old Tercel and his dad reaching over to the MP3 on his knee and hitting repeat on a favourite song so that he woke fully but kept his eyes shut and his breathing even, as his dad's voice falsettoed and fell silent.

Patrick is trying to keep the speedometer between 110 and 120, wondering what his mother and father think of him selling the house and everything else and setting out after his wife. He doesn't imagine that they think much of Anne for leaving, abandoning her son and then flying home and leaving again without even seeing Hab.

Patrick doesn't think it would do any good to try and explain that the airport that day was crazy and that Anne had thought him dead and seeing him alive must have thrown her— must have made her act without thinking.

Though he is angry with her still, he keeps defending her in his head against what everyone seems to be saying around him. They are not allowed to be hurt, not the way he is. And he cannot help thinking that there was more right in Anne leaving than in things staying the way they were and him believing all was well with the world.

The car windows shake a bit at 120 so Patrick aims for 110, thinking if his nan were alive she would tell him he had gone beyond the beyond, which she did tell him when he first left Newfoundland for the mainland to attend a Bible College. Patrick thinks that now he would not feel so self-righteous in leaving. Now he might not be as confident as Job in his railings against God.

Now he might question more whether he was actually following God's path or his own. But regardless of whose path it is, he thinks he would choose it again if only because it led to his son sitting next to him here in this old car that is badly in need of a new muffler.

Hab is proof to Patrick that God makes good things out of hurt and selfishness. But Patrick fears he has come to realize this too late. And it seems right—not fair, but right—that God's gift to him, his son, would choose to stay in the place he had abandoned long ago.

It stings Patrick that he who was born here no longer fits, while his son who was born away has engrafted himself here and found a family of choice and of blood.

Patrick knows that his mother is tickled that her grandson is staying in St. John's, even though her feckless son is off after his crazy wife. Patrick is sure that there are other words she uses to describe him better and he imagines that they too start with *f*.

She's always had a sailor's tongue, his dad used to say of her at the kitchen table, laughing and rubbing her back with his paint-spattered hand.

Hab is snoring softly, his head turned partway to the window, mouth open. Each glance Patrick steals is too long and the car warbles in the absence of his attention to the road. But his son's face, Hab's body next to his, wells up in him what he has come to call the Holy Spirit but which may also be as simple as love. It is a pounding inside him, an infilling, a fiery rush.

And Patrick wants to bless his son, to reach his hand over Hab's face and forehead and pass on a gift that is his and yet beyond him now. But he does not do this, for fear that Hab will wake and grab his hand and he will glance from the road and miss the moose striding out in front of them.

It is more Hab's waking that deters him.

So he lets his son sleep and drives on, the road passing by in a grey blur through the holes in the floorboards beneath his feet, the wind whipping up into his pant legs. He reaches over and presses repeat on his MP3 so that he can hear Amelia Curran's words again, *If in as many years I call you from the middle of it all, will you forgive me or forget that we were ever born at all?* And he sings *bye, bye* to this landscape he is racing through, thankful for his son with him but longing for Anne so that it hurts like his nan stitching his ten-year-old torn skin together with dental floss and sewing needle.

Hab's thumb out for a ride burns like the fire dripping in his mind from those industrial backhoes, like that memory of songs sung half asleep in the old Tercel or the scorch in his own heart that kept from his dad his plan to hitchhike home to St. John's after dark and not catch the bus he said he would, though now ten miles from Placentia and the sky dark and wind cold he wishes he'd had more foresight and less of a need to feel pain in his bones so the pain in his heart will have company.

Job growls and rattles as he crests a hill. The barrens stretch out pitted with ponds on either side. Patrick is imagining himself on the shore of this place like the bald and bearded man in that book Hab carries with him always. *The Winter of Remarkable Oranges.* Poetry mostly, stuff Patrick can barely make sense of; a lot of talk of music and rum and brandy and candles. But that first drawing always catches Patrick looking out to it in his

mind's eye as the man within looks out to skins strung up in barren trees, waving before him out over the water.

The look on the man's face is the look Patrick sees often in the mirror when he gets up enough gumption to shave and is forced to stand before himself naked. Dreams skinned and flapping there like the loose skin beneath his chin which he thinks a beard might help cover. But Anne hates beards. So Patrick shaves on the days that he does not hate her. Like this morning, when longing tolls like a bell out to sea and he aches to see her again and remember those strange words of poetry next to that drawing: *misery, too, must have a keel of submerged mirth.* Mirth, that fire in the belly, the earth: heat under cold stone. Of all Patrick does not understand in that book, he understood that much—that line—and the face of that weary man kneeling by water's edge.

I am that man, Patrick thinks.

Hab told him that it is Job in the picture and Patrick laughed because he had named his car after the old wisdom writer who stared out at him from the page.

Patrick thinks his derelict car seems a good second skin for now, and he is thinking of the moose head in the picture that forms out of the rock when a great black mass jumps out of the tree-lined ditch and blasts through the windshield.

Night and the wind so cold it's hot on Hab's skin that feels lacerated as when his dad hit the calf moose at eighty klicks earlier in the day and the bulk of its body came crashing through the windshield, pinning them to their seats where they stayed until a truck happened by with two men coming back from their hunting cabin and they towed the hulking thing away and pulled him and his dad out of the car wreck more stunned than broken and his dad spitting the word miracle like broken teeth.

A BLESSED SNARL

Patrick didn't even see the thing coming: just a glimpse and then the massive dark body came smashing through the windshield. Hab looked over at his dad after those two hunters had pulled the dead moose away and he could turn his neck. He didn't say, *I told you to watch for moose.* But Patrick could see it there: that stunned shock that can whiplash into anger if the wrong thing is uttered.

So he kept his mouth shut.

You're some lucky to be alive, one of the hunters said, looking in at them through the bent windshield frame.

Patrick just looked at the guy and said nothing. But he did take the hunting knife he was offered and cut Hab and himself out of their locked seatbelts. Hab did most of the talking once they were out of the wreck. He told the hunters they were headed to the Argentia Ferry and asked if they could give them a ride.

First we'll nose your wreck off to the side with the truck.

Thanks.

Least the ferry'll be cheaper without the car, hey?

The guy who said this, Len, got ribbed hard by the other guy he called Squirrely— *'Cause of his crooked eye, see?* Patrick just nodded at the grumpy guy with the lazy eye and climbed in the back of the truck with Hab. He asked if they wanted any of the moose meat from the carcass on the side of the road but they said, No, it'll be all bruised to shit.

Should we wait for the cops at least?

The two hunters seemed to get a little shifty when Patrick asked that. Squirrely said there was no point in waiting; that they'd call it in and it'd most likely be a total writeoff.

Long as you don't need the hospital, that is.

Len glared at his buddy. Patrick looked at Hab, who shook his head and looked back at his father.

I actually need to catch that ferry.

Len looked weirdly relieved: Yes. Last of the season, hey?

Exactly.

So Len and Squirrely said they would get them there. They

piled sleeping bags on Hab and Patrick in the back of the truck, and asked them not to disturb the green tarp held down by boards and bricks.

No worries, Patrick said, wondering briefly what they did not want them to see under that crinkly tarp.

Patrick's neck is killing him now, but he could not feel a thing then. He wonders if Hab is stiffening up and if maybe they should forgo the ferry and go see a doctor. But when he turns to say something to his son, Hab looks at him and puts a finger to his lips, glances from the green tarp snapping in the wind back to his father's face. His eyes are fierce in the grey afternoon, wind whipping his hair wild where they sit in the back of the truck—blankets and sleeping bags piled over them.

Patrick is realizing that it was probably dumb to leave the scene of an accident. But then again, the plates were from the old car, fished out of Fawkes Cove by the RNC. And he had not actually insured the car because he didn't think it would pass an inspection. He was just hoping it would get him to Ontario, or at least to a garage in New Brunswick.

As it is, Job didn't even get him off the island.

He remembers his foot on the brake going right to the floor. But the car would not have stopped in two hundred metres, let alone the two the moose gave them.

Patrick glances over at Hab, hoping his son will say if he's hurt, but Hab is looking away over the edge of the truck at the barrens.

Don't worry, Len had said as he hopped in the driver's seat and called out the window, we go slower than you mainlanders and we gots a moose bar on the grill!

Just drive and leave the mainlanders be, Squirrely said from the passenger's seat. They've just been in a friggin accident, or didn't you see the car?

Look somewhere else with that crooked eye. You're freakin me out.

Patrick almost said he was from *here* but stopped him-

self. Better to be thought a dumb mainlander than a dumb Newfoundlander in fancy shoes, at least this side of the Gulf of St. Lawrence.

Though the freezing drizzle is stinging his cheeks and he can hardly see three feet in front of him and it looks grim the chance of him hitching a ride, still he laughs at the memory of his dad banging on the truck window and saying he needed to pee and getting out of the box where he stood pissing over the incline, unaware of Hab hefting a boot over the box edge until Hab kicked him down the incline, him cussing and piss flying up everywhere.

Patrick does not know why Hab was grinning a while back. He was frozen by the time they reached Placentia—pee splashes iced all over his clothes and his hands from when Hab kicked him down the hill. He thinks that might be what his son was laughing at. He thinks he might have unleashed on Hab if Len and Squirrely had not been howling and giving Hab high fives through the truck's back window.

Len and his buddy drove them right up to the ferry and offered them their iPhones if they needed to call anyone about the car. The two hunters seemed a little distracted and eager to be on their way. So Patrick, a little surprised by the phones, said *no.* He told them that he didn't have insurance on it anyway. They seemed to understand that and said so long and were gone off toward town.

That was a few minutes ago. Now Hab and Patrick are standing waiting for the ferry to begin boarding. The parking lot is full of cars, and Patrick is thinking that there is something nice about being able to bypass all that line-up and walk right on, though he knows he will have to rent a car or buy another wreck in North Sydney.

He turns to Hab and realizes by the smirk on his son's lips that he must look some foolish with his bruised face, glass in his

hair still, his one sports bag of clothes, good shoes, and a tarp and bottle of baby oil, which he suddenly realizes has a crack in it—his hand slick.

I can explain the oil if you want, he says.

Don't you friggin dare.

And suddenly Patrick is blushing, thinking that his son has known all along. He is going red at the sheer stupidity of it. His wife may not even want to talk to him, let alone …

Dad?

Yes.

You know those guys were drug runners, right?

Squirrely?

The green tarp. No cops. Who does that?

Did you get their plate number?

They helped us. It didn't seem right. And they stripped the plates off Job before we left, so the cops won't be able to trace the wreck back to you. I just thought we owed them.

So …

Hab smiles at Patrick, who wonders at what his son knows of the world, what Hab sees when he looks at him, dishevelled as he is. He coughs and says, I guess I should be boarding.

Dad.

Yes.

Can I tell you something straight up?

Yeah.

Don't fuck it up this time.

Part of Patrick wants to slap his son for his dirty mouth and part of him wants to say it wasn't him who left. But he knows enough by the look in his son's eye to stay silent and nod. He wonders if it is wisdom to know when to shut up, when to listen to one's own son. After a while he wants to say *I'll try* but instead asks if he can give Hab a hug.

You can always do that.

He feels small in his son's arms, his oiled fingers in Hab's hair. He wants so badly to utter something profound in his son's ear like Gurney did to him when he and Anne said good-bye to them on their move out here. Gurney told Patrick that when he came face to face with a ferocious challenge he was to draw a line in the sand and dare the devil to cross, like that day in the woods by West Coon Lake when Gurney met a big black mother bear so he dug his steel toe into the soil and drew a line, dared the bear to cross in Christ's name, and watched as she snorted and waddled away. Patrick looks at the painted yellow line between him and Hab—their feet on either side of it, their bodies embracing over it now. He waits for words but none come. No story of his own. No wisdom to impart as he hugs his son. So he squeezes Hab tighter and then releases him, trying to look away so his son won't see the tears in his eyes.

You're catching the bus then? he finally manages to ask, scratching his neck with his oily hand and sniffing, smelling wet rock and salty kelp.

Do moose have antlers? Hab asks, smiling back at him.

Not going to live that one down, eh?

Yeah, *eh*? You mainlander you.

Drug runners, huh?

Go on or you'll be swimming, Hab laughs.

Patrick smiles at his son as he gathers up his gear from where he dropped it to hug Hab that one last time. You know, Patrick says, when I used to play hockey here there was a building that was the tallest building in Newfoundland. It's gone now. But when it was still standing Joey Smallwood was having the Confederation Building built and he wanted it to be the tallest structure, so he had them put that stupid-looking steeple on top. Get it up higher than the Americans!

Hab laughs and shakes his head.

Patrick turns and boards the ferry, and it is not until he is on deck and looking back at his son over the rail that he thinks that was the dumbest thing he could have said to Hab, who he might be seeing for the last time in a long while. He feels like a foolish king drifting away, vanquished. But the smile on Hab's face and his arm-waving makes Patrick think that his son is okay

with his awkwardness and lame stories—his failure. That Hab loves him despite everything. That there is still a chance that he might be saved.

Hab remembers standing on the wharf end of an old airplane runway, watching the ferry chug out to sea in the dark and, in that darkness, in his mind's eye, the big industrial backhoes are all about him, digging up pits where jet fuel comes up out of the earth like liquid fire, set alight by the metal buckets sparking against stone. It's the memory of pulling fire from the earth—a memory not even his, but for old archival footage—that fills him with warmth on this frigid highway after dark, ice rain spitting in his face to cover his tears, water and oil feeling like blood running down his neck, and his shadow growing long as headlights crest the hill behind him.

IV

It was the baby oil and blue tarp that did it. Not what Anne thinks Patrick was anticipating. When he showed up on the doorstep of the house she's renting a room in on Bold Street, she saw his bruised face first, his slacks and good shoes, big hockey bag, and that tarp slick from a cracked bottle of baby oil. And that's when she asked him to take a step back and slammed the door in his face.

Seriously? she thought, staring furiously at the fishing pole she'd bought a week ago, standing in the corner behind the door. *Baby oil and a blue tarp? What are we, Patrick, nineteen again? Did you come all the way from Newfoundland for some nooky? For crying out loud!*

It was all Anne could do not to yell these things.

And then came the sheepish knock at the door.

Yes?

I wasn't ... you know.

No, I really don't.

Umm ... do you know a place I can stay?

So she told him—through the closed door, counting the eyelets on her rod—where Christopher and Ruth lived on Charleton Avenue, a few streets away. That must be where he bustled off to a few hours ago because it's late afternoon, Anne's phone is ringing, and the call display reads *C & R Rhynes*.

Yes.

Uh ... Anne. This is Patrick.

Uh-huh.

I hear there are coffee shops on Locke Street.

Uh-huh.

Any you like?

Uh-huh.

Care to show me?

No not really, she thinks but she says Okay before hanging up. *What am I doing? What is he doing?* No word all summer, and then suddenly on her doorstep. She doesn't know what to do or say or think, so she goes and changes her shirt. And then she changes it again. And again and finally says, This is stupid, they're all too tight, and heads downstairs just as the doorbell rings. Charleton and Bold are a lot closer than she thought— *either that or he ran.*

But he's not puffing when she opens the door. He looks good. Fit. Clean-shaven. Still the bruises on his face, though. She wonders if he was in a fight or something.

Does he even know how to fight?

What happened to your face?

Well, hello to you too.

I just meant the bruises.

A moose.

You had a fight with a moose?

Can I tell you over coffee?

Okay, she says grabbing a jacket and heading out the door with him. She kicks her heel to get in step with him: a marching trick her dad taught her when they would tramp through the woods behind Lemming's Lake, checking deer ruts. *Right, left, right, left.* Patrick is oblivious, swamped in his own thoughts.

Anne: I meant to say you looked good, just the bruises caught me off guard.

Thanks, he says, looking askance at her and scuffing his shoes, hands deep in his pockets. You're looking ... healthy.

Anne pushes her hands deeper into her pockets so that she doesn't sock him. *Healthy? What am I? A horse? Classy, Patrick.* She wraps a fist around her worry stone in her pocket, smells

cut grass and damp leaves, looks at the tiny brick houses—
a bright red door newly painted. *Healthy?* She's clicking her
nail against the stone, starting the three-count to end the
conversation and head back to her room, when Patrick sidesteps
some dogshit and manoeuvres into another question.

So Christopher ... he's an artist, is he?

What did you think of the painting in that back room?

The Madonna?

Yeah.

Like he shot a giant yellow paintball at a blue canvas.

Weird, eh? Anne says, stepping into the eddying memories
of Kyle she associates with the painting—that older loss a
wimple below the surface of her thoughts now.

Definitely weird, Patrick says, but not as strange as Dad's.

Your dad paints?

No. He thinks the soot stain on the flashing behind the stove
in his cabin is a vision of the Virgin Mary.

You're joking.

Nope. Now you know why I haven't really stayed in touch
with him. That, and he once told me Pentecostals were a pagan
cult. Enough about Dad, though. How's life in The Hammer
treating you?

Fine enough. Got a job at a Second Cup in St. Joseph's. Get
to see all the internal postings that way. I'm looking for an office
management position. A couple interviews, but no leads yet.

A year ago Anne wouldn't have thought twice about offering
that much information, but now she feels as if she might be
giving away too much—letting her guard drop, taking Patrick's
bait. She feels out of her element, like a fish in a boat. Trying
to think of something to say is like prying a barbed hook
loose. She opens her mouth and means to inquire about Hab
but instead asks, How's life on the Rock?

Oh ... well ... I don't live there anymore, so I can't rightly
say.

So, where are you living? She tries to ask this calmly, but is
kind of freaking out that he moved and didn't tell her.

I don't know yet.

Patrick, for the love of God stop being elliptical and tell me what in the Sam Hill is going on! She's panicking and trying to breathe, gasping as if there's a boot pressing down on her neck. Patrick whistles a lark.

What do you mean you don't know yet? she asks, swallowing.

I sold the house in Paradise.

Nice of you to consult me.

Patrick looks at her like she's a fish with spiny fins that have pricked him. That's when Anne realizes she said that last bit out loud, though she didn't mean to. Well, she says, gulping, you didn't, and it was *our* house.

Right. About that. There was this thing where you left—

Nice, Patrick.

And here come the accusations, she thinks. She has been anticipating them, expecting the tight cinch of her own like a cord knotted through her lips. She has gone so far as to rehearse some of her retorts in her head. But having one come from Patrick here, outside her favourite coffee shop, a little fair-trade café with cushioned bar stools—*Why did I bring him to my favourite café?*—just pisses her off and makes her ready for a fight.

You forget about moving me to BF nowhere?

What do you mean? he says. BF nowhere. What does that even mean?

She waves off the question, not letting herself think the words. Never mind what it means, she snaps. You should've called me.

At what number?

Touché, she thinks but says: You had Christopher and Ruth's number and they have mine. Could've got a hold of me through them. Would've taken you all of, what, five minutes and pushing ten extra buttons?

Eleven.

What?

You have to dial one for long distance.

Anne sneers at him and then turns and pushes into the coffee shop, the glass door flashing the late afternoon sunlight as it swings in. The green and blue glass crystals hanging like lures in the window clatter when Anne barges through the door. Patrick is right behind her at the till.

I'll have a chai tea latté, she says, whole milk, and whipped cream with chocolate sprinkles.

Will that be everything?

And a chocolate-dipped oatcake. Patrick?

Coffee. One cream—

One sugar. And he's paying. Thanks.

Anne leaves Patrick at the counter and heads to the window and the cushioned bar stools with her oatcake, the chocolate dip melting around her fingertips. The stone in her pocket digs into her hip when she sits down because her jeans are too tight and this just makes her grumpier. She needs a few seconds to regroup and calm down her inner bitch—stop Righty from flapping unedited. *Sugar helps*. Patrick has met her inner bitch in a few fights, but she has never really told him that's how she thinks of her own temper—like a razor-toothed muskie thrashing on a steel line in a shallow river bed. Anne remembers her dad wrestling-in a fish half the size of her ten-year-old body, muttering *Calm down ya bitch* as he hauled back on the line, arms tense. It was the only time she'd ever heard her dad say that, but it stuck with her over the years, and when she'd wrestle with herself—her own flashing temper—she'd say the same thing. She thinks Patrick would probably laugh if he knew and then the bitch would flip, say something stupid.

The oatcake's nice and fresh, the centre soft and warm still. She lets a bite dissolve in her mouth, thinking of that man she met fly fishing on the shore of the Montsberg reservoir a few weeks ago. She'd asked him what he was after and he'd said *anything w-w-with f-f-f-fins*.

She had caught a black crappie and three pumpkinseeds, but she had thrown them all back, hoping to land the more elusive northern pike—something that would give her a fight, give her a reason to swear when it zinged a water-arch off her line and spit the hook.

Calm down.

She wonders if Christians are allowed to have an inner bitch. *Shut up, Lefty.*

Latté? Patrick says, setting down her drink.

Merci.

Derriere.

De rien. Patrick's Frenglish is pissing her off right now, hence the emphatic correction. Actually, a lot about Patrick is pissing her off right now. Her inner bitch is spinning her reel. *Calmly,* she thinks. *Take another bite. Now try a different tack.*

So a moose gave you those bruises?

Yeah, Patrick says inhaling, mug to his lips.

Anne hates it when he does that. *Sounds like he's choking.* All the church ladies in St. John's did it, breathed in the *yes,* and it drove her wild.

Got me right in the face, Patrick says after a sip.

You hit a moose?

Hab and I did. But—

Hab? Is he all right?

Yes, he's fine.

Where is he? Anne asks, feeling sick that her son came to her just now as an afterthought. Where is he? she asks again.

St. John's.

Anne takes a sip of her latté and reaches for her oatcake but it's all gone. *My son is still in St. John's.* The thought is like an undertow. Yet Patrick is here. *With me,* she thinks, *sort of.* That realization is a stone to the head.

Where is he living, if you sold the house? The question is a weak tail twitch.

He's got an apartment on Malta Street. He was living with his girlfriend for a while, until he found—

He has a girlfriend? Anne feels slit suddenly, gutted. *Did you know he was living with his girlfriend?* Then she turns to Patrick: Where were you? Why wasn't he living at home?

I *was* there, but believe it or not I've been pretty torn up about the whole break-up and haven't exactly been *around* around.

Anne puts her cup down too hard and splashes her drink, scalding her hand. She wants to fire back that he wasn't exactly *around* around before she left, that their relationship might as well have been a boat with the bottom out of it, but his look tells her his outburst was more apology than self-defence.

She is not sure if it's the slivers of coloured glass hanging in the window and the light shivering bluely through them or if it's that Patrick's on the verge of tears, but his eyes look like they're brimming.

What's her name? she asks. Her mouth is dry, the question a gulp of water.

Natalie.

And she's——

She's originally from St. Lola, believe it or not, Patrick says blowing his nose on a napkin and checking it before double folding and sliding it under the tilted edge of his cup. Anne thinks this habit is disgusting, but it makes her smile.

Back home? she says, trying to lure Patrick back into the conversation.

Yeah. Weird, eh?

Anne cups this idea like her latté, not sure if it's warming or burning, comforting or not. She can't look at Patrick's eyes now because it's hitting her that her son has a girlfriend—has been living with her—and she hadn't known, even though they've had a few Facebook chats over the summer months, and Hab asked her for the millionth time whether she remembers being raised from the dead as a girl and she changed the subject. She doesn't recall what it felt like to be brought back to life but she imagines it being like that burbot ling Kyle caught—hauled up out of death's mystery dark as the depths of a lake, her whole body thrashing, trying to break free. But she didn't tell him she would rather think about her son than about resurrection.

Maybe he would have told her more about his life now if she had.

What else have I missed?

Sometimes it feels as if it is only Patrick she has left and she starts to feel free: like she *has* broken away from something—that this is all a fresh start. But when she remembers Hab, her son, and that somehow she imagined her father's heart attack was an excuse to abandon him, she turns belly up—crumples like a note balled up and tossed aside.

Like the letter that came from her mom and dad not too long ago, care of Ruth and Christopher. The one she wadded up and threw in the laundry.

Dear Anne,

It is hard for me to even want to write this to you. (He's lucky he only has to dictate the letter. I have to write it for him and I'm not sure I want to speak to you either.) It's your mother's hand but my words, my hand being too shaky to write anything readable. (I think he likes playing Moses with his scribe.)

I am writing, Anne, to say that I still do want to see you despite what you've done. I am still your father and though I do not agree with choices you have made I do still love you. (As do I, but I would still strap you if I could. Are you stunned, girl?)

I would call you if I knew the number. I hear you have connected with Ruth and Christopher Rhynes, which I am happy to hear. (I don't think he's heard that Christopher's become a Catholic.)

Please call, Anne. (The number is below. You can use the calling card I've enclosed if it's long distance.) I forgive you.

Sincerely (and in hopes that you'll call),
Dad (and your mother)

Anne remembers the letter in its entirety, those last three words like a hot slap made more forceful because of the lack of her mother's marginalia—*her* forgiveness. Her silence at that point in the letter stings still. Like the idea that Anne is the only one to blame. It was her unwillingness to accept that maybe she *was* the only one to blame that made her angrier and angrier until she balled the letter up and threw it in her dirty clothes hamper. Where she forgot it, until she washed her darks and everything came out salted with shreds of paper.

She finally realizes that she is staring into her drink unblinkingly. And she has no idea how long she has been sitting like this. She can see little flecks of paper ground into the fabric of her shirt. The letter and those last three words making her itch all over, like she is wearing a burlap sack. Patrick is leaning on the counter facing the window, his empty cup of coffee being rocked back and forth in his twitchy right hand, the dirty napkin pushed to the side.

So, Patrick?

He looks up and she sees he's got coffee on the bridge of his nose, from the edge of the mug when he took his last drink. She tucks her hand into the sleeve of her shirt and reaches over to rub it off, half liking the fabric feel of habit—smooth like a fish's underbelly, the soft skin of an inner thigh. And she is surprised that he leans in to let her and that she is blushing. This is not a first date, she tells herself. And she knows that. She is not giddy. Her hands aren't talking to her as they do when she is nervous.

But this comfort ... this ...

I can write you a cheque for half what the house got.

Anne draws her arm back and stares at Patrick. *Did he seriously just bring up finances?* Five minutes ago, when he told her about selling the house, she might have tuned in, asked how much it went for but ... *seriously?*

Did I ask for a cheque?

No, but——

Well then.

Even she doesn't think she is making sense right now, but

the last thing she wants to talk about is how much the house sold for and what her share is. She doesn't want him to give her the money because that means it's all gone—their house, their stuff, everything. She wants whatever is left, even if it is money, to be in one spot. *Waiting*. Just in case. Like the valley of dry bones she has so often heard her father preach about, and she wonders suddenly if her dad will write back this time when she sends him a letter telling of Patrick's sudden visit—of his precious son's homecoming.

Patrick whistles as he exhales. No intake. No sign of life in him for a moment. He looks like an old man slumped in sleep, like her dad napping in the back of the boat, save that he is rolling his mug in his hands now, rotating the coffee-stained clay mug around and around and Anne is trying not to think of all those cups of cold coffee she poured down the drain of their house in Paradise, waiting for Patrick to come to her at the kitchen table and comment on the new slate coasters with the Celtic swirl. She remembers following that carved line along its dips and curls all the way back to the beginning.

Patrick?

About the baby oil.

Okay?

I didn't bring it expecting anything.

Oh. Then—

It just reminded me of what we once had. That's all. It was for me. To remember, I mean. I didn't mean anything by it. Okay?

She wants him to take that back but doesn't say so. She wants him to want her, even though she doesn't exactly want him right now because she doesn't know what she wants except not to be alone and awake all night tossing in bed. She keeps telling herself it's not the sex she misses but his body cupping hers and his arm under her head, but she remembers the summer afternoon he rolled that blue tarp over their bed in Peterborough and she called him *Reverend* and they laughed and lathered themselves in oil and slid against each other until

Patrick slid right off the bed and cracked his head on the radiator and she pulled him back into bed laughing and holding his head and pressing her fingers against the goose egg harder and harder so that he wouldn't come and it wouldn't be over until he said his head was splitting and she let him go and felt a warm rush inside her.

But all she feels now is cold in this café in October. She stretches out her leg, digs in her pocket, and pulls out the smooth beach stone. But she keeps it hidden in her fist.

Christopher and Ruth are okay with you staying a few nights? she asks.

Or longer, if I need.

Do you think you will?

He slides the mug away from him until it clinks against the window, then he pulls a creased envelope out of the breast pocket of his shirt. The shivers of coloured light are fading and growing still. Evening's coming on now. Patrick looks out the window but not at Anne. She wonders about the envelope as she places the stone on the counter and shoves it gently toward him so it catches his eye. He sees it but she cannot tell what he's thinking. His eyes are dark.

What church are you going to?

Always the pastor, she says, trying to make it sound more sweet than sarcastic, pulling the stone back a bit.

No, he says, breathing out, crumpling the letter in his hand. Not for now.

I go to St. Cuthbert's, she says, pulling her hand away and leaving her worry stone sitting smooth between them.

Pentecostal?

Presbyterian.

At least it starts with a P.

Anne can see a smile creep across Patrick's face as he looks at the stone, his chin down against his chest—eyes brightening. Hands folded. Then he looks up at her for the first time in a long while—with the same intensity as Christopher gazing on a new artwork. And he says *yes* and the silence crinkles around

that one word like a dropsheet in a studio, the letter in his fist, like that blue tarp around their young bodies so long ago.

Yes, she says to his yes, knowing that a lot depends on what Patrick says next.

But she is listening.

There are live embers beneath the ash in the blackened fire bin. Gerry stirs them and looks out to the sea, past Des' renovated shed. The sun hasn't risen yet, but its light suffuses the dark cloud bank on the horizon. A storm is moving up the coast from the south. Soft orange light angles north, deepening, intensifying, and Gerry sees that the sun is going to rise into the storm clouds that mirror the dark and choppy sea. He cannot tell—looking toward St. John's—where the sea ends and the sky begins. The light to the north grows weak, and Gerry imagines the sun lifting out of the ocean behind the black veil.

He blows into the bin and scattered embers glow and dim. He needs more wood so he tramps off to Des' pile of scrap lumber, significantly depleted after last night's barrel burn, when he and Hab and Natalie sipped from the bottle of wine that had been sheathed in the ratty wool sock hidden beneath Des' workbench. Hand-bottled straight from one of Joey Smallwood's personal casks shipped from France and stashed in Des' shed for thirty-three years.

Gerry had almost refused his first sip on principle after Des told them that, but curiosity got the better of him. He took a tentative mouthful and felt the wine's weight on his tongue, its heat. He pursed his lips and inhaled through the bubbling gulp. Swallowed and sucked in more air. He felt as if a gentle hand was cupping the back of his head, drawing him forward so that his nose nearly touched the bottleneck—black cherry and chocolate notes, liquorice, sweet tobacco, smoke. His tongue felt like moistened velvet.

My God.

It's a little heavy, eh? Silty.

He could have slapped Hab for that: licked the purple skim off the kid's tongue. Natalie told him to shut up and pass the wine. Gerry watched her eyes disappear behind the dusty green bottle. She drew long. Her eyes seemed to orb the fire's pulse as she held the aged wine in her mouth. Gerry thought of struck matches seen through green marbles. Natalie swallowed and he smiled.

Am I missing something? Hab asked, taking a sip of Pepsi.

I'm not even sure you should be kissing this off Natalie's tongue if you can't appreciate it, Gerry said, taking the bottle from Nat. They could all hear Des, off in the dark by the shed, snapping lengths of lumber underfoot.

I'm just saying it's not as sweet as that stuff we bottled for bonfire night.

That's homebrew, Hab.

Yeah, Gerry, I know. I'm just saying. Can I have another sip?

No, Gerry and Natalie say in unison as Gerry passes the bottle over the fire barrel to avoid Hab's grasping reach.

Gerry's fingers are nearly frozen as he sets a length of shattered board against the shed wall and kicks it. The bone-snapping sound cracks open that day in Rod's apartment, but Gerry passes through that memory like his boot through the board and finds himself standing in one of the Waterford's long halls, comparing the room number in front of him with the sweat-smeared scrawl on his palm. A doctor accompanies him because they have ascertained that he is his father's stress trigger: that it was his father's sudden awareness of Gerry's presence in the room that set him off, making him lash out with the bayonet.

Up, Gerry corrects the doctor. He lashed up, not out. I was leaning over him.

Yes, the doctor says, whispering. Do you know where he got the bayonet?

Haven't got a friggin clue.

Yes. Well, it is an odd sort of weapon to possess these days.

These days? Was it ever normal to sleep with a fuckin bayonet?

The doctor glances at Gerry and writes something on his clipboard. He should be relatively calm, he says softly after a while, clicking his pen and ignoring the question.

Gerry clenches his sweating palms, not hearing fully what the doctor says about mild antipsychotics and minor side-effects. He is led in behind the doctor, who greets his dad and introduces him.

This is your son, Bill.

His dad is propped up in bed, a light blue sheet smoothed over his skinny legs. He's wearing an open-backed hospital gown that's slipping off his one shoulder, and the front of his gown is moist around the nipples.

Hyperprolactinaemia, the doctor whispers, as if that explains something. Minor lactation: a result of the antipsychotics. Nothing to worry about. The doctor's whole demeanour seems geared to tranquilize: soft voice, insistent on the minor nature of everything, that there really is nothing to worry about. Gerry wants to stab the doctor with a bayonet, see if the timbre in his voice snaps.

He kicks through another board and looks through the window on the wall of Des' shed in front of him. He can see clear through the outbuilding's other window on the white-washed seaward wall. There's a seam in the cloudbank—a livid scar liquefied in the old glass.

He remembers leaning against the wall of his dad's hospital room, hand on hip, his thumb feeling the stitched bumps of newly healed flesh beneath his T-shirt. His dad so mellow that Gerry barely recognized him. And there was meat on the old man's bones. *This isn't the guy I watched knot his body in sweat-stained sheets.* This guy smiled pleasantly while the doctor explained to Gerry that they had diagnosed his father as having a delusional disorder.

Gerry remembers twisting the Irving ball cap—a gift for his

SMART

dad—in his sweating hands. He looked at the doctor as if he had not heard him: Diagnosed with what?

A delusional disorder, the doctor whispered, leaning in. His version of reality is, in a few key respects, different from ours. For example, he claims to have been shot at by a hunter while living in Renews. He even identified the man for police, but the man doesn't own a rifle. Your father claims a young mother found his face on an online sex-offenders identification database, and that children then began throwing rocks at him while their mothers looked on. No mother the police interviewed in Renews had any idea that a former sex offender was even living in their community. It is not uncommon, the doctor continued hoarsely, placing a soft white hand on Gerry's shoulder, for someone like your father, living alone in relative poverty, to develop these sorts of delusions over time. It is common for people with this form of psychosis to feel as if they are being persecuted, hunted down.

Gerry thought of his father's letter, mailed from Ferryland. *Did he not trust the postman in Renews? Had he walked all that way?* He looked over at his dad, who was smiling back at him, showing the blackened stumps of his teeth.

But people I talked to in Renews said they knew him.

That he lived where he did and was a bit of an oddity, yes. A townie living out around the bay would stick out any time he opened his mouth. It was really only the priest who knew him, though. Knew who he was, that is.

So that much is true, Gerry thought. Has he mentioned someone named Trudy?

Trudy? the doctor said at a slightly higher octave. No, I don't think so. Why?

Gerry didn't answer. He wondered if his dad had heard Trudy's name on the doctor's lips, if it had sparked anything in his hazy mind, if it had ignited any drug-soaked sense of guilt. He saw that his dad was whispering something and had crossed his arms limply on his lap, as if holding a fairy child. His posture and leaking nipples gave Gerry the shuddering thought

that a ghost was being nursed in those arms, in his dad's broken mind.

He saw the ugly scars slashed from elbow crook to wrist, made with the jagged teeth of broken bottlenecks. If anyone ever pushed his dad around, he'd smash the bottle he was drinking and scrape open the skin on his arms, yelling *You're a big fucker but do you think I'm afraid?*

Gerry rubs his numb fingers over the bubbled metal lip of the fire barrel Des made by cutting an oil drum with a welding torch. He feels an ache in his side and shivers, thinking of putting that Irving ball cap on his dad's greasy hair before leaving, his dad's eyes going wide, big-knuckled hands reaching to feel its familiarity. He thinks of those jagged marks on his dad's arms and that day last week he'd seen Rod again, seen him up close enough to discern a purple scar thin as a spider vein threading out from beneath his eye patch, hidden within a crowfoot wrinkle when he smiled.

Gerry stirs the ash again with a splintered length of wood and dumps an armload of slivered ends into the barrel. The ash plume makes him think of the thick cigarette haze in Rod's new apartment on Barnacle Lane. He'd had a dick of a time finding the place and had to follow Rod up from Erin's Pub one night. The lane was a footpath off Long's Hill that slit between two clusters of row houses, wide enough for Gerry's shoulders—for a shopping cart—but not wide enough for furniture, which Rod had none of anyway except a tattered, faded green camping chair. The door of Rod's apartment looked liked the entrance to a crypt, and Gerry feared knocking on it at first. He tried three times and failed before he actually tapped the glass, bracing himself in case Rod had recognized him on that day that seemed so long ago now—recognized him and remembered. But Rod only remembered *Gerry-me-buddy* and he ushered him in and offered a beer he didn't have but would go get if Gerry would spot him the cash. He told Gerry, in his croaky voice, to sit in the chair while he hobbled off to the convenience store. And Gerry sat there thinking the old drunk looked jaundiced, slack-jawed, half-starved.

He thought that he had gone to Rod's to get it off his chest. But he hadn't said anything. Even after three beers and Rod telling him about having colon cancer and shitting black bile and having to wear Depends and that's why he didn't have money this week for beer or rum, only chicken, but who ever heard of getting drunk off chicken soup?

Guilt over not saying anything stings his eyes like the wisps of smoke curling from the broken boards below. He'd had a chance to fess up and had said nothing, only listened to Rod talk about feeling green and pukey and that he was going to St. Clare's this week for tests, yes b'y, walking the whole way and that bunion no smaller than it was six months ago when that punk knocked a headlight out, which is why the patch, to cover the ugly hole. *See, I can stick my thumb in it.* Gerry winces at the memory of Rod showing him, looking away now to the sky that continues to swell with light. He remembers how he had angled that old camping chair more toward the door in Rod's absence, so that if Rod stood by the rattling fridge when he got back with beer Gerry might have a chance to make a run for it, depending on Rod's reaction to the news he was here to break.

He coughs on the spindling smoke, Rod's voice in his head asking if he wants one.

Gerry had insisted that he didn't smoke but eventually he'd taken one and let Rod light it with his own. Then Gerry held it between his second and third fingers and let it burn, adding to the air's thickness as Rod talked on about stealing a cartload of half-rotten pumpkins after Halloween.

Got them outside, he had said, and Gerry was glad for a reason to breathe some fresh air, even if it still smelled faintly of the cigarette smouldering yet between his fingers or like putrid pumpkins after Rod peeled back a tarp slick with rain scum. *If I ever lay hands on the funking puck who beat me I'll do this to him!* And Rod had pulled a splintered half of an old board from the baby seat of the rusted cart, hefted a mouldy pumpkin and tossed it in the air, taking a swipe at it with his makeshift club. But he missed, staggered, and slipped on the exploded squash, collapsing in a muddy heap at Gerry's feet. *He's wily fucker but I'm not afraid*, Rod had said, scrambling painfully to his feet and setting up another on the corner of the cart. Gerry stood back and Rod cracked it in half, spattering them both with stinking orange goo.

He handed over the stick and told Gerry to have a go at it. But Gerry kept refusing until Rod set up another pumpkin on the cart and jeered at him, calling him a pussy. That's when Gerry stuck the half-smoked cigarette in his mouth, raised the club, and burst the pumpkin open. As he did so, he thought of the skin on Rod's face breaking and blood hitting the spray-painted window, the water-stained wall.

And he shook, the cigarette quivering in his lips.

Tell him, you son of a bitch. Have the balls to tell him.

But he couldn't stop his mouth from trembling, the cigarette nub squiggling smoke in the air about his head.

We should take him together, Rod said, grinning and sliding another pumpkin into place, this one with a buck-toothed grin carved into it below a dented forehead that made the bulbous eyes look crossed. Gerry saw in it someone's caricature of a redneck bayman, but the eyes looked droopy and sad, tired.

Give it another go, Rod laughed, stepping back. And Gerry saw then the melted stub of a candle still in the jack-o'-lantern's skull. He took the club from Rod and his cigarette nib in the other hand and lit the bent candle wick. It sputtered but caught, held, and began to burn, filling the sorry eyes with light and making the goofy grin twist into a tortured scream—Rod's naked bleeding face, glassless eyes searching blindly, that creosote stain, his own soul.

As he breathes in the wood smoke from the junks of lumber in Des' fire barrel and looks out to the face of the storm cloud glowing—three lava pits, a hellish yowl—he remembers passing the club back to Rod, fully intending to tell the old drunk in that instant that it was him who took his right eye. But he had only watched Rod wind up awkwardly and extinguish the jack-o'-lantern's light.

He'd left Rod's place soon afterward, said he had to be getting home. But he knew it was because he was afraid he might let it slip. The desire to just confess burned in him wetly, hissing like snakes in a barrel, raindrops on cinders. He feels the first misting spats as the wind shifts—Des' shed no longer shielding him.

He knows he has to go back. *I will, I'll do it.* But he shakes at the thought, feels cold as the fire he can't seem to start. He had been unable to sleep on Des' couch, and he'd spent the last four hours flipping through the folk mix on Hab's MP3 player, settling on a man's whispering voice singing *we get so close, we get estranged, we get so close*, eventually deciding to relight last night's fire.

Something to do.

The empty bottle of the best wine he has ever tasted lies abandoned in the wet grass—water beaded on the green glass, smearing the fingerprinted dust in fine rivulets, patterns. Des had produced the bottle last night and said: *How about a toast to the young?* He'd explained where the bottle came from, its history, and why as a recovering alcoholic there was no point in him keeping it any longer. *Go on, drink up. Enjoy.* And he had left them to sip the fine wine while he wandered off to make more firewood, his mangy dog Jesse nudging Gerry's hand for a pat, the dog not leaving his side the whole night long.

Gerry hears the rusty latch of Des' rear door and sees the old man shiver into a jackshirt and start moving toward him.

I wondered if it was you or the young lad out here, Des says, coming to stand on the other side of the smoking barrel. Gerry thinks he means Hab but Des goes on about the kid being a pyro, and Gerry realizes that's Des' other grandson: *the crazy one.*

Just me, Gerry says, watching his own breath mist.

Hell of a sunrise for All Souls Day.

Strange bird, Gerry thinks.

Quite the story, Des says, and Gerry sees the old guy's wearing the black plastic rosary he'd left in the old tobacco tin.

Red sky in the morning, you mean? Gerry asks, being evasive.

The one you left in the can with this, Des says, touching the teardrop Christ.

Gerry looks up. He'd almost forgotten the tobacco can of old letters and the story he'd stuffed inside it. *Sailor take warning*, he thinks, seeing spears of red hurl through the sky behind Des' white and wild hair, setting the old man on fire.

I sent the letters 'cause of you, Des sighs after a while. New ones. Waiting on one response yet. The one buddy's takin me to court. Told the missus the other day. We might lose the house, everything. Imagine. At our age.

Gerry blinks: his eyes suddenly dry. The heat has gone out of him and he feels tired, exhausted—the skin wrinkled around his lashes. He hasn't slept since visiting Rod. Last night's insomnia was nothing new.

You putting me in your novel? Des asks after a while, sniffing.

Gerry shakes his head. You haven't killed anyone, he says, trying to smile. So you're not that interesting.

Des nods and slips his hands into his jackshirt pockets. He seems to be considering Gerry standing on the far side of the fireless barrel. Then: You told him it was you yet?

Gerry sees the half buried dory behind Des—his wife's new flower garden—and to his smoke-blurred, tired eyes it looks as if the old man is in the boat, watching him drown. He feels the rain coming down harder, whipped on shuddering gusts.

He shakes his head and blinks, gonging the barrel with a kick. Can't get her lit, he says, thinking that's enough of an admission. Gerry of course can't see what Des sees in the predawn gloom: the shed window behind the boy's head filling with fire flung off dark, rolling waves, refracted yet intensified, lighting Gerry's sleep-tousled hair like an icon's saintly glow, like the red hot chimney flashing the day *she* spoke in the cabin's strange chill, the Holy Mother's words misting. The older man squints and sees his own fear in the young lad's sun-dimmed gaze, but he sees those shoulders squaring in that ochre-stained sweater, the one Gerry left hanging to dry in the shed a while back.

It's taken Des thirty-three years to face himself. For all that he has thought the younger generation to be soft and strange and somehow weaker, he sees in this one now a fire hot enough to sharpen fear and turn it back on itself.

Gerry has no idea why Des is smiling cockeyed at him. He shifts and farts, wanting a coffee in hand and a warm toilet seat.

Should've blue-angeled that and got this fire lit, he laughs, seeing suddenly his shadow stretching toward Des. He turns and sees through the two angled windows the heavy red sun blaze across the water. He is blinded and warmed and confounded. Lost for words and laughing for no reason. Tears hot on his face awash in sunrise, like his dad's that morning when Gerry's blood ran out of him and his father shook and pressed this same sweater against his son's pulsing gash.

Gerry turns and sees that Des has rounded the barrel to stand next to him. He feels giddy and wary at the same time. Full and drained. He wants Des to hug him so that he can imagine the old man to be his father who sits, sedated, in the Waterford. At peace and cared for. He has stopped caring if his dad deserves any of it—the clean sheets, the counselling, the drugs that help him sleep and still the savage voices in his battered mind.

But Des doesn't hug Gerry. He moves off toward the shed and grabs a diesel can from under the eave. The violence has gone out of the sunrise, but a splash of fuel on the smouldering embers sends up a flash and ignites the broken bones of old board lengths.

The flames rise up harsh and high as the rain begins to pour down. Smoke billows thickly from the blackened barrel and Gerry remembers the taste of that thirty-three-year-old wine, cellared in a grungy sock. He had thought it to be a time bomb for Des: his last resort if sobriety became too much to bear.

But the remembered taste of it now on his tongue—the after-breath like swallowing liquid fire—cools his lips strangely as winter rain stings his wincing face. He can hear the tags on the dog's collar jingle somewhere nearby, like that faintly remembered bell ringing before the Eucharist, the cigarette voices of those three old men rasping behind him.

And he feels as if he is just now waking up.

On a recent visit to Fawkes Cove, Des had told Hab that bad things always come in threes. Hab has often thought about that since. Like when his great uncle who had Alzheimer's died of pneumonia two days before his distant cousin walked into the woods with his 30-30 and didn't come back. And then a week later, after two funerals, his dad had told him they were moving to Newfoundland.

Sometimes not that close together, but always, it seems to him now, within a year. First his mom leaves his dad for the guy she met on Facebook. Then his dad's car gets rolled over a cliff by some punk and his buddies. And then his dad hits a moose on their way to the Argentia Ferry. They were lucky on that last one but since it involves his dad, and the two had to do with cars, Hab ties them together in his mind. So that's three.

Done.

While unloading skids at Middle Cove Beach on Bonfire Night, though, Hab can't shake the feeling that something bad is going to happen. Whether it's that the wind is cold and smells of coppery salt and blood or that an evening of bonfires is coming on and the van is packed with cases of homemade wine—he doesn't know, but he feels on edge as he bends to help Gerry heft the pile of skids down to the gravel beach.

He's walking backward and stepping crablike to keep from falling over in the loose beach stones, heading to the creek that runs into the ocean. Last year it ran straight out from the riverbed to the sea, but winter waves sweep up gravel and sand

and change the path of freshwater across the landwash so that sometimes the creek snakes away across the beach to the north cliffs, like it is now. But across the stream, near its source, is a section of Middle Cove cut off from the rest, tucked behind a granite alcove, and that's the spot they want for this epic fire they've been planning.

Gerry rented the van from Home Depot earlier in the day and drove to Kent's Building Supply where his buddy Pete works, and they loaded the whole back of the long van with busted old skids.

You're not gonna bleed in it this time, hey?

Shut up, Pete.

Just sayin. It's hard to clean.

I was the one who was friggin stabbed, Gerry says, lifting his T-shirt to show off his scar.

Planning on luring the ships in? Pete had joked once they'd done and slammed the van door shut.

She's goin up tonight. That's all I can say.

Keep the fire department on speed-dial.

After picking up the skids, Gerry remembered he hadn't filled in his time sheet at the group home, so he headed over to Pennywell. As he drove, he thought of how scattered things had been for him since his visit to Fawkes Cove with Natalie and Hab. He had come away from that early-morning fire soaked to the bone and shaking, knowing he was going to wind his way through wet streets once they got back to St. John's, squeeze between those two row houses on Long's Hill, knock on Rod's door regardless, and tell the old drunk who it was that gouged out his eye and broke his jaw.

He had hyped himself up on coffee at the apartment and had even stopped for an extra large light roast at The Jumping Bean on Military Road, and then he'd drummed the walls nervously down Barnacle Lane, saying over and over in his head what he was going to blurt out the moment that door was opened. He was prepared to see Rod's smile slip. He was ready for a fist in the face. He could take it, all of it.

Standing in that dingy back alley, he could feel that splintered club tearing his ear off, smashing his face open like a pumpkin.

But when he knocked on Rod's door an old lady with yellowed eyebrows and a leathery, spray-tanned face answered it. She was dressed in a matted blue bathrobe, her grey hair oily and spiked in the slope of a pillow, a shock of pink like a middle finger on her forehead. Her robe was held loosely together by a nylon curtain cord, and Gerry could see she was naked underneath, her veined breasts drooping near her navel. He asked after Rod and she said she had no fucking clue, but she was taking clients if he had twenty bucks. Gerry thought he recognized that cigarette rasp in her voice—the memory of a late night phone call cut short.

He felt like he should wash his hands.

You staying here? he'd asked, looking at the stack of empty liquor boxes by the door, the cardboard soaked and limp.

Got a call from a friend, the lady croaked. Said I could use up the month's rent on his place if I needed it. Just so happened it was a good time for a move.

He's gone?

Gone when I got here, the old lady said, scratching herself. She lit a cigarette, and the smell of it and the smashed pumpkins conjured Rod's voice in his mind. *Gerry, me buddy.*

She drew long and exhaled blue smoke out her nose.

A blow job for fifteen, you have your own condom. She licked her lips, chapped and pink from old lipstick.

Gerry stepped back, said I don't have any cash on me, nearly tripping over Rod's upended shopping cart.

Hand job for free, you gets rid of that thing, she called, hacking into her sleeve as Gerry ran back out to the road.

He had wandered then, his chest aching with caffeine, hands twitching, until he thought of St. Clare's and the tests Rod was supposed to be having this week. But when he got there he couldn't get any information because he didn't know Rod's last name. So he'd gone back to Barnacle Lane and slipped the

rain-soaked wad of mail out of the bulging tin box, sorting mail from Walmart coupons and pizza fliers until he'd found an envelope from St. Clare's Mercy Hospital addressed to Roderick Malone. And he had wondered at Rod having the same last name all the way back to the hospital. Were they cousins somewhere way back? *That's absurd.*

When he returned to St. Clare's for the second time that day and gave them Rod's full name, he was not prepared for the nurse's cool response: I'm sorry, but Mr. Malone passed away this morning. He had—

—colon cancer, Gerry said.

Yes. I'm sorry.

Shit, he said. And then he snorted and laughed, choking on his sudden grief, remembering Rod opening the fly of his soiled workpants to show him the diaper he was wearing because he'd shit himself if he sneezed too hard. And Gerry was back in Rod's apartment then, unable to breathe in the thick smoke and scrambling to get outside, hyperventilating, chest aching, surges of acid burning his throat.

He felt this same heartburn as he tried to find a parking spot near the group home, driving the van full of skids. The sour burps were the only sensation that seemed to sting the numbness he'd felt since leaving the hospital two days ago. He knew that drinking tonight would not help his hyperacidic stomach, but he was hoping for warmth and oblivion—the dreamless, drunk sleep that was not sleep.

He had felt bloated since finding out about Rod. Like his dry skin was cracking, bursting, as if he was full of rot. A mouldy pumpkin on cart handles waiting to be obliterated. He had felt too big for his body. Awkward: like this big white van he was trying to parallel-park on Pennywell. He eventually gave up and left it parked in the road with the four-way flashers on, and ran in to deal with his blank time sheet.

Cindy—diamond nose stud and fish hook tattoo on her wrist—was on duty, in the back-room office doing paperwork, while River played *Grand Theft Auto* on mute.

Cindy? Gerry said, sticking his head in the office, trying to make his voice sound more upbeat than he felt.

Yes?

Can you put me down on the time sheet for an overnight last night and a morning on Wednesday?

Sure. Off somewhere in a hurry?

Bonfire tonight at Middle Cove. A crowd of us. You remember Natalie?

Yeah, I remember her.

She'll be there. You should stop by after midnight.

I just might.

Gerry tapped the door frame nervously, like he'd drummed the walls of Barnacle Lane, and turned back down the hall. He said hello to River, who made no response—only the tapping of the kid's thumb on the control.

Gerry got in the van, turned the starter, and jolted away, trying to outpace Rod's limping ghost in his mind. All while a digital avatar on the flat screen inside the group home beat a woman's face to a bloody pulp, and River glanced at the wooden Slugger sticking out of Liam's bag of baseball gear.

That was all earlier in the afternoon, before the sun began to set and the temperature plummeted—before Gerry picked up the cases of homemade wine from Hab's Malta Street apartment, where the wine had been brewing in big white buckets in the closet that was an old staircase drywalled off from the basement apartment: stairs leading nowhere. Hab helped load up the wine and threw in a pile of blankets. They were planning on sleeping in the van overnight after the fire, and he didn't want to be frigid.

Then the winding drive out toward the Marine Institute, and up along the forested coast to Middle Cove or, as Gerry kept calling it, The Great Guy Fawkes Altar.

No scarecrow to burn tonight.

We got enough for a friggin pyre though.

Yes we do!

Hab sometimes finds himself in Gerry's vortex, sucked into his excitement and passions—Newfoundland literature, films by the Coen brothers, Yellowbelly beer, Ethiopian coffee and homemade wine. The closet brewery was Gerry's idea a while back, though it was Hab's closet they used. No space at the Merrymeeting place, Gerry had said as he helped pour the wine mix into warm water, adding crushed partridgeberries and oak chips for extra flavour before sprinkling the yeast over the bubbly surface.

Besides, Gerry insisted, Snuggles' fur would get into everything.

So Hab's place it was.

Ever since Hab's dad had left more than a month ago, Hab has been diving headlong into a freedom and independence he's never known before. The freefall has landed him with a sprained neck from puking hard one night after a bender with Old Sam and Gerry in the graveyard between Freshwater and Bonaventure, where Gerry said he had lost his virginity.

Lisette says you're a virgin still.

What does she know? Or did she tell ya?

Hab had taken another burning swig of Old Sam and shaken his head.

She told you, didn't she?

Gerry—

I can't believe she went and told you. Here. Give me that bottle.

Hab remembers little else from that night after passing the bottle over. He remembers the ground spinning. He has tried to forget the taste of upchucked rum. Thought he'd swear off booze for a while because he felt guilty for hurling on a Christian Brother's grave, but here he is lugging cases of wine across the gravelly beach toward a rock alcove that shields their mammoth pile of skids from the general view.

The key, Gerry says to him once they've crossed the creek, is to keep a nice-sized respectable fire going until people start to bugger off because of the cold and the fact they got to be up tomorrow for work. The cops do their drive-bys before then, and that's when we pile her up and cut loose.

Will we last that late? Hab asks.

Forgot you were a mainlander.

Fuck off.

Hab shocks himself every time he swears. He's never done it growing up, and he feels the force of the word—hack of an axe in a kneecap—more so than Gerry or others he's met at school or downtown, who use the word as punctuation and to sound worldly. He immediately regrets saying it, even though Gerry's laugh is a hood pulled about his ears, keeping out the screaming wind.

Last thing's to gas it before we lights it.

With what gas? Hab asks.

Come, my young disciple, let me show you the way.

Hab thinks Gerry is in a funny mood but he follows along. At the van, Gerry pulls out a three-litre wine jug from behind the passenger seat. It's empty and there's a small coil of plastic tubing duct-taped to its side.

You coulda got a gas can, eh?

Yes, but the wine jug means I didn't have to make a trip to Crappy Tire.

You've done this before?

Siphoned gas? Sure. You never?

No.

You had a deprived childhood.

Hab half agrees mentally, but says nothing as he watches Gerry uncoil the tubing, insert an end into the glass jar and unscrew the van's gas cap with his other hand.

Gerry: Here, hold this, will ya.

So Hab holds the jug while Gerry feeds the other end of the tubing into the vehicle's gas tank. Then he takes the jug from Hab and tells him to hold the hose to his mouth and stick the end and his thumb in his lips and draw hard to coax the gas up.

Hab blows out and sucks on the plastic tube. Gas shoots up the pipeline and catches him in the back of the throat like a

spitting cobra. He spews over Gerry's boots and drops the makeshift gas line.

Gerry is laughing so hard he's crying. And all Hab can think is that he has burned himself a second esophagus. He coughs and kicks gravel at Gerry, spraying it against the side of the rental van.

Easy there! You'll scratch the finish.

Hab can't speak for the upchuck reflex he's trying to swallow. He burps petrol. His breath smells of raw crude.

Hey Hab, Gerry laughs as he fishes a lighter out of his pocket, wanna light?

Hab goes to say something but spews, splattering Gerry's sleeve.

For fu—

Shut up, Hab says, wiping his mouth. He doesn't hear Gerry's cursing as he turns and heads to the beach and the boxes of wine. He needs something to help him swallow the nasty taste, some of their sweet, juice-flavoured wine to burn it off. While his shoes are ankle-deep in beach gravel, Gerry's are near a splash of Hab's half-digested lunch, his hands holding the glass wine jug that's filling slowly with gas from the rental van's fuel tank. Gotta pay for it, Gerry thinks, so I might as well use it. Friggin Hab.

He's trying to keep his soiled arm away from him as he finishes the siphoning. Then he peels the old sweater off and rifles in his overnight bag for another hoodie. The cold he feels on his bare chest, his nipples in tight knots, is the same empty chill he has felt since leaving St. Clare's. He knew that day that he would never be able to get rid of it: get it off his chest, banish the hag. Because the only person who needed to hear what he had to say was gone, gone for good this time. No more run-ins downtown. No more house calls and nights of drinking. All that was left of Rod in this world was a damp X-ray letter from St. Clare's, an old prostitute living off his last month's rent in that back alley, and that rusted shopping cart caked in pumpkin rot. He pulls on another sweater, flings back the hood and shivers, his ribcage feeling as cold as the vaulted stone ceiling of a vacant church in November. Hollow. His stomach is empty and growling. He has not eaten anything all day, starving himself so the wine will hit him faster—take the top of his head clear off—make him crazy.

He slams the van door and heads down to the beach, dragging his dirty sweater behind him, his middle finger slung through the handle of the glass jug three-quarters full of unleaded.

Gerry finds Hab guzzling a bottle of wine, and a crooked grin slits his pursed lips and pissed-off look: Nice one, buddy.

Hab swallows and swings the bottle down.

All I need now is a smoke, Hab says, smiling with his eyes finally, imagining himself with Kyle at a back road keg-party in St. Olga, hearing his dead cousin laugh and fire off his gun into the night sky.

Gerry looks at him and *hmphs*: Some dragon's breath you'd have.

Enough to torch your short and curlies.

You'll not be getting your lips near them, I can tell ya.

Shut up.

Wasn't me that said it.

Fuck off, Gerry.

You kiss Natalie with that mouth?

I think I might, Hab says, feeling the kick of the wine more strongly than the other night at Pop's place. The smell of gas on his breath gives him a bit of a high as he looks past Gerry and across the creek, to the parking lot where Lisette and Natalie are getting out of a cab and coming down the stairs to the beach.

He shudders and feels his skin goosebump inside his clothes.

Hab is surprised at how cocky the wine has made him feel by the time the girls reach them. He walks right up to Natalie, takes her in his arms, and plants a kiss on her lips that are open to say: What the hell, Hab?

Natalie pulls back from the kiss and thumps him in the chest before spitting on the ground.

What type of motor oil you drinking? she asks.

Homebrew.

If the wine tastes like your mouth I'd rather drink sea water.

Gerry: That's just because he drank some gas a minute ago.

Gas?

Friggin guy had me siphon fuel from the tank.

Natalie turns on Gerry, who is laughing and reaching for a wine bottle in an old appliance box. It's true, he giggles, asking Hab where he put the corkscrew.

In the box, Hab says, his stomach gurgling, thinking he should find a seat. He settles himself on a rock outcropping and watches the others break up some skids and build a tepee out of shattered wood that Gerry splashes with gas and sparks with his lighter. The wind rushing in on them brings surf spray like gusts of rain, and each rush of salt air flares up the meagre fire in its tent of pressurized wood—crooked nails glowing coal red in its heart.

There are shouts and sparks and guitars in the night. Voices laughing, whooping, singing and calling out amidst the constant churl of waves and gravel, the sudden snapping of lumber underfoot.

The din flashes loud and cuts into the greater silence surrounding the bay, slashing weakly at the cold night closing in. And outside the rings of firelight, on the edge of the riverbed that runs by the parking lot, there's a boy with his face cowled in a hooded sweater. He's sweating because of his long and determined walk from town, but his breath is even, his hand shaking slightly and fisted around a wooden bat. Light wobbles on the water running by his feet, its flash and flow. But he doesn't see the peripheral light—the moon overhead showing the route he came up the river bed. A way of escape. A chance to back step. The grace of an empty road at midnight. His hood is pulled over his head like blinders on a beaten workhorse. He sees only the hellish glow straight ahead from the far side of that rock cut—sees her stumble out into the dark to take a pee in the shadows by the creek where she thinks no one is watching. He wants her to turn so he can see her face. Her eyes. One last time. Before he breaks her jaw and bashes in her forehead. Her face. Her eyes.

His thoughts wander from this to torching his mom's house to his grandfather's letters about burning down whole outport communities in the sixties for a government cheque—fishing stages and family homes. His mom crying at her kitchen table. Half a bottle of Listerine at her elbow, next to an empty plastic tumbler. Screaming about his grandfather trying to rape her one Christmas Eve. Bottles of Lithium and Clozaril empty and cracked on the bathroom floor, their contents flushed down the toilet. He'd hoped she was asleep when he lit the fire in her porch. Wanted the smoke to asphyxiate her and the fire to melt the blade of the fillet knife she'd once held against his neck while he pretended to sleep, urine seeping through his boxers and blanket and into the couch as he tried to keep his breathing steady. Like it is now. His hands raw from hefting buckets of jack-hammered stone out of his dad's basement—making a room he has no desire to live in. His shoulders ache and his fingers twitch as he rubs the back of his hand across his eyes. Blinks. Sees her across the creek shake in a squat, stand, and button her jeans. She's the reason he went to Whitbourne. She's the reason they did that to him. *Again and again.* Bruised ribs, cracked collar bone. Forehead busted on the back of a toilet.

Her.

He grips the bat tighter and waits, fingering a jackknife in his other hand. Wondering which vehicle is hers: *which one brought all those skids?*

Across the stream, Natalie feels someone looking at her in the dark, but she shrugs it off drunkenly as her own fear as she wipes her hands on her jeans and heads back around the out-cropping to the fire and her third bottle of wine in three hours.

A box is gone already and it not yet 10:00 p.m. Gerry breaks the cardboard down and pins it atop the fire with more broken chunks of skid. The fire swells like Hab's chest filling with so much love for these people—his friends—the heightened

intimacy of inebriation. But despite his own drunkenness and his second bottle of wine, Hab looks at Nat coming out of the night staggering and he's worried for her now as he's always worried about the alcohol she carries in her Nalgene and how he thinks she's started using over-the-counter painkillers to replace the Ativan she can no longer get from Sherl. So he heels a hole in the gravel and wedges his bottle upright into it before shakily stepping toward Natalie, who's hugging her bottle in the crook of her arm, her chin sunk in the high collar of her big green army coat—a knitted toque from Lisette's nan pulled down over her ears—her eyes filled with fire and water.

You coughed up the tar sands yet? she asks, giggling.

Yeah, he says burping and blowing into the wind.

You're lookin dry, sailor, she laughs, offering him her bottle.

He takes it and puts it to his lips but stops the bottleneck with his tongue to keep from drinking. He swings the bottle down and Natalie holds out her hand, saying: Give it here. But when he asks if she thinks she's had enough to drink, the smile on her face slices down and she says: I didn't know I brought my mother along. She grins as an afterthought, an effort to make light of her comment that sounded much harsher to Hab than to her.

I'm just worried about you, he says passing her back the bottle.

Keep it then, she sing-songs, and turns to Lisette who's curled up against the rock cut, her toes a few feet away from the fire and a sleeping bag spread out under her.

You seen my bag? she asks.

Sure. It's there. No, there. Yeah.

And Natalie digs her camera out of her backpack, turns and snaps a picture of Hab in his grandfather's jackshirt staring back at her out of the blurry half dark. Gerry sees the camera come out and the flash sparks a brilliant idea in him.

Hey, Nat! he calls.

Yes, me buddy, Natalie says, using Gerry's own mock accent against him.

Take a click of this, ya wannabe, Gerry slurs loudly, lurching for the glass jug of gasoline a quarter full. He pours petrol on the discarded hoodie that Hab puked on earlier and walks it onto the landwash, tucking it into him and clicking until his lighter catches the fumes. The flames shock up and make him drop it as a wave rushes in around his feet and carries the burning sweater out to sea, where it flickers like a witchlight just offshore.

The fu—

Can you see it still?

No, it's gone!

I almost burned my fuckin hand! Gerry curses coming up to them by the fire. Friggin thing. For the love—

Calm down, me buddy.

Gerry glares up at Natalie: You get the picture, smart ass?

Yes, Natalie says hiccupping.

Well take one of this too then, he says tearing at the hem of his T-shirt and ripping away a strip. Natalie plants herself and begins her photo shoot of Gerry stuffing the shirt end down the bottle neck of the gas jar and—his back to the wind—clicking the lighter against the fabric wick now gas-soaked from a quick shake of the jug. The wick flames up, and Gerry heaves the glass jar against the granite cliff, where it explodes in a shattered burst—a quickflash like gunfire. Bright shards amid rags of flame circling stones, soon to fade and hush altogether.

Wooo! You see that?

Gerry, quit being an arse and throw some wood on the fire.

Lisette, my duck, why don't you get off your ass and do it yourself?

My fucking trout, that's why we brought ya.

The fire was my idea.

Don't make you Guy fuckin Fawkes, do it?

Shii ... Gerry trails off, his head still in the back-draft rush of the small explosion, drunkenly remembering that candle nib glowing in the bucktoothed jack o' lantern the last night he saw Rod. He takes a full skid and drags it over to the fire as Natalie crouches by the boxes of wine and uncorks another. Hab watches, her last half bottle still in his hand.

Gerry, you dumbass, come keep me warm.

Why, Lisette—

Shut yer gob and come down here, she says pulling him over onto the sleeping bag so that his head falls into her boobs. But he just comes up giggling and she's laughing with him and he puts his arm around her like old friends. He snuggles into Lisette and hides his tears in the shadow of his hoodie. Natalie asks if there are other blankets, and Hab says there's a pile in the van and that he'll go get them.

He gets a soaker in the creek slipping off a stepping stone. The other fires across the beach are dying down, all but abandoned now, save one or two farther away that are starting to kindle with more wood stacked on.

Seems they had the same idea Gerry did.

When Hab reaches the van he's not prepared for what he sees. Tires slashed and sitting on the rims. Each window— all the way around—smashed in. Along with the head- and tail-lights. The back door is swung open and the pile of blankets strewn across the parking lot. One of them soaked, pissed on. The word RAT is carved into the side of the white van—the R angular and the T like a cross.

What the ...

He goes back to the fire with the dry blankets and drops them by Lisette and Gerry curled-up together. Then he tells them, and they all stagger up to the van. No one says anything for a while, until Gerry starts in about the fucking kid who fucking did this, the little fucker!

You've certainly demonstrated the versatility of the word, Lisette says, straight-lipped—her face grim but her eyes sparking.

Look at the fuckin van! Gerry yells.

It's a rental.

Yeah, but it's in my buddy's name.

He'd better have insurance then.

Gerry glares at Lisette and then storms off back to the fire.

When they all return he is piling up all the skids on the blaze, holding them square against his chest and heaving them up one on top of the other, six, seven, eight high. Then he hauls up the few remaining ones and leans them against the stack. He's working like a Viking berserker, eyes glazed and wide, muscles shaking, running his mouth off about the little bastard who vandalized the van.

And as flankers begin shooting up out of the pressurized wood, Natalie drops her camera onto Lisette's sleeping bag and runs at the fire before Hab can stop her. She toes the skid board set sideways to the stack like a ladder up to the top where the fire hasn't reached yet—a smoking pyre—and she lets out a whoop and Lisette screams *yeah baby* while Hab stands dumbstruck and Gerry scrambles for the camera to snap a pic as the flames shoot up around her legs and waist and she walks off the other side, drunk enough she doesn't realize her pants are on fire.

Nat! Hab yells rushing at her.

Gerry snaps a blurry picture of Hab tackling Natalie and her flaming pants into the beach gravel. Then Hab is swatting at her and she is swearing at him and hitting back so fiercely she doesn't smell singed denim or see the shock in Hab's eyes.

I'm fine! she screams.

Nat—

For fuck's sake, Hab!

I—

Get off me!

And he's staggering back and listening to her unleash on him about how he can't have any fun and his prudishness and holier-than-thou attitude makes her so sick she could puke. She's breathing hard and goes to stand but falls over in the gravel. Hab, for the first time, makes no move to help her stand. Telling himself she wouldn't take his hand if he offered. So he thrusts his fists in his pockets and heads up to the van, a mountain of flame rising behind him.

It is hours before the others come up from the fire to the van where Hab is laid out on his side listening to the night. He

hears a car drive in and a bit later hears Gerry and Natalie talking to a girl from the group home. He hears the name Cindy tied up in talk of a missing kid named River. The conversation fades in and out, and eventually Cindy's car revs and she drives away.

Shortly after this the others open the back door and there's talk of bedding down. Hab gets up and helps them load the empties gathered from the beach. He can smell smoke on them—like they've crawled out of a bushfire.

Wood smoke and sour wine.

Natalie's holding an uncorked bottle and the opener. Gerry and Lisette spread out blankets in the van as Hab watches Natalie pop the cork out and toss it to him. She swigs and chugs and brings down a bottle already a quarter gone.

Let me have the bottle, Nat.

She glares at him. Falls against the side of the van and steadies herself. Bats away his hand reached out to help her.

I'll walkhmme, she slurs.

You can't even stand.

I can do whhat I wants.

Then she just thrusts the bottle at him and climbs into the back of the van and tells Gerry to move over, that she'll be sleeping on that side and he and Lisette can have the middle.

Hab is sobering and wondering what's happening to Natalie and him, why their relationship is so strung out and frail. He can feel the night chill, colder for being away from the fire these past few hours. *There'll be frost tonight*, he thinks. The sky is clear and there's a ring around the moon, and he remembers his Grandpa Gurney telling him a ring around the moon meant three nights of white frost. He misses his grandpa ... and his mom—an ache pitting in his chest, cold as a deep glacial lake.

Smoke in the wind: the stink of burning rubber.

He corks the bottle and hides it in the front bumper. Then he goes around back of the van, touches Natalie's foot through her sleeping bag and feels her draw away—sees her curl up into a tighter ball.

Then he climbs into the van on the far side of Lisette, who is spooned into Gerry, who is already snoring and mumbling something, his thumb rubbing against a cracked seashell in his soot-stained fist.

He puts his back to Lisette, and it is a long while before the warmth of their bodies becomes some comfort against the November night. And then everything fades for Hab. He falls asleep watching his breath smoke in the light of the moon coming through the van's broken window.

Harsh light glaring sharp on broken glass wakes him and he sees Natalie is gone. The back of his head feels blasted out— hangover headache, and no pillow but the grooved van floor. He puts his hand to the back of his neck, thinks of his cousin Kyle's hollowed-out skull. Light livid on the horizon. Blood red. And they're minus a body. He must have been sleeping soundly because he didn't hear the door open or close, didn't hear the scrunch of shattered glass underfoot on the asphalt.

He pulls himself up and looks out the window, over to where Natalie slept, toward the ocean. Shards of glass catch the morning sun and splinter it. The beach is white with hoarfrost and scattered ash from the bonfires. Everything glistens.

The whole beach is a beacon, sun throbbing on the water.

He remembers a line by an English poet, though he can't recall her name. *Last night the ghost of a world lay down on a world.* And the hair rises on his neck, not least because of the morning chill.

He gets out of the van and goes down to the beach, thinking to find Natalie poking in the embers of the night before. Thinking that on a morning like this, where you have to squint to see, they can both forget last night and move on, like he's been trying to do ever since his dad drove to the Argentia Ferry and left to find his mom in Ontario. The mother he can't forgive and can't stop loving. He wonders if in this place Natalie has been able to move on from her past. He wonders about her and holds

his hand against the light to see her.

But she is nowhere to be seen on the deserted beach.

He doesn't know where she is or where she's gone: doesn't know as he looks over that beach of iced stones flaming at sunrise that he will find the wine bottle missing from inside the front bumper of the vandalized van. Or that they will find Natalie lying in a ditch on Logy Bay Road, beside a shard of bloodied bat, with a jagged bottleneck still clenched in her hand. Or that when she comes to in hospital in three days' time her face will be black with bruising, and he will think of his grandfather's creosote Madonna and that his pop called the cops when he woke on November sixth with a silver skull ring on his chest and the bloodied handle of a Louisville Slugger smouldering in his burn barrel—muddy boot prints leading from his newly renovated shed to his bedside—the phone ringing and Rhianna screaming that her son River had been charged with attempted murder.

Hab doesn't know that when Natalie surfaces from her coma he will be looking through furious tears at her mangled face, her one eye swollen shut and the other bloodshot and searching, finding him in the white white room. Or that she won't attempt to say her attacker's name through clenched teeth, her jaw wired shut—only *his* name, like a desperate laugh: *Haaa*—her hand squeezing his and not letting go. Her weak grip sign enough of her will to persist. God's breath ragged in her—five broken ribs. That violence a gash in his world: fractured skull, concussion. And a newfound need to pray kindled by that bloodshot eye, coal-red and blistered. Her face smouldering hope in him. Needing her to recover, so that he can believe resurrection is possible—hook him and haul him up from the depths.

He's cold now, inside and out. Chilled, and blind to all that is to come, as he turns—grinding gravel underfoot on this bright morning, his world consumed in pulsating afterimage—the memory of iced beach stones at sunrise sparking still.

Acknowlededegments

First, I would like to thank the people who read early drafts and gave very generous and helpful feedback: Samantha Martin, Annamarie Beckel, Bruce Lilly, and Jessica Grant.

I would also like to thank my two sharp-eyed editors—John Eerkes-Medrano and Leslie Vryenhoek—who ruthlessly cut, thoughtfully rearranged, and kindly allowed me to keep some things.

The beautiful cover art is by Jonathan Castellino, whose gritty photos, found at www.sacramentalperception.com, were a constant source of inspiration during the writing of Natalie's back story.

Three of the novel's four chapters are titled by artwork by Gerald Squires, Jim Maunder, and Boyd Warren Chubbs—three artists of Newfoundland and Labrador whose works have allowed me glimpses into the mystery of this place.

There were many poets, novelists, artists and singer-songwriters whose work inspired me while I wrote. Heartfelt thanks to Nathan Stretch of Bass Lions, Amelia Curran, Robert Deeble, Lisa Moore, Kenneth J. Harvey, Michael Winter, Kevin Major, Mike Gough, Jonathan Castellino, The Navigators, and Spirit of the West.

Two generous grants from The Newfoundland and Labrador Arts Council allowed me time and space to write.

Thanks to Krissy Parsley for lending me the pterodactyls, and to Emily Gushue for sharing the story of Smallwood's wine, if not the wine itself. And thanks to the folks at Northwestern for believing in Patrick.

Great Uncle Garnet Gunter—yes, I remembered the great— thank you for being a man of faith, hope, and love. Gurney's good qualities are yours, his faults fictional.

Dear Unknown English Poet, your beautiful poetry was once quoted to me in Brussels by a complete stranger and he never told me your name. But I was so moved by one poem I wanted to include a line in this novel. Please accept this as acknowledgement and thanks.

And finally, many thanks to the excellent people at Breakwater, who brought this book to print.

SAMUEL THOMAS MARTIN

is the author of *This Ramshackle Tabernacle*
which was shortlisted for the 2010 BMO
Winterset Award and longlisted for the 2011
ReLit Award for Short Fiction. His reviews
and stories have appeared in journals in both
Canada and the U.S. and his jalapeno chili
once made someone cry. Originally from
Ontario he now lives in Newfoundland with
his wife Samantha and their dog Vader.

ART CREDITS

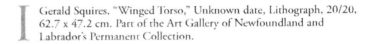 Gerald Squires, "Winged Torso," Unknown date, Lithograph, 20/20, 62.7 x 47.2 cm. Part of the Art Gallery of Newfoundland and Labrador's Permanent Collection.

 Jim Maunder, "Man nailed to a fish," 2001, © CARCC 2012

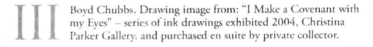 Boyd Chubbs, Drawing image from: "I Make a Covenant with my Eyes" – series of ink drawings exhibited 2004, Christina Parker Gallery, and purchased en suite by private collector.

 Samuel Martin, "Guy Fawkes Night," 5 Nov. 2010, Digital Photograph.

Sections of this novel have appeared in adapted forms in the following publications: "Running the Whale's Back" in *Image* 72 (2012); "Creosote Madonna" in *Riddle Fence* 10 (2011); and "Resettlement" in *qwerty* (Fall 2009).

1 Stamp's Lane, St. John's, NL, Canada, A1E 3C9
WWW.BREAKWATERBOOKS.COM

Copyright © 2012 Samuel Thomas Martin

LIBRARY AND ARCHIVES CANADA CATALOGUING IN PUBLICATION
Martin, Samuel Thomas, 1983-
A blessed snarl / Samuel Thomas Martin.
ISBN 978-1-55081-381-4
I. Title.
PS8626.A7729B54 2012   C813'.6   C2012-900920-2

We acknowledge the support of the Canada Council for the Arts which last
year invested $24.3 million in writing and publishing throughout Canada.
We acknowledge the Government of Canada through the Canada Book Fund and
the Government of Newfoundland and Labrador through the Department of
Tourism, Culture and Recreation for our publishing activities.

PRINTED AND BOUND IN CANADA.

 Canada Council   Conseil des Arts
for the Arts   du Canada

 Canada Newfoundland Labrador

 ENVIRONMENTAL BENEFITS STATEMENT
Breakwater Books Ltd saved the following resources
by printing the pages of this book on chlorine free
paper made with 100% post-consumer waste.

TREES	WATER	ENERGY	SOLID WASTE	GREENHOUSE GASES
20	9,228	8	585	2,047
FULLY GROWN	GALLONS	MILLION BTU	POUNDS	POUNDS

 MIX
Paper from responsible sources
FSC   FSC® C016245

Breakwater Books is committed to choosing
papers and materials for our books that help
to protect our environment. To this end, this
book is printed on a recycled paper that is
certified by the Forest Stewardship Council®.

CPSIA information can be obtained at www.ICGtesting.com
Printed in the USA
LVOW05s2022301113

363342LV00005B/709/P